Death Games

Book 8, Jon Spicer Series

CHRIS SIMMS

Other novels by Chris Simms:

<u>Psychological thrillers</u>
Outside the White Lines
Pecking Order

<u>Supernatural Thrillers</u>
Sing Me To Sleep
Dead Gorgeous

<u>Jon Spicer series</u>
Killing the Beasts
Shifting Skin
Savage Moon
Hell's Fire
The Edge
Cut Adrift
Sleeping Dogs

<u>DC Iona Khan series</u>
Scratch Deeper
A Price To Pay

Copyright © 2017 Chris Simms

The right of Chris Simms to be identified as the author of this work has been asserted by him in accordance with the Copyright, Designs and Patents Act 1988.

All rights reserved.

ISBN-10: 1541136608
ISBN-13: 978-1541136601

To that big kid I play with on a Sunday morning.

PROLOGUE

'We've got the clock towards Stockport.'

'Roger that, 873CK. You'll be clockwise on the M60. How long 'til you're on it?'

The passenger in the Tactical Intercept Vehicle was readying a large print version of Manchester's A to Z across his lap with one hand. In his other was a cappuccino. Six minutes earlier, their brightly marked BMW 330 had rolled slowly into the car park of the McDonald's beside the A57 in Gorton. Now the driver was gliding back round the curving road that led from the fast food outlet. The traffic lights ahead switched to green and his right foot sagged against the accelerator pedal. The passenger felt like he was in a slingshot as the car rejoined the main road at almost 50 mph.

'Two minutes.' He held the cup over the foot well, drips detaching themselves from its base as he shot a glance at the driver. 'Twat. If the lid wasn't on, that would be everywhere.'

The driver grinned. 'But it was.'

The radio sounded once more. '912CK, we'll take the anti-clock towards Oldham.'

'Roger that, 912CK. How long til you're on it?'

'Less than a minute.'

'Anyone else?'

'807CK, we are stationary at junction 3, can go clock or anti-clock.'

'Roger that, 807CK. Maintain your position and await further instruction.'

'Anyway,' the driver said. 'You and that stupid map.'

'You and that stupid map,' the passenger parroted back in a childish voice, placing the cup in the drink's holder to his side and then sucking foam off one knuckle. 'Nothing beats a bit of motorway orienteering, mate.'

'Motorway orienteering,' the driver scoffed. 'You were a boy scout, weren't you? Admit it.'

'Right up to Explorers.' Lifting his eyes from the map's pages, the passenger spoke towards the ceiling mike. 'Control: when did the ping come in?'

The voice on the other side of the speakers took a moment to reply. 'One minute fourteen seconds ago.'

So he's not far in front, thought the passenger. 'Could just be joining the motorway. What's the stolen?'

'A silver BMW Z3. Registration Tango, Zero, November, Yankee, Sierra.'

'That spells Tony's,' the driver murmured. 'Not Tony's now, is it? Some little scrote's got it now.' The way he mouthed the words without moving his head, he could have been talking to himself.

The passenger spoke once more. 'What's the score with it?'

'Taken in a burglary from a residence in the Northern Quarter half an hour ago. Aggravated.'

The passenger glanced at the driver's profile. That meant they were dealing with potentially violent offenders. Ones who would certainly not want to be caught. 'How many in the car?'

'We're not sure.'

Above them, the gantry holding the Automatic Number Plate Recognition camera that had registered the stolen car's plates glided smoothly over their heads. The passenger examined the road in front. In the early hours of a Friday, there was only a light smattering of cars. In fact, at that point, their main risk was from a drunk or drugged idiot driving home from a night out. The sight of a police car racing up behind them with the word 'Interceptor' emblazoned across its jet black bonnet had been known to provoke stupidity.

Speed now over seventy, the driver gave each vehicle a wide berth. As they reached the junction with the M60 it all became a question of luck. If the stolen car had stayed on the A57 by going straight across the roundabout, the interceptor's presence on the motorway that encircled Manchester would be a waste of time. If, however, the thief had decided the M60 was his best bet, they might come across him. At that point, they would take tactical control on the ground and start coordinating all other interceptor units in the area. The aim of the game was to anticipate the stolen car's movements, block its route and bring an end to the chase before it had a chance to start.

The driver hugged the inner edge of the roundabout, knowing if he kept above forty, he'd make it through the successive sets of lights as each went to orange. The towering Denton Rock sign came into view and he straightened the wheel to join the slip road onto the motorway.

Red rear lights of about a dozen cars were strung out over the next few hundred metres. The interceptor kept to the inside lane, both occupants eagerly scanning ahead for anything small, silver and sporty. Both were also listening to the open channel, their fear of 912CK radioing in a sighting on the anti-clockwise lanes nagging at their minds. That would mean turning round and trying to play catch-up. At best, they'd be the secondary unit, merely following the lead car's orders.

'I can only see members of the public,' the passenger stated.

'Yup.' The driver ghosted out into the fast lane, passed the first few vehicles then settled back into the slow lane. They started scanning again.

'Over there,' the driver stated. 'Middle lane, two cars in front.'

'You sure?'

He closed the gap with the car ahead of them in the slow lane, waited a few seconds, then strayed fractionally out for a clearer view. 'Registration says it's Tony's.'

The passenger spoke up. 'Control, this is 873CK. We have sight of the bandit, clock on the M60, about one mile from the Bredbury exit.'

Control came back on. 'Let's hear it.'

'I'm a passenger in an interceptor being driven by an Advanced Pursuit Trained Driver. We're in a liveried vehicle, at a safe distance behind a stolen car. The occupants of that car are not known to us. Exterior conditions: visibility excellent, road surface dry, surrounding traffic light. Do I have authorisation?'

'Authorisation given.'

The passenger knew the patrol car heading anti-clockwise would have already started looking for an opportunity to turn round, but he went through the motions anyway. '912CK this is 873CK, please join the clock motorway at the earliest opportunity.'

'912CK, am doing.'

The passenger was studying his map, even though he knew every aspect of the motorway system around Manchester. '807CK, are you still stationary at junction three?'

'Correct.'

'Plain or stripey?'

'Stripey.'

Good, thought the passenger. A liveried car would at least let the bandit know he was hemmed in. 'Can you get into position at the exit to the A34?'

'Yes.'

He addressed the driver. 'Enough under the bonnet to take that thing?'

'A Z3?' The driver snorted.

'807CK,' the passenger said more loudly, 'let's try and do it that way. Have the stinger ready. We'll close on him and then attempt to herd him your way. 912CK, what's your location?'

'Still a good four minutes behind you.'

They would be at junction three before the support car caught up. If they couldn't get the bandit to come off at that point, he would join a stretch of motorway that soon split into the M56 and the M60. Their job would then become a whole lot harder. 'OK, he seems happy in the middle lane at the moment. Let's stay tucked in and see what he does.'

They continued along in silence, the passenger using the opportunity to gulp back as much of his coffee as he could. The lane for the Bredbury exit began to branch off. To their relief, the stolen car ignored it. One of the cars behind it drifted into the fast lane, giving the driver of the interceptor a better view of his quarry. 'Looks like just the one person inside.'

A minute later, the ghostly blue glass sides of The Pyramid appeared to their left. The building occupied a prominent position at the exit which led into Stockport: the stolen car's last chance of leaving the motorway before junction three, where the trap awaited.

Both men's eyes were glued to the Z3, now about one hundred metres in front.

The radio came to life. 'Control to 873CK.'

'Go ahead, Control.'

'Word from the bobbies at the address where the car was taken. The house owner is on the way to the specialist head unit at Salford Royal. A nasty one, apparently.'

'Roger that. It looks like just one person driving.' The passenger glanced to the driver. 'More resources for this?

If he doesn't come off at three…I'm thinking NPAS two one.'

'Agreed.'

'873CK to control, what's the status of NPAS two one? We could do with air support if the stolen makes off.'

'Give me a minute.'

The turn off into Stockport was almost past them when the car they were using as a screen suddenly signalled left and steered up the slip road.

'Shit,' the driver breathed.

The passenger looked at the road behind them. The nearest vehicle was a good two hundred metres away. They were caught in the open.

'Think he's spotted us.' The driver's voice was tight. 'He's starting to accelerate. Definitely spooked him.'

'Still a couple of miles to junction three,' the passenger replied. 'Light it up?'

'No time for anything else. And turn the dash-cam on, will you? I want this recorded.' The driver flicked his controls and the siren started its painful shriek, blue light surging like a force field around their car.

The Z3's speed increased, but not recklessly so. Accelerating across into the fast lane, the interceptor driver rapidly closed the gap, hoping his position out wide would encourage the stolen car to make a dart for exit three.

'873CK, the bandit's seen us. We are now in pursuit, attempting to herd him off at your junction.'

'912CK, we are three minutes behind.'

'Is the stinger ready for deployment, 807CK?'

'Ready.'

'OK. We're thirty seconds off, max.'

The Z3 was refusing to budge from the middle lane, despite the interceptor getting closer and closer. Signs for exit three appeared overhead.

'You've got no chance,' the driver mocked. 'Take the exit like a good boy.'

They were now almost level.

'What's he doing?' the driver mused.

The passenger could see the silhouette of the driver's head. Short hair, thin neck. 'Juvenile?'

A verge sign appeared. Junction three, half a mile. They were within twenty metres of the stolen car. The driver glanced back, face lit for a split second by the flash of the interceptor's roof lights. Fourteen or fifteen. Sixteen at most. And he looked petrified.

'873CK to Control, solitary male occupant. Appears to be a juvenile.'

'You're sure?'

The passenger sucked breath in through his nose. High speed pursuit of juveniles was not permitted; on being chased, many started to treat it as some kind of challenge. It was just too dangerous. 'Yes.'

'Terminate the pursuit.'

Their speed immediately began to drop and the passenger slapped the flat of his hand against his knee. 'Bastard!'

The driver had to steer left as a row of bollards started to angle in, blocking off the fast lane. Some kind of roadworks up ahead. He turned the lights and siren off. As exit three went past, the Z3 was sixty metres ahead, the distance opening with every second.

Then his brake lights showed red.

He swerved between the bollards into the closed-off fast lane. Workmen clustered on the central reservation straightened up in surprise as he steered towards a flat bed truck with a single light revolving on its roof.

The interceptor driver's eyebrows lifted. 'What the fuck is he doing?'

A workman, the strips on his orange tabard and trousers shining silver, began to wave both arms above his head.

The passenger pointed. 'They've taken out a section of the central barrier. He's not going to – '

The Z3 aimed straight for the gap, rear lights juddering as it crossed the rough strip of ground separating one flow of cars from the other. Headlights of at least five vehicles were heading in the opposite direction. Now across the central reservation, he entered the closed-off fast lane on the other side and started to nose the vehicle into the middle lane.

Directly into the path of two cars, both doing about sixty.

The driver of the interceptor involuntarily hunched his shoulders. 'Oh Christ.'

The first car jinked into the slow lane and was past the danger in a blink of an eye. The second car – suddenly presented with a vehicle blocking its way – hit its brakes. A split-second of tyre squeal before it connected with the Z3's rear. The bang was like an artillery cannon going off. Fragments from both cars flew outwards. The impact caused the approaching car to veer into the fast lane, directly at the missing section of central barrier. Somehow, it passed between the workmen, all standing like mannequins. Its front left tyre hit a sack of gravel and reared up.

The vehicle began to flip.

For the passenger in the interceptor, everything slowed as a couple of tons of out-of-control metal came tumbling directly at them. The somersaulting car completely filled the windscreen and he squeezed both eyes shut in anticipation of the impact.

A heart beat of deafening silence.

With a crash, it landed on the lane behind them. His eyes reopened. The stolen Z3 looked like it was on ice. Revolving with a leisurely grace, it made its way into the slow lane where an oncoming van crumpled its front end. Locked firmly together, both vehicles ploughed onto the hard shoulder, metal grating as they made contact with the barrier beyond it.

Forty metres behind the interceptor, the car that had missed them by a whisker slid to a halt, wheels pointing up at the night sky. Other vehicles were slamming on their brakes. Several low speed collisions created an erratic rhythm of lesser bangs.

'Holy shit, Steve,' the passenger said, head still pressed firmly back against his seat. 'How did that not hit us?'

'Fucked if I know.' The driver was unwrapping his fingers from the steering wheel.

The passenger cleared his throat and spoke up, voice shaking. '873CK to Control, we have a multi-car collision, both sides of the M60 between junctions three and four. You need to matrix it, red X across all lanes, repeat all lanes, in both directions. The entire motorway needs to close.'

'Roger that, 873CK.'

He twisted in his seat. The car that had come through the gap in the barrier looked like something from a scrap heap. 'We'll need ambulances, both sides of the carriageway. Members of the public involved, possibly Highways workmen, too.' He turned back to view the far side of the motorway. 'The bandit is demolished. Send Trumpton – we'll need cutting equipment.'

'Roger that, 873CK.'

'Paul,' the driver stated in a quiet voice. 'Tell me the dash-cam was on record.'

The passenger understood what lay behind the question; he needed to know they were covered. Footage from their car would prove – indisputably – that they had followed the rules of pursuit correctly. The passenger checked the device; its side light was glowing green. Their careers were safe. 'Yup.'

Steve breathed out. 'Thank God.'

Paul reached for his seatbelt. 'I'll take the car behind us. Second unit can't be far off.'

The driver nodded. 'I'll hop over the other side.'

Paul climbed out, sounds suddenly sharper. From the far side of the motorway he could hear a man's shrill screams. Squealers weren't the immediate concern; it was the injured and silent they needed to worry about. He glanced up at the nearest gantry; a red X was already flashing on each screen. Exhaust fumes mixed with the sour smell of burnt rubber. Further down the motorway a siren was getting louder. Probably 912CK. What little traffic there was on his side had now formed an untidy barrier across the lanes about fifty metres from the upturned car.

He jogged across the tarmac, tool belt jangling and clinking. The wrecked car was a saloon, dark green in colour. From somewhere beneath the front wheels came a rapidly slowing tick. Unclipping his torch, he crouched down at the driver's door and shone the beam into the dark interior. Black drips cut through the bright ray. For a second, he feared it was fuel. No, not fuel. Blood. He could smell it. Taste it on his tongue. He lifted the beam and needed a second to process what it had illuminated. A torso was suspended from the seatbelt. He slid the beam down. Smashed-in skull. Arms hung limp. He reached through the remains of the window and felt at a wrist. No pulse. Movement. Another person, slumped against the roof on the passenger's side. A hand flapped slowly back and forth.

Standing up, he reached for his tunic radio. '873CK to Control. We have one fatality on the clockwise lanes, one injured. Not sure how bad.'

'Life is extinct?'

Knowing his answer would spark the involvement of all sorts of agencies, including the Independent Police Complaints Commission and Internal Affairs, he said, 'Life is extinct. Checking the other casualty now.' He walked quickly round the vehicle, fragments of glass crunching with each step. On the other side, he raised a palm. 'Stay in your vehicles, please! Get back inside, now!'

A few drivers from cars that had pulled up retreated to the open doors of their vehicles. He could see at least one mobile phone trained on him as he went down on one knee. The man inside was about thirty. He'd managed to get the door partly open. He looked Greek, maybe. Dark eyes were unfocused as he pawed at the nonexistent window.

'Sir, can you hear me. Sir?'

The man grunted as he tried to push his way through the gap.

'Sir, it's OK. An ambulance is on its way. Can you hear me?'

He appeared not to. Fingers curled round the empty window frame and he began to tug desperately at it.

'Hang on.' The officer grabbed the edge of the door and pulled. It creaked open another few inches and the man immediately wormed his way out. Trying to raise himself onto all fours, he began to retch.

'Sir, you're safe. It's OK.' He placed a hand on the man's shoulder. 'You're safe there.'

He now started trying to stand. Jesus, thought the officer. Is he hearing anything? 'Sir, it's better if you – '

Almost on one knee, the man began to keel over.

'I've got you, I've got you.' Draping one of the man's arms about his shoulders, Paul managed to walk him towards the hard shoulder. He noticed the man's other arm swinging uselessly about. 'Let's sit you on the barrier here. The ambulance will be with us soon, OK?'

Groggily, the man began to look around. He coughed. On the far side of the motorway, the screaming had grown more shrill. The officer looked across: orange flickers. Vehicle fire. Oh fuck. 'Stay there!' He pointed at the man's chest. 'Just stay there!' He span round and ran towards the central barriers.

The workman who had been waving both arms above his head was now sitting down, legs stretched out before him. He was examining the sky with a serene expression.

Not wanting to lose seconds running back to the gap in the barriers, Paul climbed over the metal railings. Steve was at the driver's door of the Z3, attempting to get it open. Flames were coming out from beneath the stoved-in front of the van, oily smoke churning upwards. A workman in an orange tabard was struggling to get a fire extinguisher started. It let out a brief, explosive whoosh. Paul remembered hearing a dolphin surface. It had been off the coast of Cornwall. Their family holiday last summer. He wished he was back there.

'Won't open,' Steve cursed.

Inside the car, the teenager continued to shriek and yell. 'Get me out, get me fucking out, get me out!' He kept turning to look at the flames licking the shattered windscreen.

Paul moved to the back of the car, removed a bulbous-headed tool from his belt and put the rear window in with a series of quick blows. 'This way! Out here! Come on!'

The lad scrambled back over the seats. His arms emerged and Paul grabbed one, hauling him clear of the vehicle. As he flopped down on the tarmac, Steve took hold of his other arm. They marched him a safe distance up the hard shoulder. Behind them came more sounds of dolphins surfacing. Lots of them. The fire extinguisher had obviously started working.

A siren that had steadily been growing louder cut off. Second unit, finally. Paul looked to his right to see Derek and Ian clambering over the barrier.

'Any other casualties?' Derek called across.

'Check the lorry driver, I think he was alone,' Paul shouted back. 'And the Highways workmen, I'm not sure if any were hit. You got him?' he asked Steve.

'Yup.'

Paul turned round. He needed to get back to the upturned Honda and box things off. People were out of their vehicles again, but staying close to them. He ran back to the interceptor, opened the boot and removed a foil blanket, a roll of police tape and a stack of bollards. As he jogged in the direction of the flipped car, he noticed a snack-sized bag of carrots. A carton of orange juice. Stuff flung from the interior as it had rolled. A mechanical arm, about a foot long, with propellers on the end. Another one, then the rest of it: a drone. A camcorder, the outer casing broken open and the lens shattered. He skirted round the vehicle. The man had gone. Paul looked left, right, then behind him at the wreckage. No sign of him.

'Excuse me!' He started towards the queue of stationary traffic. One of the watching drivers pointed towards the screen of shrubs beyond the hard shoulder.

'He ran off down there.'

CHAPTER 1

'Mmm, I love shiny things.' The Weapon Inventory Officer wiggled his fingers in the air, like a kid who couldn't decide which type of toy to pick. 'Don't you love shiny things?'

Detective Constable Jon Spicer gazed down at the open weapons box in the car boot. At the back was a baton gun with a variety of 38mm rounds: ones for disrupting a vehicle's tyres, ones for filling a room with crystallised CS gas and ones just for knocking a violent rioter flat on his back, unable to do anything but gasp.

Next to that was a Glock 17 handgun, with a selection of tools that could be attached to the rail beneath the barrel. Of these, Jon could only ever see himself using a tactical light if the building he was entering was dark. The laser attachment just annoyed him and the window breaker was, in his opinion, crap.

The front part of the slide-out tray was taken up by the main item. Jon let his eyes linger. There was no denying it; the dull gleam of firearms sent a tingle down his spine – and the MCX had a special allure. Most of his training had been spent with a G36c, a decent enough assault rifle. It certainly had served the interests of firearms units up and down the country well enough. But rumours were swirling that the carbine was about to be replaced by a different model – and just as Jon was sent to do the Specialist Firearms course, the MCXs had arrived. Lightweight and modular, they looked the absolute business. A couple of spare magazines were embedded in the foam casing beside it. Jon flipped them out and dipped them by sliding a thin length of metal in beside the bullets. Each time, it stopped at the 30 mark. Satisfied the magazines were full, he replaced them and lifted up the grab-bag. Inside would be another seven magazines for the MCX, two for the Glock and six stun grenades. The seal that tied the bag was intact and he checked the issuing number against the one in the WIO's book. They matched.

The officer looked up at Jon's face. 'All your bits and pieces present and correct?'

'Looks it to me, cheers.' He jotted his signature at the base of the page.

'Lovely. Now you need to set a number for the combination lock. Four digits. Most people do a family member's date of birth.'

His wife's face appeared in his mind, swiftly followed by Holly's and Doug's. Unwilling to favour one child over the other – even in his head – Jon leaned forward and punched in 0511. Fifth of November. Alice's birthday. 'Done.'

'OK, back we go. Where's your desk?' the WIO asked, short steps taking him to the corner of the indoor parking area. The set of keys dangling from his belt was very loud.

Jon took one last look at the small arsenal that lay before him. He couldn't quite believe he had responsibility for it. What the hell, he thought, are Greater Manchester Police thinking? He slammed the boot shut and followed the other man. 'Apparently. Nick...bollocks, can't remember his sur – '

'Grant?'

'That's him.' Jon cursed himself: first proper day in the new job and his inability to remember names was already embarrassing him. 'He's sorting me out.'

'Good-o.'

The man's blustery manner was beginning to grate slightly. Jon wondered what part of his training he'd messed up to be landed with the role of WIO. A large white van with BT OpenReach markings started reversing out from a row of commercial vehicles on the far side of the garage. Impressive, Jon thought. They'd even etched some graffiti in the grime that coated the rear doors. No way anyone would realise that was a surveillance vehicle.

The WIO was stamping his way up a set of metal stairs. They led to the door into the main facility. 'Where is Granty?' he called over his shoulder.

'Not sure.' Jon took the stairs two at a time. 'We were on our way to find you, then he got a call.'

The WIO held his card to a panel and the door clicked. 'Don't forget.' He pointed to the sign above the panel.

No tailgating! You must swipe your own card each time you enter or exit.

Jon went to hold his own card against the reader. The lanyard hadn't been designed for someone his height and he had to bend forward slightly. Immediately beyond the door was a brightly-lit room. Mirrors lined one wall, lockers the other. Two dishevelled-looking men were sitting before the mirrors. A petite Latino-looking woman in jeans and a white shirt was using a spatula to smear what looked like wet clay into one of the men's hair. On the floor beside her was a case full of bottles, tubes, pastes, brushes and pads. Like Alice's make-up bag, Jon thought, but on steroids.

'Christ, Alan,' the WIO said loudly. 'You remind me of me after my stag night.' An approval-seeking glance was sent in Jon's direction. 'Right messy, it got.'

The other man raised a cut-down Costa Coffee cup. 'Spare some change, mate?'

The WIO flicked two fingers. 'Get a job, crack-head. This big bastard, by the way, is DC Jon Spicer.' The WIO was carrying straight on towards the far door. 'He's Specialist Firearms, joining Granty's lot by the sounds of it.'

Jon reached out and quickly shook their hands.

'Alan.'

'Guy.'

'Good to meet you.' Jon directed a quick glance at the girl doing their make-up. 'You had me fooled.'

'Cheers.' As she ran a hand through her jet-black hair, he was struck by the colour of her eyes: bright blue. He hurried after the WIO, wondering where she could be from. Brazil, or somewhere like that, maybe?

'So,' the WIO was holding open the door. 'Did I hear mention that you've joined us from the Major Incident Team?'

Here we go, Jon thought. Tongues have been wagging. 'That's right.'

They set off down a long corridor. 'But fancied the Counter Terrorism Unit instead?'

Jon readied the response he had prepared. 'Racing around after proper bad guys – who wouldn't?'

The WIO sent a brief look sideways. Jon felt the man's eyes lingering on his ear, or rather the top of it that was missing. 'I heard you gave a very good account of yourself over in Ireland. What was it? Five blokes in a dog-fighting gang you took on?'

Jon wanted to sigh. The episode had cost him his position in the MIT, a role he had loved. It had also cost him the rank of Detective Inspector. Now here he was, busted back to Detective Constable. Mind you, he said to himself for the thousandth time, if the Counter Terrorism Unit hadn't come calling, he'd be in uniform: a constable at over forty-years-old. 'You make them sound like a proper outfit. They weren't.'

'Not what I heard. I heard they were about to – '

'Jon! Sorry about that.' Nick Grant had stepped out of a room further along the corridor.

Thanks Christ, thought Jon. 'No problem.'

The officer nodded at the WIO. 'Michael shown you to your car?'

'All signed off,' Michael said before Jon could speak. 'Detective Constable Spicer, maybe continue this conversation next time we meet?' He took a left turn.

Nick waited a moment. 'So, you've met Michael,' he announced quietly.

Jon gave a nod.

'Right prick, isn't he?' Nick grinned. 'Don't worry: we all know it.'

Jon smiled uncertainly. 'Well, he did seem a bit...'

'Full of himself?' You wouldn't have thought he totally bollocksed his SFO course would you? I'll give you the gory details sometime. You'll piss yourself. Anyway, this call I took. There's been a nasty RTA out on the M60.'

'I heard something on the radio earlier, on my way in. They've had to close both sides?'

'That's the one. Just past junction three. One fatality, a few others injured. You're wondering why they want us?'

'Yup.'

Nick started walking him back to the garage area. 'Turns out one of the vehicles had false plates. Not only that, there was a drone on board. They also checked the glove compartment and found some maps with handwritten notes on. Some weird language.'

'Have they identified the dead guy?'

'Negative. He had no identification. None whatsoever. There was also a passenger in his car. A male who needed to be dragged from the wreckage. He's done one, despite his injuries. Fled.'

'Interesting.'

'DCI Pinner wondered if you fancied tagging along? Me and Hugh Lambert need to collect the drone's camera, then secure any other interesting evidence and the like. You did plenty of that in the MIT, I assume?'

'Years of it.'

'Great. Hugh's meeting us downstairs. We'll go in my car.'

CHAPTER 2

As the new detective and Nick Grant strode purposefully back through the room known as the departure lounge, the female was snapping shut the clips on the box of theatrical make-up. 'You're good to go.'

The officer she'd been working on stood and frowned at his reflection. Grime was etched into the wrinkles of his forehead. His eyes appeared sunken through lack of sleep. 'She's got the touch. That's bloody ace, cheers, Iona.'

'My pleasure,' she replied. 'I'll let you put the effects box back, I've got a meeting to make. And be careful out there.' She hurried back into the main part of the building, checking her watch as she went. Almost eight. Damn it, she said to herself. She couldn't stand being late.

She darted into the women's wash room, grateful to be among the few female officers in the CTU: never a problem with crowded facilities. Standing before the row of empty sinks, she washed the smears of make up from her fingers and sneaked a quick look in the mirror. Her oval face was framed by hair that hung to her shoulders. On starting in the CTU, she'd had it cut in a very short bob. Big mistake. She was aiming for businesslike, but ended up – in her opinion – more like school kid.

Up in the main operations room, she swung past her desk, snatched up her daybook and continued towards the murmur of voices coming from one of the two meeting rooms at the far end.

All seats at the central table had been taken. Seeing some photocopied sheets on its corner, she took one and then slipped into a spare chair near the door, eyes going to the clock up on the wall. Seven-fifty-nine. Just made it.

A moment later, DCI Martin Weir looked up. 'OK, everyone.' He waited as conversations rapidly died away. 'This package is part of a wider thing resulting from foreign intelligence. It's a mop-up operation, basically. The dead guy on your top sheet is a British citizen.'

Iona took a moment to study the image. It was of a man's face and shoulders. He appeared to be laid out on a concrete floor with the camera pointing straight down at him. Most of the long black hair was caked in blood. The face was puffy; bruising had forced both eyes shut, his nose was a shapeless lump and his lips were so swollen, the skin had burst open in several places.

'He was captured recently by militia forces our government has been funding out in Syria. He was the only survivor from a group of four Isis fighters. During interrogation, he gave up some information that the Syrian guys passed to us. It's got merit.'

Merit, Iona thought. Corroborated by secondary sources, therefore more than the desperate claims anyone being tortured would come out with.

'A couple of years ago, Isis forces over-ran an Iraqi Army base near Tikrit. The Iraqis, in their rush to get the hell out, left behind eight surface-to-air missiles. FIM-92 Stingers which can be shoulder-fired by a single operator. A great deal of effort has since gone into getting these back.'

No wonder, Iona thought. Allied forces in the region relied on having total domination of the skies. Isis didn't –

as yet – have an airforce. But ownership of several Stingers dramatically altered the balance of power.

'Next sheet,' her senior officer instructed. The sound of rustling paper briefly filled the room. The page was filled by a grainy image of a desert crater. 'That's a satellite image of what was an Isis command post in Western Iraq. The bomb that took it out is believed to have destroyed six of those missiles. One other missile was handed over in return for a senior Isis figure American special forces snatched close to Mosul last year. The whereabouts of the last missile has remained a mystery, until the guy you were just looking at was taken. Turn your sheets again, please.'

The image below was of a healthy-looking male, probably mid to late thirties.

'This is our man, during happier times. Name: Feiz Atwi, formerly of 33 Richmond Grove, Longsight. He's from quite a large extended family here in Manchester. Originally, they came to this country from Lebanon – displaced during its civil war in the 1980s. He has one sister. The dad has two brothers, one is married with two sons, one married with one son. The mum has a sister who also lives close by: she married a Lebanese man, called Gibran Yared. You'll find all this in the family tree in the file.'

A voice came from the back. 'Was Feiz Atwi known to us?'

'To the CTU, no. To local bobbies? Yes. I'd classify him as a nuisance; low-level stuff like driving without insurance, threatening behaviour, handling stolen goods. Similar situation with his cousins.'

'But nothing to suggest Feiz was developing any radical views?' Iona asked.

'Not until he showed up in Syria. So, he gets himself captured and, during his questioning, mentioned that an attack was being planned. This attack involved the use of the final Stinger missile.'

He paused a moment before continuing.

'You're all aware, I presume, of our Royal Family's tradition of sending their younger members to serve in the armed forces?'

Now the entire room was hanging on his words.

'At present, we only have one prince who's on active duty. Currently, he's on his second tour out in Afghanistan.'

Harry, Iona thought, sitting back. Oh my God, they're going for him.

Her senior officer looked around the room. 'During his first tour a few years back, the prince made a few ill-advised comments about video games.'

'It was a PlayStation,' Iona found herself saying. She glanced up to see a dozen stony-faced men turning in her direction. 'Sorry.'

'No, you're all right,' Weir replied. 'Go on.'

As the silence grew louder, she searched her memory for the details. 'Erm, well – he's an Apache gunship pilot with the British Army, isn't he? While at Camp Bastion, he gave an interview to the British Press. In it, he said that operating the controls and weaponry systems of an Apache weren't that different to playing on a PlayStation. Didn't he actually use the word 'game'? Something like 'taking bad guys out of the game or similar?'

Her DCI raised a thumb. 'Ten out of ten, Iona.'

'Bloody swot,' the male officer next to her grunted with a good-natured grin. A few other colleagues chuckled in agreement.

'Isn't his older brother, William, something to do with helicopters as well? Coastguard or something?' someone near the door asked.

'The Duke of Cambridge?' Weir replied. 'Yes, I think he is. But he's here, in Britain, so not a concern. Harry, however, is. The bad guys he talked about were none too pleased with his videogame analysis. They saw his comments as trivialising a religious and historic conflict – now they see a chance for payback.'

A dark-haired officer at the end of the table half-raised a hand. 'So why not just get him the hell out of the country?'

'He refuses. Top Brass agree with him, as it happens. Two reasons for that. One, they fear it will be construed as a retreat of sorts. Don't worry – he won't be exposed to any real risk.'

Among the general murmurings, another voice rang out. 'How can that possibly be guaranteed?'

Weir lifted a hand to bring silence back to the room. 'He never really has done anything risky, to be honest. They don't let him near any real action. Now all his flights are off: reconnaissance, everything. Second reason for not pulling him out is that, thanks to the intelligence from Feiz Atwi, the missile's location is now believed to be known. I've not been given details, other than it's currently within Isis-held territory in western Afghanistan.'

'Then why not call in an airstrike and vaporise it?' the same dark-haired officer at the end of the table demanded.

Weir sat back and shrugged. 'How should I know? Anyway, we now get to what our involvement in this is.'

You've already said, Iona thought. Mopping up.

'A thorough assessment of the entire Atwi family – and their associates – is now required. In Manchester, that consists of the people on the next sheet.'

Iona flipped the page and cast an eye over the various photos. Some looked like they'd been gleaned from workplace personnel files, others were shots taken on the street. Which meant surveillance was already running.

'As mentioned, the family live mostly around Manchester,' Weir announced. 'Three days ago, we put static observations in place outside the homes of all immediate family. Those cameras microwaved in the exterior images you can see. Now, there's nothing to suggest any of these people are – or ever have been – in contact with Feiz since he vanished from this country and popped-up in Syria. But you know how these things are;

we need to hold informal interviews with them all. Their phone and internet records are currently being accessed, so you'll have some means of cross-referencing responses. Any shady stuff comes out, and we pass it back upstream to MI6.' He put his set of sheets to one side. 'Personally? I'm not expecting much – but let's get it done, anyway.'

As people began to get up, he raised his voice. 'Last thing: do not reveal the fact their relative is dead. If they want to know why you're asking questions, give them a line about him appearing in an Isis propaganda video. Fran here will let you know who you're interviewing, along with all the background notes you should need. Iona? Can I have a quick word?'

CHAPTER 3

Sunlight glared through the rest-lounge windows. The double-glazed surfaces did little to dull the sound of a huge helicopter taking off outside.

Seemingly oblivious to the air vibrating around them, a group of men continued to laugh. They were slouched in a semi-circle of armchairs, each one in green flight overalls. Facing them was a single plastic chair taken from the operations room next door. The man sitting in it was hunched over, as if in pain.

A member of his audience sat back and shook his head. 'It's not happening, Robbo. No way.'

Robbo spoke through gritted teeth. 'Come on, come on.' Both hands were tightly gripping a tiny set of controls.

'You took too long on the slalom,' someone else giggled.

Robbo was entirely focused on the toy helicopter hovering at knee level before him. A red and blue light on its undercarriage winked alternately as he manoeuvred it beneath a table. Seconds later, it emerged on the other side.

'He's done the tunnel! He's done the tunnel!'

Several eyes flicked nervously to the score chart on the wall. Topping it was a piece of paper that read 'Murray the Magnificent' (3:02). Then came 'Gently Does It' (3:04). Below that was 'Red Devil' (3:05). Other nicknames formed a column below the top three.

'Get in there,' murmured Robbo.

Now the helicopter outside was a distant throb, the high-pitched whirr of the toy could be heard. It approached the final obstacle: an upturned bin. Someone had painted a large red dot at the centre of its circular base.

'He's gonna do it. He's gonna bloody do it.'

Fingers making minute adjustments to the match-like joysticks, Robbo positioned the tiny helicopter above it. His lips moved in silent prayer.

The audience was now beginning to sit forward, laughter evaporating.

'Time?' Someone demanded.

A stopwatch was raised. 'Two minutes forty-six.'

'Sweet Jesus.'

Robbo cocked his head to each side. The toy was lined up: now he just had to land it. Bit by bit, he dropped it lower. Fifteen inches above the bin. Ten. Five. Three.

A voice announced, 'Two minutes fifty-five.'

Robbo winced as the machine dipped fractionally to the right. He tried to gain height but a rotor caught the edge of the bin. The engine stuttered and the toy tumbled to the floor.

The room erupted.

'No, no, no.' He kicked both feet out and raised his chin to the ceiling as grown men danced about with glee.

'You shat out! You shat out!'

'Buckled!'

'Could not handle it!'

'Loooo-ser!'

The stop watch was positioned above his face.

'Two minutes fifty eight. Could have been top, Robbo, could have been top!'

'Bollocks.' He placed the controls on the table. 'Who's next?'

The man with the stop watch consulted his sheet. 'Oh, this'll be good. It's the turn of our real, live, genuine member of the Royal Family: Howie.'

'Why's he called Howie?' Robbo asked quietly.

'Come on Robbo, think. Howie. House of Windsor. Yes?'

'Ah,' he smiled. 'I get it.'

'Thank God for that,' the one with the stop watch looked over at a slender man who was on one foot, dancing a little jig. 'Howie? You're up.'

CHAPTER 4

'Carnage. Total carnage.'

In the back of the car, Jon nodded. As soon as they'd joined the motorway, gantry signs had told them it was closed at junction four. Traffic was being diverted off before then, and all surrounding roads were now gridlocked.

They'd made their way along the hard shoulder at little more than ten miles-per-hour. Closer to the incident itself, cars were trapped; unable to carry on, unable to go back. Drivers had abandoned their vehicles to sit on the side barrier. Jon studied them as they crawled past: most seemed entranced by their smart phones. No one, he thought, talks anymore.

A uniformed traffic officer waved them to a stop and approached the side window. Nick had the blue lights behind the radiator grill silently flashing, so the officer knew they were something official. 'Gents?'

'CTU,' Nick announced, holding up his badge.

The man pointed. 'Parking's to the side of the first ambulance.'

Once out of the car, Jon tried to get a better impression of what was happening. Too many Chiefs, he thought.

Too many Indians as well. Officials and their vehicles were everywhere. Fire and Rescue Service, Paramedics, traffic police, several people in fluorescent bibs, others in white overalls. 'The full circus,' he stated.

'Even the clowns,' Nick shot back with a sliding glance at several men in suits. The group was observing the scene with a detached, managerial air.

The grown-ups, Jon thought. Senior ranking officers, or maybe IPCC. Pains in the arse, whoever they were.

They signed in and made their way to the inner cordon. Beyond the line of tape was the crash scene itself. A white van, blackened by smoke, was being winched clear of a BMW Z3 with a crumpled bonnet. The way its front tyres pointed inwards, the car looked like it was curtsying to the larger vehicle.

'That's where he came through,' Nick's partner, Hugh, said, looking at the gap in the central barrier.

Like Nick, he was somewhere in his early thirties, but about six inches taller and with a thinner, more angular, frame. As was usual when he first met someone, Jon had found himself categorising the man according to potential rugby position. Winger, he was tempted to conclude. Fast on his feet and useful if his team got him the ball when he was in space. But there was also the hint of strength in his wiry physique, and Jon wondered if he'd be better at second row. Nick, shorter and stockier, he had down as a fly-half. More of a decision-maker.

'The iffy car is on the anti-clockwise lanes. We need to be on the other side,' Nick announced.

They made their way round the perimeter and climbed over the barriers. Jon examined the lanes: there it was, a dark green Honda lying on its roof.

'Wonder how trampled the scene is,' Hugh said.

'Looks like the traffic officers backed-off, at least,' Nick answered, leading the way. They flashed their IDs to a uniform and ducked beneath the tape marking the inner cordon. They passed an abandoned Interceptor vehicle beside a line of workmen's bollards marking off the fast lane. If that was the lead pursuit vehicle, Jon mused, the driver and passenger would be long gone; whisked back to the station for a day of form-filling and interviews with every bastard under the sun.

Someone had put evidence markers by a few items scattered across the empty lanes. A bag of ready-sliced carrots. A drink carton. He spotted a broken length of plastic that ended in a small rotor: an arm from the drone. The rest of it was ahead. They were now within metres of the upturned saloon.

Another perimeter had been put around the car itself. Three figures in white forensics suits were beside the vehicle and Jon could see blood smeared across the road surface. The body had already been removed.

He looked at the stretch of motorway behind them. People were lining the rails of the A34 where it spanned the motorway. 'We could do with a tent,' he observed. 'To go over the vehicle.'

'Good point,' Nick muttered, glancing about. 'Who's even in charge?'

Hugh called out. 'Have we got a crime scene manager?'

One of the people in white suits glanced over. Seeing three men in jeans, trainers and casual tops, the figure headed across. 'That'll be me,' a female voice announced.

Jon recognised the voice and looked round: Nikki Kingston. They'd worked on a couple of cases together when he'd been in the Major Incident Team. Nearing the men, she flipped the flimsy hood from her head. Thick auburn curls sprang out. Still got the cool hair, Jon thought.

'Jon Spicer,' she smiled. 'Should have guessed you'd show up sooner or later.'

'How's it going, Nikki? This is DI Nick Grant and DC Hugh Lambert, Counter Terrorism Unit.'

She frowned. 'So who's got this, them or you?'

Jon cringed inwardly. She doesn't know about my career change, he realised. 'I'm with the CTU now, Nikki.'

'You are?' Her eyes sparkled. 'Finally pissed-off the MIT bosses too much? Kicked your arse out, did they?'

'Actually, they did.'

Her smile wavered then fell. 'Really?' She searched Jon's face. 'Sorry, I wasn't trying to – '

He waved a hand. 'It's fine. DI Grant's in charge. What've you got for him?'

Her eyes stayed on his for a split second longer. He knew what was going through her head. How come Spicer is assisting detectives far younger than himself? Wait until you hear my rank, Jon thought, stepping away.

To his side, Nikki started to speak. 'OK, you'll see the driver's body is no longer in situ. Not our decision, I'd like to stress. We've made a start on the vehicle's interior...'

Jon circled the car until the far verge came into view. According to the report that was relayed to them en route, the passenger had to be helped across to the barrier. Then he'd vanished. Jon wandered over to the hard shoulder. Beyond the barrier was a mass of low bushes and young trees. The slope fell away quite sharply. He lifted his gaze; the residential streets of Gatley would only be a few minutes' walk away. Immediately before him was a lightly wooded swathe of wasteland. Visible above the tree tops was a clock tower. What, he wondered, was that doing there? The derelict hospital, he realised. Manchester Convalescent Home.

It had closed in the late nineties and, since then, was occasionally targeted by developers. But nothing had ever happened, and gradually the austere Victorian building had started to crumble and collapse.

To his right, the empty motorway lanes separated out immediately beyond the A34 flyover. If I was fleeing a scene, Jon thought, it certainly wouldn't be in the direction of more roads. He headed left, towards the cars stuck behind a line of temporary barriers. The vegetation to the side of the motorway opened up enough to reveal a stream. Something, Jon thought, that would feed the nearby Mersey as it meandered its way towards the Manchester Ship Canal to the east of the city. A natural obstacle to anyone on foot. He started to turn round.

'Excuse me! Hello?'

He glanced in the direction of the voice. A man was looking over with a frown on his face. One hand was bouncing impatiently on the barrier's upper edge.

'We've been stuck here bloody ages. No one's telling us a thing. Can you?'

Jon lifted a hand in apology. 'Afraid not.'

The woman standing next to him spoke up. 'They said we'd soon be turning our vehicles round. Going back to junction two, or something. That's what they said earlier.'

'They're probably still waiting for traffic levels to die down before they do. I'm sure someone will let you know...' His eyes moved back to the clock tower. The derelict hospital's grounds were massive. The person who fled would have had to –

'Well, can you ask?' The man's voice again. His tone was insistent, and angry. 'I mean this is bloody absurd. I work on Saturdays.' He gestured at his car. 'I need to be on my way!'

Jon couldn't hear himself think. 'As I said, as soon as it's feasible – '

'Can you lot not appreciate that?'

Irritation tickled the back of Jon's neck. 'You lot? Who is you lot?'

The man swept a hand towards the crash scene. 'All of you just milling about, over there. If that upturned car was dragged to the edge of the carriageway, we could all get past.'

Count to five, Jon said to himself. Nice and calmly. What was it with some people? The man had obviously seen a body being taken away. He knew someone had died in the crash.

'Seriously,' the man continued. 'Can you not have a word with someone?'

Jon glanced past the man. Knew it, he thought. Knew he'd be driving a BMW. 'We've all got jobs to do, Sir. Let us do ours, then you – '

'No. I've been patient. Patient is not getting me anywhere. I'm tired of patient. What I want – '

'Sir, you're not listening. I said – '

'No! You need to listen.'

Jon held a hand up. Enough. 'Sir, the best thing you can do is shut up, OK? Get back in your car, close the door and stay in there.' He held eye contact.

The man blinked. 'Well, really...that's...you can't say that. What's your name?'

Jon took a step closer. 'DC Spicer.' He said it like a challenge.

'Right...well...' The man was retreating towards his vehicle. He opened the driver's door. 'I shall make a note, in that case.'

'You do that.' Jon turned round and walked back to the cluster of bushes. He stepped over the barrier and picked his way down the slope. Soon, he came to a fence topped with rusty strands of barbed wire. Turning right, he followed the perimeter of the old hospital's grounds to a corner. A slip-road off the motorway was immediately in front. Keeping beside the fence, he followed it to a pair of padlocked gates.

He looked up the driveway. The abandoned hospital was like something out of a horror film: he pictured dank basements and dusty attics, lonely rooms at the end of long corridors. Standing a good five metres higher than the rest of the building was the clock tower. Its roof tiles were stained green and, the way their curved lower edges overlapped reminded him of fish scales. Old and rotting. The clock face itself was mostly smashed through. Chipboards covered all the ground floor windows.

Springing from various nooks and crannies were clumps of vegetation: buddleia bushes or something similar.

Jon couldn't see the man who'd fled the crash trying to hide out inside the building. For a start, he'd have had to scale the fence – and, according to the report, one of his arms was injured.

On Jon's side of the fence there was about ten metres of driveway before it joined a road that, he guessed, curled round to merge with the A34 and the outskirts of Gatley.

He examined the grass to the sides of the disintegrating asphalt. Among the usual items of litter he spotted a shrivelled condom. Then another. And another. By pacing about, he was able to count over a dozen more. He also spotted baby wipes and some balled-up tissues. Many were too white to have been there long. It figured, he thought. The spot was secluded, but easily reached in a car. Perfect place for prostitutes to bring their punters. He wondered if any business was being done around four o'clock, when the crash had taken place. Probably was.

The wide strip of insulation tape completely covered her mouth. Her cheeks ballooned out then collapsed as she tried yelling again. He rose up to slam a fist into her temple. Air and mucus shot out from her nostrils and her head lolled to the side.

He crouched back down and then it was just the sound of their ragged breathing in the tiny bedroom. Only able to use his right hand, he reached for the roll of silver tape and wound it round both her ankles. As she came to, she began trying to kick out with her legs. He sank back on his haunches and observed the tape as it flexed and strained. She couldn't rip that. A brown bear couldn't rip that.

Grimacing with pain, he got to his feet. Holding his injured arm close to his chest, he circled round the back of her seat and checked the tape on her wrists.

Eyes wide with terror, she could only stare ahead as the man dragged the chair into the narrow gap between the bed and the wall. Now she couldn't tip it over, either.

Almost as an afterthought, he took the roll of tape off the bed and wound more round the rear leg of the chair and the radiator pipe.

Using one finger, he hooked the edge of the curtain back a fraction. Weak daylight. Dawn. The street beyond the window was quiet. Over the road, a man was arranging boxes of produce on a display stand at the front of his store. Onions, carrots, peppers, aubergines, potatoes and beans. The shop was just like the ones back in Shali.

Satisfied with how things were arranged, the shop owner walked back towards the store's entrance. The view of him became obscured by a red Porsche Cayenne parked directly outside. The man looked at it. Last night, in the dark, he hadn't realised it was such a bright colour. That wasn't good. People would notice such a car.

He needed to move it, but how? He had only managed to get here by forcing the woman to drive him. Once she'd parked, he'd tightened his choke hold until she'd lost consciousness then dragged her into the flat.

Things had gone so badly wrong. The pain in his head was regular and sharp. His shoulder felt like a hot skewer had been thrust into the joint and left there: he didn't want to admit to himself it was dislocated. Beside him, the woman's breathing was fast and shallow. He eased himself down on the bed and stared at the ceiling. I need rest, he thought. Just for a little while. Gradually, his eyes closed.

CHAPTER 5

His phone went off. 'Spicer here.'

'Jon, it's Nick. Where did you go?'

'Down the embankment by the side of the motorway. Wondering about this man who fled the scene.'

'Right. One minute you were here, the next...You see anything?'

'Not really. My guess is, from here, he's walked it into Gatley.'

'So worth asking a few questions around there?'

'Could be, yeah. What are you up to?'

'Going over the contents of the car. You bobbing back up here?'

'On my way.'

He found Nick and Hugh crouched beside the camcorder. Both now wore latex gloves. The machine looked like it had bounced some distance across the asphalt; the outer casing had come apart and the lens cap was missing. Hugh raised a camera of his own and took a couple of shots.

'Definitely from the upturned Honda?' Jon asked, bending forward.

'Seems so,' Nick replied, eyes on the piece of equipment. 'Best thing we can do is bag everything up and get it back to base. Let the techies at it.'

'How about the drone?' Jon asked. 'Have you recovered the camera for that?'

'Yup,' Nick replied. 'Along with some other interesting items.'

Back at base, they all slipped on gloves and spread the haul out on an examination table in a second-floor room.

Jon took a seat and surveyed the items: the various parts of the drone, a Sky-Eye IV that looked quite expensive. In an evidence bag next to them was the camcorder and its case, that had been found wedged beneath the vehicle's passenger seat. Beside that was a mobile phone, found in the jacket of the dead driver. Jon's gaze went to the end of the table where the maps from the vehicle's glove compartment were lined up. One had been folded open at the coastal area around Wylfa, the nuclear power station on Anglesey. In the blue expanse of sea at the left-hand side of the page, a few words had been written in black biro. They certainly weren't English – but neither were they Arabic or Russian. Whatever the language, Jon thought, it's not a well-known one.

Hugh was leaning over the sheets, camera clicking away. Next to him, Nick lifted the camcorder and fiddled with the controls. 'Either the batteries are dead or it's bust.'

'Looks like it took a bit of a clattering,' Jon stated.

'Yeah. One for the tech boys.'

Jon glanced at his watch. Almost eleven already. And no point in me sitting here, he thought, with a quick glance round the room's sterile white walls. He stood and went over to the window. Immediately beyond the security fence at the rear of the building was the Manchester Ship Canal. He studied the slowly moving brown water. Follow that upstream, he realised, and I'll be back in the city centre in two minutes. The urge to be out there was an itch. 'I'm not doing much good here. How about I have a nose round Gatley? I could check any taxi places and all-night garages. Gone four in the morning, a bloke with an injured arm? Good chance someone spotted him.'

'More than happy for you to do that,' Nick murmured, attention still on the camcorder.

'Probably worth contacting Manchester black cabs, too: see if any were flagged down in the area.'

Nick gave a nod. 'Good point. Put someone on that, can you, Hugh?'

Jon caught a flash of irritation on the other man's face.

'Yes, boss,' the other detective replied.

'Do we know where the two from the Interceptor were taken?' Jon added. 'The passenger who helped the mystery man out of the crashed car; I wouldn't mind having a quick chat – '

'No chance,' Hugh cut in. 'They'll be buried. IPCC, IA, crash scene investigation: the queue will go right down the corridor at Longsight.'

'Longsight? That's where they were taken?' Jon headed towards the door. 'I'll give it a go. Probably'll love a break from all those suits.'

Nick looked over. 'Ten out of ten for optimism. Let me know how it goes.'

Longsight was the main police station for the city centre. Jon had worked out of it numerous times during his years with the MIT: the specialist unit had several rooms at their disposal there. As he trotted down the steps into the Counter Terrorism Unit's parking area, he fought the temptation to check his vehicle was still in its space. It'll be there, he told himself. No one will have borrowed it. No one can get at the weapons box. Stop bloody fretting.

Because he had to avoid the M60, getting to Longsight station took almost thirty minutes. Once inside the main building, he headed straight for the canteen. A uniform, barely in his twenties, came round the corner. Seeing Jon, he almost stopped in his tracks.

It's like being an outlaw, Jon thought sadly. 'Excuse me, the Interceptor driver and his passenger? From the big RTA on the M60 earlier on. Do you know where they are?'

The constable licked his lips and looked to the ceiling. 'Upstairs briefing rooms. I think the driver is now in with IA.'

'Thanks mate.' Jon stepped aside and the man scurried by with an uncomfortable look on his face.

Jon ducked into the canteen, got two brews from the machine, along with several sachets of sugar and a stirrer. Up on the first floor, he spotted five men in suits sitting outside Briefing Room 3. Not slowing down, he made a bee line for the door and looked through the glass.

A knackered-out-looking officer was writing away at a table. Jon gave a quick knock then began to push the door open with his elbow.

'Hang on a moment,' one of the waiting men said. 'We've been – '

'Just taking him in a tea,' Jon said, raising the cups in explanation as he backed in. 'He's been on shift since yesterday.'

The man hesitated enough for Jon to raise a foot and kick the door shut. He turned round. 'Brought you a brew.'

The person was looking up with a confused expression. 'Right...OK.'

'I figured it wouldn't have crossed the minds of the twats out there.'

'Yeah,' he agreed, sitting back. 'It hadn't. Who are you?'

Jon plonked the drinks down then dropped the sachets and stirrer between them. 'DC Jon Spicer. I'm with the Counter Terrorism Unit.' He waved at the form the man had almost completed. 'It's not about the pursuit.'

The officer laid down his pen with a look of relief. 'Is my driver, Steve, out yet?'

'Internal Affairs are talking to him, apparently. Sorry, what's your name?'

'Paul.'

'Was the dash-cam in the car turned on, Paul?'

He nodded.

'Then you're in the clear. This,' he flicked a hand at the paperwork, 'is just a formality.'

The man appeared like he wanted to believe it. 'Except the lad we were after was so young.'

'Control had terminated the pursuit, correct?'

'Yes.'

'So you'll be fine. Trust me.'

The man tore the top off a sachet. 'You're here about the iffy car?'

'Yeah – the guy you helped out of it. The one who vanished.'

'It was bizarre. Last thing I expected.'

'What was he like, this bloke?'

'Late twenties, early thirties. Short black hair, lightly tanned complexion.'

'Ethnicity?'

'Not sure. Romanian? Albanian?'

'Why do you think that?'

'He reminded me of that footballer. The one who's always boasting about being God's gift.'

'Not sure who you mean.'

'Zlatan, is it? Zlatan Ibramo-something or other. He's got a long curving nose, eyes set quite deep, prominent forehead.'

'Did he speak?'

'No.'

'Not a word?'

'Nothing.'

'According to the report relayed to us, he was injured.'

'Apart from looking like he'd just been in a cage with Conor McGregor?'

Jon smiled. 'Something about his arm?'

'As I helped him over to the verge, I could see his left arm was hanging awkwardly. Dangling.'

'What sort of shape was he in, physically? Fat, thin, average?'

Paul considered the question. 'Certainly not fat. In good shape, thinking about it. I had my arm round him. Yes, very good shape. Solid. And he was getting out of that car, no question. He was groggy, could hardly stand – concussed, I'm pretty sure – but that wasn't stopping him.' The officer paused. 'You think, to manage that, he had military training, maybe?'

Jon ran a hand across his chin. 'That's what I'm worried about.'

CHAPTER 6

Jon's phone was pressed to his ear as he made his way across the car park at Longsight station. 'It's Detective Constable Spicer.'

'You can use first names, Jon,' Nick replied.

'Right.' He patted his pockets with his free hand, momentarily panicking that he'd mislaid the keys. What if someone had...He caught site of the car just as his palm caused metal to chink in his jeans.

'Still there, Jon?'

'Sorry, yes. I've just chatted to the passenger from that interceptor, the one who – '

'Good going. How did you get in to see him?'

'Ways and means, as they say.'

The DI laughed. 'Go on.'

'The man who fled appeared Romanian or Albanian – lightly tanned. Resembled a footballer called Zatlan, or something.'

'Zlatan Ibrahamovic? He's Swedish, but his dad's from Bosnia.'

'Him, anyway. He didn't speak. According to the officer, the fact he was able to make off from the scene was a feat in itself.'

'How so?'

'The car had flipped and rolled: the bloke had mushy legs, was groggy and his left arm was injured.'

'OK. So you'll have a wander round Gatley?'

'Yes.' Jon thought about the condoms littering the grass at the turn off into the abandoned hospital's grounds. 'That and something else. There's a chance a spot nearby is where sex-workers are taking their punters. Someone may have seen something.'

'Sounds worth a shot. I'll leave you to it. Oh, and Jon? They've just reopened the motorway, so no need for any more side-roads.'

'Bonus.'

The nearest mini-cab place was above a Top-Toppings pizza outlet beside Gatley train station. The owner stated that the last person who'd climbed the stairs into the cramped little office to ask for a cab was just after 4.30 am. A lone male. Jon had felt a brief tingle of excitement. But the person had been black, dressed smartly and with no injuries.

Next, Jon checked the station's ticket office. The man behind the counter said it closed at nine in the evening. A side gate gave access to the platform after that but, after midnight, no trains actually stopped at the station.

Back out on the street, Jon looked around, imagining the place at after four in the morning. Ghost town. Every shop would have been dark and empty, traffic lights flicking from green to red for no reason.

You've crawled out of a car, he thought, leaving all your stuff behind. And you're injured. You don't want to be staggering around in the open. The sound of nearby sirens are filling the air. His mind went back to the fenced-off driveway of the old hospital. Where working girls did what they had to do.

By the time he dropped off the Mancunian Way and joined the flow of traffic moving along the A6 towards Piccadilly Station, a light rain had started up. He looked to his left;

the wide border of grass that flanked the road was now covered by a motley collection of tents. Clothes lines had been strung between the few spindly tree trunks. Sleeping bags, towels and items of clothing hung limp in the fume-filled air. The owners were probably all in the city centre, begging. A group of four men squatted in the porch area of a larger tent, a pan balanced on a small cooking stove. Manchester's own Jungle, thought Jon. Migrants, asylum-seekers and the homeless, reduced to this. What is happening to the world?

At the junction with Fairfield Street, he hesitated. It's been so long since I worked the city centre in a uniform, will they still be there?

He turned right, driving for the wasteland of industrial units, breakers' yards and lock-ups that lay behind the city's main train station. After patrolling the criss-crossing streets for a few minutes, he saw a female form standing in the shadow of a railway arch off Temperance Street.

You're not there admiring the fine Victorian brickwork, Jon thought, pulling up. He locked the car and tried the handle to double-check before ambling in her direction.

She'd sussed him well before he started reaching for his ID.

'I'm moving,' she said, stepping out into the light drizzle, arms crossed over a flimsy coat. She was somewhere in her thirties, he guessed. Her short skirt revealed bare legs that were mottled purple. She looked freezing.

'Don't be on my account,' he replied. 'I've only got a question, if you can help...'

The artificial lines of her eyebrows lifted as she stepped back out of the rain. Jon ducked in beside her and turned to face the road. 'There's this place near the motorway by Gatley. Sort of a side road. It's being used by working girls.'

'Gatley? Other side of the M60?'

He nodded.

'Bit of a way, that.'

'What I was thinking. Where do you reckon the girls using it would be coming from? I mean, you're not going to drive all the way out there from round here, surely?'

'Probably Burnage. They've been cracking down in Withington, since it turned posh.'

'Burnage?' Figures, thought Jon. For a start, it was straight along the A34 from Gatley. 'Any particular part of it?'

'Just drive about. Where it gets near Levenshulme.'

'Great, cheers.' He stepped back and looked off down the road. There wasn't a car in sight. 'It's quiet.'

'Yeah,' she said in a tired voice. 'I'll give it a bit longer and then I'm off to bed.'

'Good luck.'

He drove as fast as he could out of the city centre, aware that, as the day wore on, fewer and fewer girls would still be out. When he got to Burnage Park he turned left and got lucky almost straight away: four females, sheltering beneath the trees that lined the edge of Cringle Field.

He pulled over and climbed out, ID open in his hand. They watched his approach, faces showing a mixture of emotions as they spotted his badge. Irritation. Frustration. Trepidation – at least on the one who looked youngest. 'It's all right,' he called out while still several metres away. 'I'm only after some information.'

Their postures softened slightly and all eyes seemed to go to the tallest girl with a dark ponytail who was standing nearest to him.

'What information would that be?'

Her Irish accent took him straight back. Memories of Siobhain – the girl who'd lured him over to Galway and then manoeuvred him into a confrontation with a criminal gang involved in dog-fighting. 'I'm wondering if any of you use a particular place near here. For taking a punter.'

'What particular place is that?' She'd crossed her arms and was stepping from foot-to-foot as if to keep warm.

'It's off the A34 – only a few minutes from here in a car. Just after you cross over the M60, there's a side road; it leads to the driveway of this massive hospital that's been closed down.'

'The spooky thing?' The question came from a girl with dyed blonde hair.

Jon regarded her. 'Big clock tower, but all the faces on it have been smashed in.'

'That's it!' She turned to the others. 'Have you not seen it? Well creepy.'

Heads shook. The Irish girl's ponytail swayed.

She continued speaking to her mates. 'One time, this guy suggested going there. It was nearly dark, but you could just make it out at the end of the drive. Shitting myself, I was.'

Jon gave a cough. 'I'm wondering if anyone was over there last night. Early hours of the morning.'

'Kelly liked using it,' the blonde haired one stated, ignoring Jon to address her mates.

'That where she liked to go?' the Irish girl asked. 'She kept that quiet.'

'She can have it all to herself, no joking.'

'Does Kelly work round here?' Jon asked.

The Irish girl glanced at him. 'Usually. I've not seen her today.'

'She were here last night.' This came from the youngest-looking girl.

Nice strong Lancashire accent you've got there, Jon thought. 'What time was that?'

'Midnight. I saw her then. She were with Julie. By that girl's school over there.' She nodded in the direction Jon had come.

Levenshulme High School for Girls, Jon thought. 'But not since then?'

She shook her head.

'This Kelly, do you know her surname?'

That got him an incredulous look.'

'What does she look like, then? Age, height, hair colour – that kind of thing.'

The girl bit on her lower lip as she thought about it. 'My height, brown hair with some blonde bits. How old is she? About thirty?'

'Thirty?' The Irish girl laughed. She looked at Jon. 'And another few years. Very thin, she is. Usually, she's in high heeled black boots and a little yellow puffa jacket.'

'Don't suppose any of you know how I could contact her?'

'What's it about?' the Irish girl asked. 'Do we need to be worried?'

Jon understood the question. Had someone been attacked? Are we in danger, too? 'There's a chance she saw something, that's all. Someone fleeing from the scene of a car crash.'

The Irish girl shrugged, attention switching back to the road. The others were starting to turn away, too.

'How about the girl she was with? Julie, was it?'

The youngest of the three nodded. 'She sometimes works through the day. If she's desperate.'

'Come back tonight,' the Irish girl said. 'Sure they'll both be out tonight. Saturday, isn't it?'

'OK.' He reached for a card, then remembered he hadn't been issued any by the CTU. Checking his wallet, he pulled out one from his time in the MIT. After crossing the number out, he scrawled his mobile across the top. 'Here – my number.'

The Irish girl pocketed it without a glance. 'Grand.'

'Ignore everything but the number in biro.' He wondered whether to ask the youngest one exactly how old she was. But he'd lost their attention. The only thing he was doing now was getting in the way of business. 'Thanks for your help,' he called over his shoulder, setting off back to his car.

CHAPTER 7

'Put him in bay three, please.'

The orderly nodded, elbows flexing as he began to push. The gurney glided silently though the usual cacophony of sounds filling the Accident and Emergency Department at Manchester's Royal Infirmary.

Quickly scraping her black hair back, the nurse re-tied it with a maroon hairband then studied the screen before her. The computer banded patients according to a traffic light system of colours: ones who'd progressed through to red needed to be seen within the hour if the hospital was to meet government-set waiting-time targets.

Currently, the screen was dominated by green and orange. For late morning on a Saturday, we're doing well, she thought. After lunch, the sports injuries would start to appear. Footballers with twists and sprains, rugby players with dislocations and concussions, hockey players with broken fingers.

She glanced at the wall clock. Time for my break, she thought. The one from nearly an hour ago. 'Darren, OK if I grab a breather?'

The senior nurse glanced up from his spread of patient notes. 'Go for it.'

She walked along to the next bay where another band five nurse was working. 'Maria, are you OK to cover me? Nothing urgent needs doing.'

The Philipino nurse smiled serenely. 'That's fine.'

She walked behind the main desk and into the staff area. Her locker was in the corner. Once she'd retrieved her phone and a bottle of water from it, she looked around for a seat. Frank the Delivery Man was standing before the vending machine, making his selection.

She crossed to the opposite corner, sank gratefully into the nearest chair, kicked her Skechers off and put her feet up on the opposite seat. She started checking her Facebook page. Saturday night and she had nothing lined up. She came off shift at five. Normally, there was no way she'd be staying in – not with being off work tomorrow. Normally, she'd be furiously making plans. Nicole and Judy were going to the new Japanese place in Didsbury. That was an option. Shamin had suggested a cycle ride: no thanks. Marcus had a spare ticket for the Funk n Soul Club at Band on the Wall.

'Elissa, how's you?'

She suppressed the urge to groan. Frank the Delivery Man was harmless, but he couldn't take a hint. And the last thing she wanted was to be making polite chit-chat. She looked up with a smile. He was standing before her with that cheesy grin of his, a coffee in one hand, a Kit Kat in the other.

'Hi Frank. I'm fine, thanks. You?'

'Mmmm, not so bad.'

Her eyes strayed back to her phone. 'Good to hear it.'

'Having a little break, are you?'

'Yeah, just a quick one.' She brought up Marcus', post, wondering if the ticket was still spare. It would be fun. You should try, she told herself. Try to be the person you once –

Her seat shifted as Frank flopped down beside her. 'Traffic was terrible on the M60. There'd been a crash near junction three. The whole thing was closed. Luckily, I came off at junction nine of the M6, went up to the M62 and came into the city that way. I mean, it adds on a good twenty minutes, that. But no other choice with the M60 out.'

Reluctantly, she placed her phone face down in her lap. 'I bet. Many more deliveries to make?'

'Stepping Hill. After that, more portable Nitrous Oxide canisters for the North West Air Ambulance.'

'That's not too bad, is it?'

'No.' He examined his cup, pursed his lips and blew a crater into the layer of foam.

'So, what's the gossip?'

He thought for a moment. 'Not much really.' He lowered his voice. 'No change to the schedule of our celebrity friend out on – '

She widened her eyes at him and he stopped speaking.

'Sorry.' He checked no one had been in hearing distance. 'Oh, me and the missus are going to an agricultural show at Chatsworth on Sunday. About twenty shire horses are going to be there in a ploughing competition.'

'Sounds interesting.' She flipped her phone back over, wondering about the ticket once again.

'Elissa Yared?'

She looked up. A female, about her age, in jeans and a purple gilet with a white shirt beneath it. Black hair and bright – piercingly bright – blue eyes. Amazing eyes, Elissa thought. 'Yes.'

The woman gave a quick, almost apologetic smile. 'Detective Constable Khan. Really sorry to interrupt, but is there any chance...?'

Elissa watched those brilliant blue eyes shift to Frank – and stay on him.

He stared back for a moment, then blinked. 'Ah, right.' He turned to Elissa. 'I need to get going anyway. I'll drink this in the van.'

'OK, see you about, Frank.'

As soon as he was clear, Iona pointed to the seat he'd just vacated. 'Mind if I sit down?'

'Be my guest.' Elissa took her feet off the opposite chair and sat up straighter.

'I hope I didn't interrupt anything – but you didn't seem that, you know –' She glanced at the door Frank had just walked out.

'That obvious, was it?' Elissa sighed. 'He's all right – just I was in the middle of doing something.' She waggled her phone.

'Don't let me stop you,' Iona replied, starting to unzip a small attaché case.

'Are you sure? Cheers.' She started typing a swift reply to Marcus, asking if the ticket for the Funk n Soul Club was still free. Her finger moved towards send, but she didn't touch the screen. She tried to decide if she could face it.

'Plans for the weekend?' the detective asked.

She placed her phone to the side, message unsent. 'Yeah. A friend has a spare ticket for this funk night –'

'Band on the Wall?'

'Yes.' She looked at the officer. 'You know it?'

'Bloody love it.'

'It's great, isn't it?' She pictured herself at the venue. Usually, she ended up dancing non-stop. Keeping that image in her head, she reached for her handset and pressed send. 'Fingers crossed I haven't missed it.'

'Absolutely,' Iona replied. She let a second pass then opened her notebook. 'OK, Elissa, there's nothing formal about this; background enquiries, that's all. They concern a relative of yours.'

Elissa's smile faltered. 'I thought you were here about someone who'd come in for treatment.'

'No, it's about your cousin, Feiz Atwi.' Iona watched the nurse's face carefully.

'Him? He left the country ages ago.'

'Do you know of his whereabouts since he left the UK?'

She pursed her lips. 'You know I do. I've been spoken to before. Questioned. He went out the Middle East to join Isis.'

'Are you aware of which countries he's been to?'

'No, but I'm guessing Syria. Why?'

Iona jotted the essence of her reply down. 'As I said, it's just routine stuff. We think he features in a recent propaganda video.'

Elissa looked queasy. 'You don't mean...not one of those ones where the poor prisoners...'

'No,' Iona interjected as soon as she realised where Elissa's suspicions were leading. 'Nothing like that.'

'Where is this video? I mean, is it on the internet? Will everyone see it? His mum and dad, they've been spat at, you know? On the street, people spat at them when news first got out about Feiz.'

Iona was cursing the badly-considered choice of cover story. 'No, there's no cause for concern. The footage was, I believe, seized by a foreign intelligence agency. It won't be made public.'

Elissa didn't appear particularly reassured.

'Since leaving the country, has your cousin made contact with you?'

She shook her head. 'No.'

'Has he ever attempted contact? Social media, maybe. Even just a text.'

'No. I've explained this before; I didn't know the guy.'

'How about other people you know. Has he been in contact with anyone?'

'I'm not aware of it.'

'Not even his immediate family?'

'The Atwis? They disowned him. Bilal and Furat, his mum and dad, they gave an interview to the Manchester Evening Chronicle, they were so ashamed.'

'I'm aware of that. But has he contacted them in any way since?'

'They haven't said. Which part of the police are you from? Is it the Counter Terrorism Unit?'

Iona was careful to keep eye contact. 'Yes.'

Elissa thought about that for a few seconds. 'It was men before.' She glanced up. 'Who came to see me. That sounds sexist, I know. But...it was.'

'OK, Elissa, I need you to think very carefully about this. Phone records, internet use: it can all be checked. It's better you tell me now of anything you might have heard. Even the smallest thing.'

'What, you'll be going through my phone records?' Elissa sounded outraged.

Iona didn't want her turning hostile. 'If communication from Feiz is tracked to this country, that might happen. I wanted you to realise that.'

'No one's heard anything, I'm ninety-nine percent sure of that. Someone would have said if they had, I'm certain.'

Iona noted her responses down. 'What are your views?'

'How do you mean?'

'You said Feiz' parents were ashamed when he left to join Isis. How about you?'

'Ashamed?' Her eyes drifted for a second. 'More sad, actually. Feiz wasn't ever political. He was just a bloke who lost his way. He couldn't find work – nothing long-term, anyway. So he decided to join Isis.' She shrugged. 'Now he's stuck. Even if he wanted to get away, where does he go? Back here, he'll just be arrested. He's ruined his own life.'

Iona kept writing. 'And Isis. How do you feel about them?'

'What? Would I like having to wear a hijab? Pack in my job and stay at home? Be forced to watch daily beheadings in Piccadilly Gardens?'

Iona glanced up to see Elissa looking at her with arched eyebrows. 'OK. As I said, it's only background stuff.'

'Really?' Elissa replied aggressively. 'Are you sure about that? You know about my brother, don't you?'

Iona nodded: it had featured in the notes she'd been given back at the office.

'Tell me what you've heard,' Elissa demanded. 'What the official version currently is.'

'He was killed almost a year ago when the hospital he was in was accidentally struck by a missile – out in Afghanistan. He was there as a doctor, working for Medics International.'

'Accidentally struck, was it?'

Iona was about to reply yes, but paused. 'That's what the report said.'

'Who fired that missile?'

'I...I don't recall.'

Elissa nodded. 'That bloody figures.' She looked down at her lap then glanced around the room. 'He used to work here. Not in this department. Paediatrics. We shared a flat together.'

In Didsbury, Iona thought. 4a Cattermere Avenue. You still live there. Alone, now. 'It must have been very hard for you, what happened.'

Elissa bowed her head. 'It still is.'

Iona found herself studying the side of the other woman's face. She looked lost. No, worse than that: she looked bereft.

Then a double blip came from the woman's phone. She flipped it over to see the screen and smiled briefly.

'Did you get the ticket?' Iona asked, closing her notebook.

'I did,' Elissa replied.

Iona stood. 'Well, enjoy it. And thanks for your time.'

Elissa watched the detective go. A video of Feiz; was that the truth, or were they fishing for something else? She wondered whether to ring Aunty Furat to see if the police had called on her yet.

She felt unsettled and anxious knowing the stress that was caused to Furat when police came knocking at her door. The elderly woman would be beside herself, certain there was other news about her son. Stuff being held back. Lying in a dark bedroom: that would be how the wretched woman would probably spend the next day or two. Battling a migraine.

Raising her phone, she looked at Marcus' message. She didn't feel like going now. She tapped out an apology: a family issue had just cropped up.

Iona was about to get back into her car when she saw the parking ticket pinned beneath a windscreen wiper. Had the attendant been trained to ignore police notices that were propped on dashboards? Good luck chasing that fine, she thought, unlocking the vehicle and tossing the ticket onto the passenger seat.

Right, next on the list. She slid the sheets from her attaché and the names she saw caused her heart to sink. Bilal and Furat Atwi: Feiz's parents.

When Weir had pulled her to one side at the end of the briefing, it had been to tell her the job of interviewing them was being given to her. He had asked as if it was some kind of favour: a female officer knocking on the door would be far less intimidating for the couple than a male.

She double-checked the address. Park Crescent, Rusholme. A stone's throw away from the Curry Mile, the stretch of road a little way out from the city centre that was bordered on both sides by dozens of restaurants, sari shops, jewellers and confectioners selling brightly-coloured Mithai.

As she started the car, she thought about the woman she'd just interviewed. They were within a year of each other's age. She seemed nice. A little worn out, but, part-way through a Saturday shift, that was only to be expected.

Besides, Iona thought – nurses, teachers, police officers: we're all permanently knackered, aren't we? Or was Elissa more than tired? Sad? Even depressed?

Iona found herself hoping she enjoyed it at Band on the Wall; a carefree night of dancing would do her good.

When Iona pulled up outside the house, the first thing she saw was a woman standing at a ground floor window. She was staring out with a worried look on her face. The woman's hair was silver.

As the front door opened, Iona raised her ID. 'Furat Atwi?' The woman was probably in her early fifties: a bit young to have gone so grey. She nodded apprehensively. 'I'm Detective Constable Khan. Could I come in for a quick word?' For a moment, she thought the lady was about to lose her balance.

'Is it Bilal?' she asked, one hand seeking out the door frame.

Iona frowned. 'Your husband? No, I'm here to – ' She paused. 'What's the matter?'

'I don't know where he is! I thought, for a moment, you were here to...'

'No, no. Could I come in so we can talk?'

The lady beckoned her into a spotlessly neat front room. The wallpaper's heavy floral pattern was broken by several framed photos. Shots from family events. She quickly spotted a portrait of Feiz in a school blazer and tie. Hair in a neat side-parting, he was standing at the front of the house with a nervous expression on his face. First day at secondary school? Iona sat in a peach-coloured armchair.

Furat took the chocolate sofa alongside it. 'I don't know where Bilal is.'

'When did you see your husband last?'

'Yesterday. In the morning. He was visiting a client, but said he'd be back by the evening. Now he won't...' Her voice started to waver. 'Every call goes to his answer phone.'

'Where was this client he was seeing?'

'I don't know.'

'Did he drive there?'

'Yes. He has a silver Mercedes.' She started struggling to her feet. 'The registration will be here, I can – '

Iona lifted a hand. 'That's fine, Mrs Atwi. You can fetch it in a moment. How often does he go on overnight trips?'

'Never. He always comes back, however late. And he rings me. He always rings me. Something must be wrong!'

'When did he last call you?'

'In the afternoon, at about six.'

'And everything was fine?'

'Yes. He said there'd been a delay, so he'd be a bit late.'

'But you don't know where he was calling from?'

'No.'

'What line of work is he in?'

'He imports. Fruit and vegetable, mainly. He has contracts to supply lots of restaurants. And quite a few academies and colleges.'

'Local ones?'

'Yes. Some in North Manchester. One or two out towards Liverpool, I think.' She looked towards the window. 'I don't understand this.'

'OK, try not to worry, Mrs Atwi, I can make some calls.' She turned to the photos massed on the wall above the television. 'Is your husband in any of these pictures?'

The woman nodded.

'Which one is the most recent?'

She stared back with a fearful expression.

'I'm not saying anything's happened, Mrs Atwi. But it's always helpful to have a recent photo – for making enquiries.'

She turned. 'This one. Our holiday from last year.'

A heavy-set man with bushy eyebrows was standing in front of a jetty. Cornwall, Iona guessed. Somewhere like that. The day looked hot, but he was wearing dark brown trousers and a polo shirt with all the buttons done up. Waves of thick black hair undulated sideways across his head, sunlight catching on each crest.

Iona stood and took out her phone. 'May I take a photo?'

'Yes.'

As she scrolled to the camera option on her phone, she contemplated whether to go into the questions about the son. No, she decided. Not now. 'And if I can have the registration of his car and a number I can reach you on, that would be great.'

CHAPTER 8

Jon turned into the industrial estate where his section of the CTU was located. The building they occupied was at the end of an avenue. Apart from a cluster of antennae and dishes sprouting from the roof – and the double strand of razor wire topping the perimeter fence – nothing indicated anything out of the ordinary.

Jon showed his ID to the man on the front gate and was waved through. Half-way up the interior garage stairs, it occurred to him he had no idea where his desk was. If he even had one. He wandered up to the second floor office where items from the crash scene had been laid out. No sign of Nick or Hugh. He scanned the table, quickly spotting that the mobile phone, camcorder and drone camera were all missing. Tech department was top floor, Jon thought, heading for the stairs.

He found the two men in a large open plan room that looked like a gadget-geek's idea of paradise. Workstations were dotted about, most with at least two monitors on. Small clamps were set at regular intervals into a work bench that ran along the far wall. Lining the wall above it were shelves and racks full of gear. The far corner was occupied by a booth with large windows. A silver pipe emerged from its roof into the ceiling and Jon guessed the white door giving access to it would be part of an airlock to ensure the inner area remained free from any contamination. His nostrils were tickled by the smell of iron filings.

Nick and Hugh were standing behind a bald-headed man. He was sitting before a screen, gazing intently at it as his right hand nudged a mouse around.

When he saw Jon approaching, Nick lifted his chin. 'How goes it?'

'Not a lot, so far.'

'Black cabs got back to Hugh.'

The other officer didn't take his eyes from the screen. 'No one picked up a solitary male with obvious injuries from the area.'

Jon clicked his fingers. 'Oh well, worth a try.'

'Oh,' Nick said. 'The car with false number plates? The chassis number came back from DVLA; it matches a car that was stolen from Leeds over a week ago.'

'Leeds?' Jon said. That suggested a degree of organisation and pre-planning. The humming noise coming from the screen lifted in pitch. 'This footage from the drone?'

'Yup,' Nick replied. 'Carl here got us in. It's just been trees and fields so far, like they're practising.'

Jon watched as the camera's view gradually lifted. It cleared the tree in the foreground and empty countryside opened up. Now the view rotated round. Distant buildings. A string of pylons and, beyond them, a spire. The image tilted and the horizon appeared. Next came clouds, then only blue. Several seconds passed as wind buffeted the device's microphone. Then clouds reappeared, followed by another glimpse of horizon. Momentarily visible on it was a faint mass of thin chimneys. Jon pointed. 'That was...can you pause and go back? Just to where we could see the horizon.'

'Sure,' Carl answered. The footage went into a jerky rewind.

'There,' Jon said, a forefinger directed at the screen. 'Isn't that Stanlow Oil Refinery?'

Nick craned his neck. 'Good spot. Hugh? What do you reckon?'

The other detective had crossed his arms. 'Maybe.'

Jon opened his mouth to ask what he was on about. There was no maybe about it. He cleared his throat instead. 'You pass it as you go along the M56_towards North Wales.'

'Which would make sense,' Nick stated. 'The RTA was on the M60 just where the M56 rejoins it. I think you could well be right.'

Noticing Hugh Lambert's lack of response, Jon kept quiet.

'Let's continue,' Nick said.

The footage resumed, camera tilting down at one point to reveal a nearby stretch of dual motorway.

'Looks like the M56 to me,' Carl stated.

The device descended quite quickly, the sky slowly shrinking to a thin band at the top of the picture. Soon, it had been pushed completely out as fields filled the screen. Jon remembered reading an article written by a sky diver whose parachute had failed to open. It was this gradual replacement of sky by land that had registered most in his mind as he had fallen. Eventually, all he could see was green, rushing closer and closer and...he'd woken up in hospital, arms and legs in plaster, tubes all over the place. A fir tree had saved him: he'd connected with its tip and then ricocheted down through the branches.

The camera was now at house height, and dropping all the time. A voice spoke, faint and muffled. The drone bumped down and a mesh of out-of-focus grass filled the screen.

'Is OK?' The words were spoken by a male, his accent heavy.

'Yes,' another man replied. 'Not as difficult as I thought it would be. I press here? To turn it off...' A blob of pink smothered the view. Part of a hand? The image cut.

'How much more footage to go?' Nick asked.

Carl tipped his head to the side. 'Another thirty-five minutes.'

'May as well make ourselves comfortable, then.' Nick pulled up a chair and Hugh followed suit.

'Mind if I bob down to the main office?' Jon asked. 'I wouldn't mind getting on the system. See if anything's showing on the overnight log for Gatley and the surrounding area.'

Nick glanced up. 'You're thinking of the man who fled?'

'Yes.'

'Go for it.' He pointed at the two evidence bags besides Carl's elbow. 'We've got the phone and camcorder to go, yet.'

Jon stepped back then paused. 'Er...have I got a desk?'

Nick sighed. 'Desk? Desk? Is there no end to your demands?' He grinned. 'Fair point, mate. Main ops room, far left hand side. Yours is about half-way down.'

'It's easy to spot,' Hugh added with a smirk. 'It's the one covered by everyone else's crap.'

Figures, Jon thought, heading for the door.

The main ops room had three rows of desks running down it. Unlike the Major Incident Team, which was divided into teams known as syndicates, the Counter Terrorism Unit operated to what was known as the silo approach. Each officer could work independently or as part of a loose group brought together according to the skill-set required for that particular operation. If the operation demanded it, the entire branch could be involved. The system allowed small jobs to run alongside larger ones, so keeping every officer busy.

As Jon stepped through the doors, he noticed a couple of photocopying machines to his left. Next to them were metal cabinets stacked with reams of printer paper.

Less than half the desks were occupied. Sitting at some were detectives in plain clothes, sitting at others were uniformed officers. All were quietly working. Jon made straight for the left side of the room. That'll be it, he thought, spotting a desk that was home to an assortment of folders, old print-outs and discarded vending machine cups. He quickly cleared a space in front of the computer, sat down and turned the computer on. As it booted up, he fiddled around with the seat's controls, trying to find the lever that controlled its height.

A voice behind him spoke: 'On the left. Next to where the backrest connects.'

He glanced round. A young bloke in chinos and a pale blue shirt was pointing at the chair.

'Cheers,' said Jon. He lowered the seat to a height that allowed him to get his knees beneath the desk. Then he spun the chair round and held a hand out. 'Jon Spicer.'

'Peter Collier, civilian support.'

They shook hands and Jon turned back to the computer while speaking over his shoulder. 'What do they keep you busy with, Peter?'

'I'll help anyone out on this row of desks, if they need it. Internal enquiries, file retrieval, checks on the system, any bits and pieces like that. Mine's the end desk, by the photocopiers.'

Jon glanced over his shoulder. 'A useful person to keep on side, then.'

The younger man grinned, obviously glad to feel appreciated. 'Feel free to give me a shout.'

Jon guessed he had just turned twenty. Short haircut, smooth skin and enthusiasm radiating off him. Here's me, he thought, old enough to be his dad. 'Tell you what, Peter. Can you check for any cars reported as stolen last night? Early hours of the morning – after half-three, from an area, say, one kilometre in diameter from junction three of the M60. Start south of the motorway around Gatley, then look north of it around Didsbury. That OK?'

'Definitely,' he said, hand brushing nervously at his lips. 'by the way, Sir – '

Jon flicked a hand. 'No need for sir. Jon's fine.'

'OK. I just wanted to say...' Redness was spreading across his cheeks. 'What you did over in Ireland? I think that was...' He clenched a fist and held it up. 'It took guts.'

Now Jon felt his cheeks grow warm. 'Cheers.' The other man quickly retreated and Jon stared at the computer screen. It was obviously common knowledge throughout the CTU. The upper part of his left ear – or what remained of it – tingled as it always did when he was embarrassed. His mind flashed back to the car park by the pony auction place. When they'd ripped it away with a pair of pliers, his face had been pressed into tarmac that was strewn with straw and dung. He glanced in the civilian support worker's direction. If you'd seen the state of me after that beating, he thought, you wouldn't think I was so tough.

He opened up the PNC and checked on the Missing Persons list for the Greater Manchester Area. He wasn't sure what he was expecting to find, but the man had got away from the vicinity of the car crash somehow – and it hadn't been by public transport. Nothing weird reported around Gatley. Next he tried Greater Manchester division's incident log. He knew the boundary separating the division of South Manchester from Stockport ran right through the area he was interested in, so he checked both logs for any car-jackings or other unusual reports. Nothing again. Maybe the guy had walked it – in which case, roadside CCTV was going to be the best option. And, from previous experience, he knew trawling it was mind numbingly slow, very costly and probably wouldn't be approved – unless evidence emerged that the two men were up to something serious.

Hearing movement, he looked back to see DI Grant striding towards him, a grin on his face. 'More from the drone footage!'

CHAPTER 9

'Yeah?' Jon rose to his feet.

'Where's Collier?' Nick asked, slapping a piece of paper down on the desk.

'Not sure.' Jon glanced about. 'He was just here.'

'No matter,' Nick replied. 'They managed to film themselves – one of them, anyway. Here's a still.'

Jon looked at the image. It was out-of-focus, but he could make out a man with thick, wavy black hair. Judging by the jowls and double-chin, Jon guessed he was about fifty. Maybe older. His bushy eyebrows were tilted; the expression on his face was tentative, as if by even touching the drone he might damage it. 'Nice selfie,' Jon stated matter-of-factly.

Nick snorted. 'Reckon it's the one who did a runner?'

'No – too old. And his hair's not short enough.'

'So it's the fatality, then.'

'Looks like it.'

'Hugh's sifting through the remaining footage. In the meantime, we need this copied and circulated...' He looked about for their support worker.

'Leave it with me,' Jon said, lifting the sheet of paper up.

'You sure?'

'Yeah, it's no problem.'

'OK, thanks. I need to nip upstairs and bring the branch manager up-to-date. If this thing merits further work, it'll be to focus on this.' He rubbed a thumb and forefinger together. 'Whatever this pair were up to, they needed money to be doing it. Someone, somewhere has put up the funds.'

Follow the money, Jon thought. The trusted technique for any investigator. Nick set off across the room and Jon approached the photocopiers. They were a damn sight more modern than the ones he was used to. Everything's shiny, he thought, in the CTU. The bloody thing didn't even have buttons: just a touch screen. He squinted at the menu, trying to work out where, among the complex mix of symbols, was the one he needed to just do a few copies. Was that, he asked himself despairingly, too much to ask?

Someone came through the doors and he looked to his side, hoping to see Peter Collier. But it was the really short girl with the bright blue eyes. The one who'd been smearing brown crap into a detective's hair.

'Stuck?' she asked.

He flapped a hand over the screen. 'No green button. What was wrong with a green button?'

She smiled. 'Just stick it in the slot on the top. How many copies do you need?'

'Twenty should do,' he replied, thankfully stepping aside. How tall, he wondered, is she? The top of her head was about level with his elbow. He watched her slender finger as it made contact with the glass; the machine beeped in response, as if appreciating the deftness of her touch. It began to whirr and the sheet he'd placed in the top slot was sucked out of sight.

Jon put his hands in his pockets. 'You're not just an expert with the eyeliner, then?' He glanced down at her, quite pleased with his turn of phrase.

She gave him a questioning look.

'Before – you were putting make-up on two detectives. Do you help out in here, too?'

'Kind of,' she said, looking back at the machine.

Jon hesitated. Had he trodden on her toes? Her reply had been a bit short. 'So how many of you are there in civilian support?'

She bowed her head for a second then turned fully to him and held out a hand. 'We've not been introduced. Detective Constable Iona Khan.'

Detect – ? Jon felt the floor shift. Oh my God, Spicer, you have just made such a tit of yourself. 'When I saw you out...I assumed, you know, that...' Her hand was still out. It was like a child's. He made sure to grasp it lightly and was surprised by the strength of her shake. 'I'm sorry. I feel like a right twat...I mean idiot.' He knew he was bright red.

She hunched a shoulder. 'At least you didn't mistake me for a cleaner.'

He searched desperately for something else to say. But every comment he came up with would just make the hole deeper. Glaciers could have formed by the time the machine came to a stop. At bloody last, he thought.

'They all get spat out here.' She reached to the side of the machine and took the sheets out from a tray. Glancing at the top one, she shot him a look.

Jon's hand was outstretched. All he wanted to do was grab them, say his thanks and scuttle back to his seat.

'Who's this?' she asked.

'Not sure, yet. It's a still from some drone footage. Why?'

She handed him the sheets, took out her phone and brought up an image. Her glance went from her screen to the sheets and back again. 'What do you reckon?'

Acutely aware how much he towered over the other detective, Jon moved back a fraction. 'About what?'

She held her phone up so he could see the display. A man's pudgy face filled the screen. Wavy black hair, heavy eyebrows, somewhere around fifty. He looked at the photocopies in his hands. Same bloke.

He came to with a start. A woman's face was almost above him. Her mouth was covered by tape. Wide, terrified eyes stared down at him. He blinked, utterly confused. Who was she? Where was he? He turned his head. A bedroom. I'm lying on a big soft bed. There was a roll of silver insulation tape in his hand. The same type of tape covering her mouth. I've been asleep, he realised.

It made him angry to realise the woman had been watching him while he had slept. While he'd been vulnerable. He wanted to shove his palm into her face, to forcibly avert her gaze. He tried to sit up. A grinding in his left shoulder made him fall back with a gasp of pain. She looked away, breath starting to speed up. Who was she?

Slowly and carefully, he raised himself into a sitting position. He had to cup his left elbow with his right hand. Every movement made him want to yell. What time was it?

With his right hand, he reached down to just above his ankle. He realised he was wearing trousers. Denim jeans, dark blue. His fingers traced the outline of his knife, safe in the neoprene sheath that hugged his shin. He got to his feet and waited for waves of dizziness to pass. He looked at the woman. A little yellow jacket, black boots and a short skirt. He could see her legs, right up to her thighs. Tight loops of tape attached her hands to the chair. More of it had been wound about her ankles. The edges of her nostrils were rapidly flexing and she'd squeezed her eyes shut. I must have done this to her, he thought. Why?

He checked the tape was secure then shuffled from the bedroom. A short corridor. A room at the end. Cautiously, he looked through the doorway to see if anyone was in there. Empty. He stepped carefully into the room. There was a mirror on the wall. He saw himself in the mirror and his eyes widened in shock: his hair was cut short and his beard was gone. There was a large bump above his right eye. Some minor cuts across his forehead and right cheek.

He was wearing an orange top with three buttons at the collar. He stepped closer to the mirror. Small words on the top said Lacoste. Who had bought him this top? These jeans? On the wall above the mirror was a clock. Both hands were pointing upwards. Beyond the net curtains it was daylight. Almost noon, then. He stood in the middle of the room and willed his memory to work.

It was obvious he was in a different country. Where he was from, no woman dressed like the one in the other room. Which country? It was cold. The room had a gas fire. There were shelves, but they were all empty. In the corner was a television and below it an Xbox. The packaging for the machine lay in the corner. He knew, somehow, he had thrown the packaging there and plugged the Xbox in to the television.

Where, he wondered, is my phone? As he looked around, a dim image flickered in his mind. A trainer, the heel of it crushing a mobile against tarmac. He looked at his feet; he was wearing the same type of trainer. He closed his eyes and glimpsed his own hands prising the phone's casing apart. A SIM card was snapped in two then thrown away. It disappeared in long grass. He'd thrown the pieces of his phone further down the slope. I destroyed my phone. Why did I destroy my phone? What happened?

The window looked out on to a street. The kind of street you got in a city. On the far side of it was a grocery store. It looked similar to the kind from back home. Even the name: Mega-Mart. Where am I?

A car went past and he glimpsed a sticker on its rear. GB. Great Britain. I'm in Britain. The realisation released a mass of memories. They flooded his mind, chaotic and unordered. A sliver of sky, viewed upwards from the floor of the lorry carrying boxes of peppers. Red, yellow, green. Arriving by ferry in a place called Hull. Seagulls, large as eagles. Their shrieks jabbing down from the grey sky. He saw a wide road. The green Honda waiting for him at a place where lorries parked. He had never seen so many lorries.

Where was the man called Bilal, the one who had been in the green Honda? The one who was helping him? He could recall another stretch of coast. Driving to it had taken some time. A drone: he had been teaching Bilal how to fly a drone. Abruptly, he knew why he had come to this country.

The realisation of what he'd been sent to do caused his heart to pound.

He breathed deeply and tried to calm himself. Think! Night time. Travelling fast, in the dark. A line of little mirrors set into the middle of the road. They were the eyes of cats, Bilal had said. It was a good name. Then…then…nothing.

One of the cars outside caught his eye. It was bright red. It seemed familiar. Did I drive that car? He couldn't have: his shoulder was too painful. He could barely lift his arm. Did the woman own the car? The one in the bedroom? He thought that could be right. He had been in it; he was able to remember the smell of its leather seats. He concentrated on the memory of that smell and another image briefly emerged. Sitting behind the driver's seat with his forearm across the woman's throat.

She knows, he thought. She knows what happened to me.

CHAPTER 10

Jon gulped down the last of his sandwich and stuffed the balled-up wrapper into one of the empty vending machine cups taking up the end of his desk. Should tidy that lot up when I get a minute, he thought, following Nick and Hugh into a meeting room.

The detective inspector took the seat at the end of the table. 'OK everyone, sit down anywhere. This won't take long. First up, this is DC Jon Spicer. As one of the new intake of SFOs, he's responsible for knackering all that overtime you've been enjoying of late.'

Jon acknowledged the good-natured dig by inclining his head: recent austerity measures by the government had drastically reduced the number of Specialist Firearms Officers nationwide. Then the Home Office had decreed the threat from terror attacks warranted a big increase in the number of officers trained to use deadly force. But the government, keen to avoid an embarrassing u-turn, had sat on its hands for a while. The result was that the few SFOs still on the force had been inundated with opportunities for overtime. Jon was among the first batch of new SFOs to have been trained-up, and one of only six selected to bolster the CTU's recently-formed Armed Response Unit.

The detective opposite him leaned back in his chair. 'Good to have you onboard, Jon. Not a moment too soon.'

Heads nodded round the room.

'Right, let's bring you up-to-speed on this,' Nick announced. 'To my right on the wall behind me is a photo of Bilal Atwi, the fatality in the RTA on the M60 in the early hours of this morning. The car Mr Atwi was driving had been stolen from Leeds one week ago and then fitted with false number plates. Also travelling with Atwi was a male occupant who fled the scene. Among other items recovered from the car were the remains of a drone. Now, it could be the two of them are just a couple of minor criminals, travelling in a stolen, using their flying toy to scope out landed properties with a view to burgling them. It happens.'

Jon glanced about: all eyes were on Nick. Everyone in the room knew that wasn't the case.

'However,' the DI continued, 'footage from the drone's camera shows Stanlow Oil Refinery in the background.' Nick's glance stopped briefly on Jon. 'A map also recovered from the crashed car had some handwritten notes in a foreign language.'

'Arabic?' someone asked.

'Actually, no. We're still waiting on what they are. The notes were written at a point on the map that's within two kilometres of Wylfa, the nuclear power station on Anglesey. So we're looking at the possibility they were undertaking reconnaissance for some kind of attack.'

'Who is this Atwi character?' the officer sitting next to Nick asked.

'He appears relatively clean,' Nick answered. 'Of more interest to us is the son, Feiz.' He pointed a thumb at the wall behind him. 'Next to Mr Bilal Atwi is a picture of that son: he recently met his maker out in Syria. Feiz Atwi joined Isis almost three years ago. He was captured by a Syrian group opposing Assad who subjected him to some heavy questioning, as you can see. What Feiz coughed up has sparked a separate operation, called Stinger, that a team reporting to DCI Weir is handling.'

Jon's mind went back to the discovery at the photocopiers. Realising they were dealing with the same individual, he and the female detective had sat down to compare notes. She was undertaking routine background checks. When he asked what they related to, her answer had taken him completely by surprise. A stolen surface-to-air missile in Afghanistan? Jesus...he was looking at nothing more than a nicked car and suspicious behaviour on the M60. He zoned back in to what Nick Grant was saying.

'Weir's team is trying to establish if any links exist back to the wider Atwi family here. Worst-case-scenario is some kind of active terror cell is here in Manchester.'

The detective opposite Jon shifted in his seat. 'I'm never convinced about our Royals doing stints in the armed services. If they limited it to official ceremonies in all the regalia, fine – we wouldn't have a problem. This active duty stuff: it's asking for trouble.'

A crop-haired officer with a mass of tattoos on his forearms sat forward. Definitely ex-armed forces, Jon thought, as the man started to speak with a Welsh accent.

'My old man? He was serving on HMS Invincible during the Falklands war back in the 1980s. Remember that kicking off? Prince Andrew was also serving aboard the Invincible, flying helicopters. Sea Kings. They were all shitting themselves, convinced the Argies would target their ship because it had Royalty on it.'

Nick sat back. 'Seems flying helicopters runs in the family.'

'Queen and Country, isn't it?' Hugh Lambert chipped in. 'Helping out their mum.'

The comment drew a few smiles.

'Anyway, it is what it is,' Nick said. 'Weir's team will continue to question members of the wider family.

Analysis of their phone and internet usage has been prioritised. Us lot? DCI Pinner is overseeing our operation: we'll be taking a much closer look at this car crash. Upstairs are trying to access Mr Atwi's phone along with a camcorder, both recovered from the crash. Drone footage is being studied to establish where it was taken. We will be going over Mr Atwi's business dealings: if there is some kind of terror cell, was he helping to finance it? Last thing is the mystery man who fled the scene. Jon?'

He straightened up. 'Firstly, it appears he's injured his left arm. That's according to the passenger of the interceptor that was first at the scene. The officer helped him to get clear of the wrecked Honda. Our mystery man was badly dazed, probably concussed – but the officer didn't have time to make a proper assessment before he vanished. I've checked taxis and trains in the immediate area: no joy.' He sent a questioning glance at Nick. 'In case he was on foot, I believe CCTV cameras are...'

Nick waved a hand. 'Being taken care of.'

'The only other thing, then – and it's a shot in the dark to be honest – is the chance he was seen passing a nearby location that's being used by working girls. I've been asking around – '

'Oh, yeah?' Hugh Lambert chuckled. 'Questioning them in the back of your car?'

A few of the other officers started to grin.

'Thought he looked flushed when he arrived back earlier,' Lambert laughed.

Jon regarded the other man in silence. Eventually the other officer's eyes made their way back to him. 'What? Just a joke, mate.'

'Right,' Jon replied. 'Hilarious.'

The door opened and Carl, the techie from upstairs, poked his head in. 'Nick, you asked to let you know straightaway if I got anything.'

The DI beckoned. 'What is it?'

'A still from the camcorder: could be the other person from the car.' He edged his way round the table and placed a sheet down before Nick. 'Basically, whoever was filming decided to get a bit of the drone. Mostly, it's close-ups of the thing being readied for take-off. Looks like they're in a field, next to a big chunk of rock with a tortured-looking pine tree beside it. He steps back at one stage and zooms out slightly. Catches the other man's head. Less than two seconds' worth – this is the best image.'

Jon stood up for a clearer look. A leanly-built man was crouching over the drone, head bent forward. He was wearing an orange polo top and his short black hair was being stirred by a light breeze. At a guess, he was thirty. 'Could I see that?'

Nick slid the photo across. 'Does it match the description from the interceptor driver?'

Jon sat back down and studied it for a second. Because the man was leaning forward, most of his face was hidden. But Jon could make out a broad forehead and the bridge of a strong aquiline nose. 'Can't see who else it could be.'

Nick clenched a fist. 'Ace. We need the interceptor driver to see a copy and confirm it, but good stuff. Carl, any luck with the phone?'

'Not as yet.'

'OK, everyone, we'll work out who's doing what. This knocks aside any other stuff you're on for the time being, so get out there and clear your decks.'

As everyone began to get up, the officer with the Welsh accent appeared at Jon's side. 'You been shown the gym, yet?'

Jon had read the facility had something down in the basement. 'No, I heard it's good though.'

'A few of us head down at the end of our shift. It's got a proper boxing ring. You ever done any sparring?'

Jon thought back to his rugby-playing days. Cheadle Ironsides had taken on an Australian coach for a couple of seasons who incorporated punch-bags into the training sessions. Jon remembered the dead weight of his arms after only two minutes of pounding away at the thing. 'A bit.'

'Come along. Let off a bit of steam with the lads. You'll enjoy it.'

'Cheers, I will.'

'Kieran Saunders, by the way.' He held out a hand.

They'd started to shake when Jon's phone started up.

'I'll let you get that.' The other man dropped his hand.

'Right, see you later, cheers.' Jon fished his handset out and looked at the screen. The number wasn't familiar and he was about to press call divert when something told him it was worth taking. 'DI – ' Swiftly, he corrected himself. 'DC Spicer here.'

'It were you before, out Burnage way?'

He knew immediately who it was: the youngest of the three prostitutes he'd spoken to earlier. 'Yeah, it's me.'

'That Julie, she's back. The one I said was working with Kelly last night.'

Jon waved in Nick's direction, then lifted a thumb. 'I remember.'

'Kelly takes them to that mental-place that's shut down. Her.'

'And Julie's there now?'

'Aye. On the corner, next to that school.'

CHAPTER 11

He re-entered the bedroom with the knife in his hand. The fat blade was four inches long, before narrowing suddenly to a cruel point. She saw the weapon and the muscles in her neck bulged, tendons flexing in and out as she strained backwards in the seat.

A fine row of serrations ran along the upper edge of the knife. He looked at her throat, at the ridged cartilage showing beneath her skin. He knew from experience that a rapid sawing motion would open her neck up in a few seconds. First the muscles, then the gristle of the windpipe, swiftly followed by the jugular veins and carotid artery. The hiss and spray that followed.

He placed the knife on the bed and raised a finger to his lips, hoping the gesture was a universal one for quiet. She seemed to understand, judging by how she went still. He removed imaginary tape from his lips then pointed to her mouth. He raised his eyebrows in question.

She nodded.

He stepped closer. Moisture was making her skin glisten and there was a sharp smell coming from her. He half-peeled off the upper layers; that was the easy part. When he reached the layer attached to her skin, it would be different. Her flesh seemed welded to the material's tacky underside. As he pulled harder, the skin stretched like rubber. Tears appeared from her closed eyes.

He yanked sharply and part of the tape came away red with blood. Her head jerked back and she gasped through the bloody corner of her mouth. His hand stayed poised before her face, but she didn't try to scream.

He made a clicking noise with his tongue, as if calling to a dog.

After a few seconds, her eyes opened.

He opened his mouth to speak, then stopped. How to say it in English? He didn't know. 'You.' He pointed to the window and then gripped an imaginary steering wheel. 'You?' He pointed to the floor. 'Yes?'

She stared back at him.

He repeated the actions again. 'You?'

Her head shook and she tried to say something from the side of her mouth.

He couldn't understand the words. He raised and lowered his hands, trying to get her to speak more slowly. Instead, she spoke faster. He heard the word please. She kept saying it.

The only words he knew were things like hello, please and thank you. In school, he had been taught Russian. He also knew just enough Arabic to get by. He tried Russian. 'Chto sluchilos?'

She continued to babble at him, chin now wet with blood.

That only left his native tongue, which was hardly spoken beyond the Caucasian mountains where he grew up.

Her voice was getting louder, more shrill. It was no good. He smoothed the tape back in place, glad to put an end to her noise.

In the front room, he raised a hand to his face and pressed at his temples with a thumb and forefinger. Trying to squeeze his memories free. After a few seconds, he squatted before the Xbox. He could recall the people teaching him how it worked. He could clearly picture the childish game they'd shown him: the brightly-coloured dragons that lived in a mountain-top world, high above the fluffy clouds. There were lots of caves for storing gold coins and other treasure. The dragons flew around and could speak to one another and he knew that was how he was meant to keep in contact. He knew all this but it still did no good. As a means of communication, the game was useless – unless he could remember the words he needed to log on.

CHAPTER 12

As she pulled up outside Furat Atwi's house once again, Iona took a nervous breath in. Why, she asked herself, do I always get these jobs? You know why. Your boss had said as much: women's work. Begrudgingly, she admitted it hardly suited the majority of her colleagues in the CTU.

Her mind jumped back to the giant new detective who'd been trying to photocopy the image of Mr Atwi. On first seeing him enter the departure lounge, she'd sighed inadvertently; another SFO who would be equally at home working the doors of a nightclub. Probably ex-army. An opinion made stronger when he'd shaken hands with the other two detectives while hardly noticing her.

Then she'd found him struggling with the photocopier. At the time, she thought it was lucky he hadn't started trying to press the controls: his bloody great fingers would have probably cracked the touch screen. But he'd been genuinely mortified when she'd revealed she was a fellow officer. Others would have just tried to laugh it off.

'So you're happy to take the lead?' The question had come from the family liaison officer in the passenger seat. A lady with long, dry brown hair and a slightly elongated face.

'She'll be focused on me, so I suppose I'd better actually tell her,' Iona replied. 'Feel free to jump in as soon as I have, though.'

'Of course. However you'd like to play it.'

As they walked up the front path, Iona could see there was someone else in the front room. She knocked three times and stood back. When the door opened she was surprised to see the nurse from Manchester Royal Infirmary's A&E.

'Hello,' Iona said. 'Elissa, isn't it?'

'Yes, hi there.'

Furat Atwi appeared behind her in the corridor. Dread and hope seemed to be pulling her features in opposite directions. Her mouth wouldn't move properly and her words came out slightly slurred. 'Have you found Bilal?'

Iona gave a non-committal nod. 'May we come inside?' Her eyes caught on the nurse's. You've guessed, she thought. You know what's coming.

They filed into the front room, no one speaking.

Iona glanced at Furat. You poor woman, she thought. Your husband and your son: both gone. She knew it was best to get straight to the point. As they all sat, she thought it was good the niece who worked as a nurse was also present – she'd have plenty of experience dealing with emotional trauma. 'Mrs Atwi, there was an accident on the M60 in the early hours of this morning. One person died at the scene and I'm so sorry, but we believe that person was your husband, Bilal.'

Furat stared back in silence.

Iona's eyes flicked down and she saw the woman's fingers were tightly gripping those of her niece.

'Why?' Mrs Atwi whispered.

Iona didn't understand the question. She glanced at the FLO for help.

'Why are we sure,' the FLO prompted gently.

'You don't know, not for certain,' Furat suddenly announced. 'So don't come here, into my house, and tell me that my husband is...' Her voice was wobbling, cracked notes forcing their way in. 'You can't! You don't know!'

'When I was here earlier, I took a photo,' Iona replied. 'We were able to compare that...'

The woman started to swallow back air, face now white. Her lips trembled. 'This...no...it can't...'

'Aunty Furat,' Elissa began to rub the woman's hands. 'Aunty Furat?'

Iona needed to be out of the room. She got to her feet. 'I'll fetch a glass of water.' As she walked softly down the corridor a low wail began to gather strength. By the time she'd reached the kitchen, it was a howl.

Her own fingers trembled as she turned on the tap. She looked around. To her side was a shelving unit lined with glasses. She had half-filled one when the nurse appeared next to her.

'You're sure it's him? Uncle Bilal?'

Iona nodded. 'I'm so sorry, Elissa. Were you close?'

'Oh my God, she won't be able to handle this.' She took the glass from her hands and left the room.

Iona ran her fingers through her hair and then followed her. The FLO was now beside Furat on the sofa. The stricken woman was leaning back, legs out straight, arms limp at her sides. She continued to draw in great ragged breaths as the FLO murmured quietly.

'Aunty Furat?' Elissa asked. 'I have some water for you.'

She closed her eyes and shook her head.

The FLO nodded at the low table and Elissa put the glass on it without a word.

Iona moved back to the doorway and signalled to Elissa. The two of them returned to the kitchen.

Iona closed the door behind them. 'Elissa, there are some things about the accident that are odd. I'm afraid it's raised some questions...ones for the police.'

Elissa looked in the direction of the front room. 'You don't mean you're going to try and – '

'No – nothing will be asked of your Aunt. Not while she's so upset. How well did you know her husband?'

'He's part of the family. Why?'

'Were you close?'

'No, not especially. He's old fashioned. Women and men – there should be a distance.'

'So how often did you speak to him?'

'Very rarely – family gatherings. What was odd? I don't understand.'

'Do you think he was hiding anything? Perhaps to do with his business?'

Elissa crossed her arms. 'I don't understand why you're asking – '

'The car he was in, the one that crashed: it wasn't his Mercedes. It was a different car.'

'Where's his Mercedes?'

'We don't know, as yet. However, the car from last night was being driven by your uncle, even though we have reason to believe it wasn't his.'

Elissa looked confused. 'Really? Aunty Furat said he was on business.'

'Did he sometimes go on business trips with other people?'

'I wouldn't know. I doubt it. Was he not alone, then?'

Iona thought how to frame her reply. 'He was the only fatality at the scene.'

'He wasn't with a woman, was he?' Elissa whispered. 'Please tell me this wasn't some kind of...he wasn't cheating on Aunty Furat?'

Iona shook her head. 'No woman was with him.'

Elissa frowned again. 'I can't understand what he was doing, if he wasn't in his Mercedes.'

'Did your aunt ask you to come here?'

'Sorry?'

'Your Aunt, did she ask you round?'

'Yes, she rang me. After your earlier visit, she started worrying. I thought she would be calling about the video of Feiz. But she told me Bilal had gone missing so I came round as fast as I could.' She gestured at the door. 'Can't these questions wait?'

'Yes. Of course they can. And I've mentioned nothing about her son. I don't think that should be mentioned at this point.'

Elissa nodded her agreement.

'The FLO can go with your Aunt for the formal identification and stay with her for as long as she needs.' She paused. 'Are you OK, Elissa?'

'What, me? Yes.'

'OK. I need to go, but I wanted your aunt to be aware, myself – or a colleague – will need to speak with her soon.'

CHAPTER 13

'Is it Julie?'

The girl turned and looked Jon up and down. 'Amy said you'd want a word.'

Jon glanced along the leafy street. All the other girls were gone. Julie looked like someone just coming off a night shift: desperately tired. Some habit you've got to feed, he thought, noticing the long-sleeved top that covered her forearms. 'Amy finished for the day?'

'That or she's got a job on. You wanted to know about Kelly?'

'I do. Basically, if she was stood here with you around four in the morning last night. And if she wasn't, where she might have been.'

'She wasn't with me. Not around then. I tipped-up at just gone three. We were chatting for a bit. Half an hour, easily. Yeah, then this big car – hang on – '

She twisted her face into a smile then stepped nearer the kerb as a vehicle being driven by a man approached. It slowed down momentarily, but then carried on past.

'Fuck. That's you, that is. No-one'll stop while you're standing – '

Jon had taken his wallet out. He peeled off three tens. 'That do? One minute, then I'm gone.'

She took the money. 'Big car. Red: one of those posh four-wheel drive things. Looked brand new. I know the make, just can't think. Anyway, it cruised by a couple of times before stopping. Must have been nearly four when she went off in it.'

'And you've not seen her since?'

She stared at Jon for a second then shook her head. 'This is about that motorway smash, yeah? In case she saw something to do with that? You're not covering up something to do with Kelly? Something bad?'

'No, I'm not covering up anything. You say this car was big. Like a Range Rover?'

'No. Smaller than those things. One of those curvier ones.'

'You mean less bulky than a Range Rover?'

'Yeah, faster-looking.'

That ruled out a Volvo, BMW or Audi, then. Something more sporty. 'Maybe a Porsche Cayenne?'

'That's it! Porsche. Dead expensive.'

'What about the registration? Or driver? Get a look at him?'

'Windows were smoky. Or it was dark inside. He whistled her over.'

'And that was that? She jumped in and off they went?'

'Yeah.'

'Which way?'

'That way.' She tipped her head to the left. 'She would have taken him to that spot near the hospital. Always does, if they don't have somewhere of their own.'

'OK, cheers. Don't suppose you have any way of contacting her?'

'No. Just chat with her round here and that's it.'

'What was she wearing last night?'

'Yellow jacket. Black boots and skirt.'

'Right. Did Amy give you my card with the phone number on?'

She patted her thigh. 'Got it.'

'When you next see her, get her to call me, could you? Another thirty for you, if she does.'

'Yeah, sure. Like you'd come back to pay me.'

'I would, actually. That's a promise.'

She met his eyes for a second then shrugged. 'OK.'

'Cheers.' Back in his car, he called base and asked for Peter Collier. 'Any joy on cars stolen around Gatley?'

'I've literally just come off the system. Nothing in the time-frame you gave me, I'm afraid.'

'You're sat at a box now?'

'Yes.'

'Just go back on the system, would you? Have a look for anything involving a red Porsche Cayenne, recent model.'

'No problem. Shall I call you back?'

Jon didn't want anything else the civilian support worker had to deal with getting in the way. 'I'll stay on the line, thanks.'

'OK. Hang on.'

Jon sat back. Further up the road, he could see Julie's stick-thin frame lurking between the trees. All alone in the woods, he thought. What a life.

'Jon? It's Peter. One Porsche Cayenne, described by the owner as Flame Red, was reported as stolen from the city centre last night.'

'Really?' He reached for his pen. 'Where from?'

'Outside the casino by the Printworks. He said he'd parked it at ten, but it was gone on his return at five o'clock.'

Jon winced. Could the person who stole it then have gone cruising for prostitutes? Stranger things went on in Manchester on a Friday night. 'Have you got the owner's name and address?'

'Right here. You might recognise the name.'

'Why's that?'

'He plays up front for Bolton United.'

'Football?' Jon made a face. 'I couldn't name you more than two players in England's team, let alone Bolton's. Which division are they in?'

'Jesus, you really don't have a clue. Promoted to the Premiership last year. You honestly didn't know that?'

Jon was used to the confusion his lack of football knowledge caused. With Manchester City, Manchester United, Liverpool, Everton and Blackburn all so close, football was a failsafe source of conversation for most in the region. 'Rugby, mate. That's my sport.'

'Ah – you prefer just punching the other team.'

Jon studied the assortment of bumps and grooves in the skin of his knuckles. Mementos from his playing days. 'There's a bit more to it than that. We also kick, gouge and head-butt.'

The other man laughed.

'Where's he living, then?'

'Out in Lymm.'

Very nice, Jon thought. He'd played a few good matches against Lymm RUFC in his time. The place was out in rural Cheshire and rather pricey. 'Bloody footballers; they're paid far too much.'

'The house is called Pine Lodge,' Collier replied. 'I get the feeling it isn't small.'

'No, me neither. And what's he called, this footballer?'

'Wilfred Iwobi.'

Jon glanced up. The only customer who'd gone into the minicab place in Gatley at around four-thirty in the morning had been described as black. 'African is he?'

'Nigerian, yes.'

'Interesting.' Jon started his engine.

CHAPTER 14

Elissa stood in the front room of her flat with tears running down her cheeks. Her chin lifted with a brief in-draw of breath before another sob racked her ribs. She let it die away in its own time. With the back of her hand, she wiped at her eyes. She sniffed loudly. Come on, stop this. Be strong.

The hold-all on the coffee table was fully unzipped, contents exposed. A wash bag, rammed with items. A couple of sets of clothes; practical stuff. Jeans, a hooded fleece, t-shirts, a sweatshirt, a rainproof top. Loads of socks and underwear. Lying on the items were two framed photos. Her eyes welled up as she reached down and took them out. She turned and carefully placed them back on a shelf, outstretched fingers trailing uncertainly as her hands lowered.

The CDs on the next shelf caught her eye and she bent forward to survey them with affection. Memories of certain songs, points in her life that withstood the flow of time. Several books were lined up next to them and first her gaze, then her fingertips, caressed them. Never Let Me Go. The Curious Incident of the Dog in the Night-time. A

Life of Pi. Of Mice and Men. Her smile grew wider. Why've I kept a GCSE text?

She straightened up and moved towards a cabinet. The Naff Nick Nacks was what they'd called it. Her and her brother Tarek. She grinned at the twee ornaments gathered over the years from family holidays in seaside towns along Britain's coast. A pair of pink grinning pigs. A porcelain thatched cottage. A thimble with a picture of a windmill. A pepper pot with an outline of a crab and the word Cromer. It had started out as a childhood joke between her and her brother. The collection numbered seventeen. Seventeen summer holidays spent together, as a family.

There was no object for the previous summer.

A thought struck and, repeating the holiday routine her brother had so carefully maintained, she turned the TV and DVD player off at the mains. In the kitchen, she did the same with all the appliances. The fridge and freezer she left on, unwilling to let perfectly good food go to waste. She wondered what would happen to it.

She studied the spider-plant on the windowsill. The thing had lasted years; first in her room at nursing college, then at her parents' and now here. She tried not to think of its green leaves turning dry and yellow.

Back in the front room, she breathed deeply. She felt her pockets: over eight-hundred pounds. All the cash she had in the flat. She reached down for the hold-all's zip, but stopped half-way through closing it. Quickly, almost guiltily, she retrieved the two photos and placed them back inside the bag. One was of her brother, sitting on a see-saw, legs outstretched, mouth wide with laughter. The other was of her mum and dad, walking on a beach, arms interlinked, sunlight dappling the sands of Scarborough beach behind them. It's for you, she told herself. I'm doing this for you.

The walk took her less than ten minutes. Uncle Bilal had never actually said it was the address he'd be using, but a recent throw-away comment about council rates he'd made allowed her to guess he still owned the anonymous ground-floor flat.

On the way, she stopped at a small park, sat on a bench in the corner and took the back off her mobile phone. The SIM card was dropped down a drain, the phone itself tossed into the brown water of a deserted boating lake.

He'd bought the flat years ago as an investment, had even offered to rent it to her when she first qualified as a nurse. But, by then, she'd agreed to share with her brother. That had been fortunate as it saved her from admitting to Uncle Bilal that she really didn't want to live on a run-down street in Longsight. By now, she guessed, he would have changed the deeds so his name didn't feature. And taken what other measures were needed to ensure it couldn't be connected to him.

The holdall was making her right arm ache as she walked slowly along the road. Looking about, she saw the neighbourhood bore all the hallmarks of a low income area. Independent shops with cheaply-produced signage. Faded colours and dated fonts.

Paradise Phone. Fax / photocopy / mobile accessories / phones unlocked.

Ismail Hair Salon.

Nafees & Sons, specialists in sarees and dress fabrics.

Kwality Shoes.

Aleezy Fried Chicken.

A to Z Convenience Store.

Glasses 4 Less – opticians.

K.W. Fashions. Bridal Wear, Loose Garments and Shalwar Kameez.

At first, she wasn't sure if she'd got the right number. What was a bright red Porsche Cayenne doing on the drive? Maybe, the people who owned the flat above had parked it there. Or someone nearby, taking advantage of a driveway that was never used and a flat that seemed unoccupied. All the curtains were drawn.

She carried on, checking right to the end of the road for Uncle Bilal's Mercedes. It wasn't there. Wherever he'd left the vehicle, it was a safe distance from the flat. She walked back, this time turning up the short drive. She took the folded-up piece of paper from her pocket. As she lifted the flap of the letterbox it made a creaking noise. She resisted the temptation to crouch down and peep through.

Instead, she fed the paper into the opening. Before it was fully through, she lowered the flap, trapping the paper. Its corner poked out, starkly white against the tarnished metal.

She knocked softly and waited. As she expected, there was no reply. Turning an ear to the door, she closed her eyes. Was that movement? She couldn't tell. But then she heard a faint rasp and opened her eyes. The tiny triangle had gone. She counted to thirty then knocked again, even more softly.

There was a series of metallic clicks as the lock slowly released. Her pulse surged as the door opened a few inches. The corridor beyond was unlit. Nothing in the slice of darkness moved. Behind her, the silence of the street pressed at her back. She heard a car's engine. The vehicle passed by, noise fading. She cleared her throat and was about to say something when the door opened wider. A hand and forearm emerged and, for an awkward moment, she thought he wanted to shake hands. Strong fingers locked on her wrist and she allowed herself to be yanked into the shadows beyond.

CHAPTER 15

Jon halted at the set of closed gates. They were wooden and six feet high. Mounted on the right-hand post was a camera. A small placard on the immaculate grass verge read, Pine Lodge. Sure enough, towering above the perimeter wall were the branches of several pine trees.

He lowered his window and reached out to press the buzzer. A good thirty seconds passed before a voice spoke. 'Yes?'

Sing-song intonation somehow sweetened the word.

'Jon Spicer, Greater Manchester Police.' He raised his badge in the direction of the camera. 'I have some news about your stolen Porsche, sir.'

'You have found it?'

'It would be best to come in and tell you.'

'Yes, of course. Sorry.'

A whirring noise started and both gates started to swing in, gradually revealing a short drive of grey paving blocks, well-tended lawns, several rose bushes and a large pond. The drive led to a turning circle before the property itself. What did they call this style of house? Jon asked himself. Stockbroker chic or something?

Front steps led up to more of a portico than a porch. Roman pillars supported its overhanging roof. Mullioned windows. The building was attempting an old-world grandness, but the materials were all brand new. It just didn't work. Not the balcony above the front door, not the elaborate chimneys, not the oversized oak front door with enormous brass ring.

He let it fall against the wood and the echo of a pleasingly solid thud filled the hallway on the other side. No need to do that more than once, he thought. The slap of footsteps soon got closer and the door was opened by a tall, slender black man in a sweat-top and tracksuit bottoms. He was in bare feet. Looking up, Jon detected a hint of anxiety in his smile.

'Mr Wilfred Iwobi?' Jon extended a hand.

The man hesitated for an instant then lifted his own hand. Jon felt uncertainty in his grip. Definitely nervous. Which would figure, Jon thought: when he'd rung VIP Cabs in Gatley, the driver had said his passenger from the previous night had asked to be dropped at a bus stop about half a mile up the road from Pine Lodge. 'May I come in?'

'Yes, please. This way.'

As they crossed a smooth, marble floor to a side room, Jon said, 'Nice place you have here.'

Wilfred flicked the fingers of his hands. 'It is too big, but I didn't know this when I first came. My agent: he found it for me.'

'How many bedrooms does it have?'

'Six, but it is just me here.'

They had entered a lounge of some sort; a pair of cream leather sofas, beige carpets, fresh lilies in a huge silver vase. The place looked like a show home. Wilfred shifted a set of controls to the arm of the sofa and sat down. Jon noticed the flat screen TV set into the wall above the fireplace. The frozen image was of a race track viewed through the windscreen of a vehicle. Before it were several high-performance cars: an Aston Martin, a couple of Ferraris, what looked like a Bugatti.

The hearth was filled by a carefully-arranged pile of fir cones, some sprayed silver, some purple, some their natural colour. Jon could imagine the estate agent's patter: continuing the pine motif from exterior to interior, so creating a relaxing sense of unity and blah-de-blah.

Wilfred gestured at the other sofa. 'So, you know where my car is?'

'Not exactly, sir.' Jon produced a notepad and pen. As he sat, the leather felt cool through his trousers. 'But there has been a sighting. You reported it as stolen from outside Belugio's, by the Printworks, between ten in the evening and five in the morning?'

'That is correct.'

Jon lifted his eyebrows and smiled. 'Much luck?'

The man looked confused. 'Luck?'

'On the tables. Did you come out on top?'

'Oh.' The man tilted his head. 'A little bit, yes.'

'Good stuff. Not many do.'

'No, not many.'

'So, you left at five, only to find the vehicle wasn't there?'

'Yes.'

Jon pretended to jot something down. 'Do you still have the keys?'

'The keys?' White flashed at the corners of his eyes as he looked momentarily away. 'No.'

'Where do you normally keep them: jacket, trousers?'

'Trousers. Maybe they were stolen from me in Belugio's?'

'In which case, the casino should be alerted. CCTV in those places is exceptional. I imagine they could pinpoint the exact moment you were pick-pocketed.'

'Really?' He didn't look overjoyed at the news.

'How did you get home, sir?'

'Pardon?'

'When you discovered your vehicle was missing, how did you get home?'

'Oh, a black taxi.'

'One you flagged down?'

'Yes.'

'And you were home by, what, six? A bit before?'

'A bit before, yes. Maybe twenty to six.'

Jon sat back. 'Sir, I should warn you now, lying to the police and falsifying a stolen vehicle report is a serious matter. Would you like to tell me the truth?'

'The truth?' He frowned. 'That is it what I am doing – telling you the truth!'

'No, sir, that's not what you're doing. How about I tear this page out and we start again?'

'I don't know what you are talking about. You came here with news about my car, but now – now this.' He jabbed a finger at Jon's notebook.

'Sir, you claimed your car had been stolen. Whether you like it or not, by making that report, you've started a process.'

He gritted his teeth and waved both hands at Jon. 'Pfeesh! Go! Get out! I am not talking to you anymore.' He reached for the controls. The action unfroze and the roar of an engine filled the room.

Jon glanced at the massive screen. Normally, he thought, I'd just turn the thing off, but he had no idea where the bloody thing's power button would be. Instead, he got up, stepped over to the skirting board and pulled the mass of plugs from the wall. The screen abruptly died.

'What the hell are you doing?' Wilfred's mouth was open. He looked left and right, as if seeking support from imaginary witnesses. 'This is un-fucking-believable!'

The swear word came out with a hint of Mancunian and Jon had to hide his grin as he sat back down. He thinks I'm a bloody football referee. 'A car from VIP Cabs in Gatley dropped you at a bus stop about half a mile from here at four-fifty-two this morning. Now, I can retrieve all the CCTV from Belugio's and find out when you really left that place, if you were there at all. Obviously, things will start to become a lot more formal if I have to do that.'

'I will call my agent. He...he will come. You must speak to him, not me.'

'Wilfred, this isn't something your agent can fix. This is a criminal matter. If you want your agent, fine, tell him to meet you at the police station on Plymouth Grove in Manchester. Or...' Jon tore the blank page from his notepad, folded it over and put it in his jacket pocket. He lifted his pen and looked at the other man.

Wilfred sat forward, head dipping for a few seconds. He looked up. 'A man attacked me and stole my car.'

'A man? Where was this?'

'I do not know, exactly. Near to the motorway.'

Now Jon did start taking notes. 'The M60?'

'Yes.'

'When?'

'About four o'clock in the morning.'

Christ, thought Jon. It was a carjack. That's how he got away. 'I take it you were stationary at the time? Your car wasn't moving?'

'Yes – I had parked. It was in a little turning.' He licked his lips. 'I was listening to some music.'

Course you were, Jon thought. At least you're not trying to claim you were just walking your dog. 'Mr Iwobi, I have reason to believe you weren't alone. That's not a problem, but it is important. Do you understand? Whoever was with you in the car, that's not something that needs to go any further than us.' He looked at Wilfred and saw the shame on his face.

'You mean, you will not...not need to tell anyone what I was doing there? Back home, my family, if they – '

'No – I can't see why we'd need to. Were you in the casino that night?'

He nodded.

'And you left at what time?'

'After three o'clock. I drove round for a bit. I don't know why. I was bored, I didn't feel tired. Here,' he looked up at the ceiling. 'Here is empty. I sometimes drive around, to see the drunken people holding onto each other, walking home.'

Jon suddenly realised: the man was lonely. Desperately lonely. Outside the football club, he probably had nothing. No friends. Family thousands of miles away. His best pal was a bloody PlayStation. 'So you're driving around...'

'...and I saw these ladies. One stepped forward and nodded at me. She waved. I do not know why I stopped. But I did stop.' He lowered his head once more. 'I did stop.'

'She directed you to the little turn-off?'

'Yes. And we had not been there long. There was an almighty sound. A big bang. She said it was from the motorway nearby. She said there might be sirens, but only up there – not where we were. I didn't want to stay, but she said it was fine, we would be safe – but this was not so. Soon after, my door opened very suddenly. A man pulled me.' Wilfred lifted a hand and gripped the collar of his sweatshirt tight. 'He pulled me like this, right out of the car. When I sat up and looked, he was in the back. He had a knife and he was telling the girl, he made her sit in my seat. The knife he pointed here.' He pressed a forefinger to the side of his neck. 'She closed the door and they drove away.'

The point of Jon's pen hovered over the page. 'He forced her to drive off in your car?'

'Yes. His arm – the left one – I think maybe he could not use it. That is why he made her.'

Christ, Jon thought. We need to locate that Porsche; he's got a hostage.

CHAPTER 16

Iona pored slowly over the news report on her screen, interest piqued by Elissa Yared's comments on the circumstances of her brother's death. Whoever had put her police file together hadn't done a good job: none of the report's findings featured in it. All the file mentioned was how Tarek, the brother, had been killed in Kunduz, Afghanistan, when the hospital he was working in had been accidentally hit by an American missile strike. US forces had claimed the hospital grounds were being used by the Taliban to fire on nearby Afghan armed forces.

But the article on her screen told a very different story. It claimed the attack was not only unprovoked, it was premeditated. The Medics International hospital was a protected facility – and the Americans had been repeatedly given the facility's GPS coordinates. A spokesman from the organisation had stated that the American military's claim that the hospital grounds were being used by Taliban fighters was absurd. Why, in that case, had the helicopter's Hell Fire air-to-surface missiles been aimed only at the main hospital building? Eleven Medics International staff and fourteen patients had been killed. Many of the sick people had been burned alive in their beds. Tarek was one of five doctors to lose his life.

Following the attack, investigations by the United States, Nato and Afghan government had found no wrong-doing on the helicopter crew's part. Medics International had rejected the findings as being a sham and had demanded an independent international investigation. This never happened and, almost two years after the event, the US military had quietly exonerated the helicopter crew and army personnel who had been in charge of the operation.

Iona printed the article out, added it to a couple of others then made her way into the meeting room. This time, she was able to grab a place at the corner of the table. Moments later, DCI Weir called for quiet.

'OK, everyone, here's where we are. Internet records came through a couple of hours ago; nothing suspicious so far on the ones that have been analysed. Some phone records are taking longer – or they are from certain providers.' He consulted his sheet. 'Adrian, you'll be getting the ones for Ashraf Atwi tomorrow; Iona, you should have ones for Elissa Yared by end-of-play.' His head turned. 'Ritchie, same for the ones on your list. Now, interviews: has everyone seen the people on their list?'

Nods from round the room.

'Good. Let's start in the corner. Iona?'

She placed a hand either side of her daybook. 'I saw Elissa Yared in her workplace at the MRI, where she works as a nurse in the Accident and Emergency department. Nothing gave me cause for concern. I then went to the address of her aunt and uncle, Bilal and Furat Atwi. As we now know, Bilal was killed in the crash on the M60 early this morning.' She glanced about to check she still had the room's attention. 'Things from here are looking a little murky. I don't think the wife had any knowledge of her husband's whereabouts or what he was up to.'

'Why do you say that?' Weir asked.

'When I first got there, she was extremely anxious. Thought I was there with news on his whereabouts, in fact. When I later returned to inform her of his death...' Iona shook her head. 'She didn't fake her reaction. I realise that doesn't mean she's in the dark about whatever her husband has been up to, but, well – I'd be surprised if she knew. In her present state, she's not able to be questioned.'

'When will she be?' Weir asked, noting something down.

'An FLO is with her; she'll let me know. Apparently, a doctor came out to give her sedatives because she'd started to hyperventilate.'

Weir's eyes were narrowed. 'Anything else?'

'Yes. When I returned to break the bad news, Elissa Yared, was there.'

'The nurse at the MRI?' someone asked.

'Correct.'

'What's her connection to the Atwi family?'

Weir gave a cough. 'Elissa's mum is Bilal Atwi's sister. The mum is called Bushra Yared, following her marriage to a man called Gibran Yared. It's also worth pointing out that Gibran Yared was a Maronite Christian, also originally from Lebanon.'

'Was?' someone asked.

'He died recently, as did the mother. Back in the 1980s, they fled during the Lebanese civil war and came to Britain. Everyone clear so far?'

Another question came back: 'What religion are the Yared children, Elissa and Tarek?'

'None, as far as I know,' Weir replied. 'Iona, your thoughts?'

'No obvious sign of Elissa being anything. The aunt, Furat Atwi, had summoned Elissa for some company. I tried to talk to Elissa about her uncle Bilal in a bit more detail, but she didn't really know him. Contact was, according to her, very rare.'

'Did you believe her?' Weir asked.

'Yes. Well...almost.' She glanced about, knowing that hesitancy did you no favours. 'I think so...but I'd like to see her phone records to be sure. And I've also done a bit more digging into her brother's death in Afghanistan. The file didn't provide much depth.'

'He was helping treat Taliban wasn't he?' someone replied.

'That's what the file might lead you to believe,' Iona answered, reaching for a photocopied sheet. 'Actually, the US military claimed there were only Taliban fighters hiding in the hospital's grounds. But the organisation – Medics International – disputes this.'

'But not whether Taliban were receiving medical assistance in the hospital?' Weir asked.

'That's not the point,' Iona replied. 'Even if they were, you can't bomb hospitals. Under international law, it's a war crime.'

'I don't see where you're going with this,' Weir replied.

Iona lifted another sheet. 'The incident has never been properly investigated. In fact, it was swept under the carpet – which left question marks over exactly what Tarek was doing out there.' She looked at the colleague who'd spoken before. 'You said just now he was helping the Taliban. I doubt you're the only person who suspects that. The father spent the last months of his life campaigning for an independent investigation in order to clear his son's name.'

The officer at her side looked up at the sheet that depicted the family tree. 'When did he die?'

'The father? Three months ago. Heart attack while protesting outside the Houses of Parliament. Here.' She held up another photocopy. 'An article on his death from the Evening Standard.'

'And her mother?' Another officer asked.

'Died within two months of learning her son had been killed out in Afghanistan. Natural causes.'

Weir tapped his fingers against the table. 'So you're saying what, Iona?'

'The Yared family seem very respectable and law-abiding. The son was a doctor, the daughter a nurse. Neither have any kind of police record. OK, they're linked to the Atwis through marriage, but I don't think the connection is anything more than that.' She shrugged. 'I just wanted to flag it up. As a family, the Yareds all seem to be dying, one way or another.'

CHAPTER 17

As Jon settled into his seat, he could hear a hum of voices coming from the meeting room next door. It sounded pretty animated in there. He started going over his notes once again, knowing it was likely his findings would be kicking off the meeting.

Around him, colleagues were pulling up chairs, low conversations rippling about.

'Right, quiet everyone! I want to get going on this.' The man who'd spoken was DCI Pinner. He had short, grey hair that had thinned on top. Though he appeared about fifty, he had the hungry, slightly intense look of a fitness fanatic about him. Hill running or something similarly horrible, Jon suspected.

DCI Pinner and DCI Weir jointly managed the branch of the CTU Jon was in. To go above them, you'd have to travel to the main office, located in the headquarters of Greater Manchester Police, over in Central Park.

'First things first,' Pinner said. 'An update on the situation in Afghanistan. We received word about an hour ago: the surface-to-air missile should be secured very soon. It's been tracked to an industrial storage facility. They're going in some point in the early hours, Afghan time. That's about eleven in the evening here. Right, DC Spicer, isn't it?'

Jon nodded. 'Yes, sir.'

'Away you go, then.'

'Thanks.' A table-full of faces was looking in his direction and, to Jon's surprise, he felt his heart flutter. He tried to use the trick of focusing on a point just above their heads, but more officers were standing behind the seated ones. 'As you know, I've been following-up on the mystery man who fled the scene of the RTA.' He looked down at his notes. 'It was possible he'd made his way past a secluded parking spot frequented by prostitutes and their punters. It now seems that, despite being injured, he commandeered a vehicle that had stopped there.' He glanced up. 'Basically, he dragged the driver out at knifepoint and forced the working girl to drive him from the scene.'

'Carjack and kidnap,' someone said with a whistle.

'That woman we only know as Kelly. Now, it could well be he's holding her hostage: I've checked the system and no female's come forward to report being involved in a carjacking.'

'She wouldn't, would she?'

Jon recognised Hugh Lambert's voice, but couldn't actually see the man. 'True,' he replied. 'I also left my number with a girl she chats to, but there's been no sign of her back on the street so far, either.'

'And the car?' DCI Pinner asked. 'The one that was taken?'

'A brand new red Porsche Cayenne. It belongs to a fairly well-known footballer.'

Several people immediately asked who that was.

Jon checked his notes. 'Wilfred Iwobi.'

Voices – and several guffaws of laughter – broke out. A Bolton United supporter was swiftly identified and mocking comments started raining down on him. The man sat, red-faced, head shaking slowly. 'Dirty bastard. Scores with prossies, but not on the pitch.'

Pinner let it continue for a few more seconds. 'Right, you've had your fun, now shut it!' He looked about. 'First, we find that Porsche. Second, we start taking this thing a tad more seriously. That means extra man-power out in the field and extra support back here. Personally, I like the sound of this mystery man less and less. As you're aware,' he nodded at the end wall, 'DCI Weir's heading up another team looking into the dead driver; let's keep lines of communication across the office open. OK, more on the items recovered from the crash scene. Nick?'

'Yup,' DI Hutcher replied. 'All the footage from the drone's camera has now been analysed and, from the locations that have been indentified, they drove out along the M56 and A55 into north Wales. That's a long way just to find a quiet spot for some flight training, which is what the early footage suggested. The final few minutes are of a stretch of coast on Anglesey. It's within a few kilometres of the Wylfa Nuclear Power Station.'

Jon glanced about; concerned looks were being exchanged around the room.

'Wylfa closed down in 2015,' Nick continued. 'It's now described by the outfit in charge as being in the 'defuelling phase'. That means there's still a lot of nasty shit on site – in the reactors and in reactor safe-stores. Interestingly, since it officially closed, security levels have been reduced to the legal minimum. In essence, that's a few unarmed civilian guards.' He looked over at Pinner.

'Thanks Nick. There were also some handwritten additions to the map recovered from the vehicle. That's come back in. Turns out, it's a Caucasic language, found only in the mountainous area in the south of Chechnya. This area is where many of the worst attacks on Russian military came from. The fighting was particularly vicious, and required Russian Paratroopers to take the Chechen soldiers on.'

Jon thought about the comments made by the passenger from the Interceptor: how the man had somehow regained his feet, despite all his injuries.

'We've sent the image we have of him upstream. MI6 will liaise with their contacts to see if anyone recognises this bloke. As I said, I'm liking the sound of him less and less. Lastly, we've got the mobile found on the RTA fatality. Hugh? What have you got?'

Lambert, who'd been lurking somewhere behind Jon, stepped round to the end of the table and raised a printout. 'OK, there were over two-hundred contacts in his address book, but many of them show no recent activity. Of the numbers he has been calling recently, fourteen feature over five times. Most of these appear to be business contacts – catering managers at educational establishments, for example. There were also private numbers for three people: a Nigel Parrit, an Elissa Yared and a – '

Jon's lower back muscles twitched as he went upright in his seat. 'What was that second one?'

Lambert paused. 'You what?'

'Sorry to butt in; the second name you read out.'

The other officer dragged his eyes back to the print out. 'Elissa Yared.'

Jon turned to DCI Pinner. 'That's the niece of Bilal Atwi. She's already been interviewed by a detective in DCI Weir's team.'

'And the last name I was about to read out,' Lambert said wearily, 'is another relative who's also – '

'But she lied,' Jon said, getting to his feet and moving towards the door, eyes on his DCI. 'Can I get the detective who interviewed her in?'

Pinner spread both palms. 'Looks like you already are.'

Hugh Lambert stared at Jon's back, his report now hanging uselessly at his side.

The man's low voice was little more than a whisper. 'I don't believe this, Howie. Bloody Cottage pie. Again.'

'Really?' Howie swivelled in his chair. By pushing hard at the edge of the desk, he rolled himself right across the smooth floor of the Operations Office to the table beside the door. 'Cottage pie is my favourite.'

'No way? Your favourite?' The older man left the lid open. 'You can have mine, then.'

Inside the hotlock was a stack of tinfoil containers, their edges folded over waxed paper lids that were marked, CP. Hot, moist air rose into his face as he peered in. 'Lovely.'

His colleague had returned to his station. 'What a whiff,' he quietly sighed.

Two monitors were slightly angled in to make a shallow V across the desk. On the left one, Anglesey formed the centre-point of a satellite image. The weather systems surrounding the island were being continually updated. As it had been for days, the Irish Sea was calm. Inland, some light cloud lay across the higher parts of the Snowdonia National Park. The immediate risk of weather-related incidents was negligible. The other screen was filled by words and numbers; a long range weather forecast that detailed the likely temperature and direction of any wind, along with its speed. Again, there was no cause for concern.

As he often did when the weather was warm, the Prince contemplated his younger brother out in Afghanistan. How hot would it be over there? A lot more than here in Wales, he thought. That was for sure.

He took a container out, picked a fork from the jar of plastic cutlery beside the hotlock and used its handle-end to prise the foil edges back. Inside was a thick layer of mashed potato. 'It's Shepherd's pie, not Cottage.'

'What's the difference?'

'Cottage pie should be topped by a layer of sliced potato. Like tiles on a cottage. And it'll be beef. Shepherd's pie is lamb, with mash on top.'

'Such good breeding.'

Turning the fork round, he broke through the fluffy layer into pink sloppy mush dotted by bright green peas. 'Oh yes.'

'Gives you rank farts, that dirge.'

'Like I care,' he said, starting to shovel it into his mouth.

The other man watched him with a bemused expression then shook his head. 'The finest education Britain can buy – and look at you.'

Cheeks bulging, he grinned back.

'What's the pudding, can you see?'

He lifted the lid and peered in once more. 'SCC?'

'Sponge cake and custard? Sponge cake and custard!' He pumped a fist. 'Get in!'

A klaxon started up and both men turned to a different monitor. On the wall, a whiteboard outlined the Search and Rescue team's roster for the next four weeks. Each person's nine shifts per month as First Standby were written in red. Shifts started at 19:00 hours and lasted through to that time the next day.

Footsteps pounded out from the rest lounge and across the corridor. Dan, radar operator for the current First Standby crew, shoved his head into the Operations Office. 'Scores on the doors, Howie?'

He placed his meal alongside the hotlock. Beside him, the printer had already started to chatter. 'Coming through.'

Dan looked over at the other man. 'Whispering-Bob? Any likely changes to current conditions?'

'Fine and clear,' he murmured. 'As per.'

Howie tore the sheet of paper off the printer and thrust it at the radar operator, who snatched it from his hand.

'Cheers!' Dan's footsteps faded.

As the klaxon bleated on, Howie crossed into the rest lounge and walked over to the windows that looked out across the runway. The crew were going over pre-take off checks on the Sea King helicopter, assisted by several ground engineers. Dan, the rad-op, came into view, head down as he scanned the print-out. Satisfied their on-board fuel load was sufficient for the mission, he waved away the ground engineer holding a pump-hose.

With a long-sigh, Howie turned round and surveyed the room. Half-finished drinks. Open newspapers. Semi-completed crosswords. All the signs of hasty abandonment.

Not long, he thought, until my next shift as First Standby starts.

CHAPTER 18

In the dim light of the corridor, Elissa got slowly to her knees and raised both hands. 'Friend? I'm a friend. Yes?'

The point of the blade was so close to her face, she couldn't have focused on its tip, even if she tried. Instead, she sought out his eyes, realising words alone weren't going to convince him. It hadn't occurred to her he wouldn't speak English.

He looked at the piece of paper again. His face was haggard and strained. She wondered how he could cope; his left shoulder was almost certainly dislocated and that alone would be enough to send most people desperate with pain.

She tried again, pressing a finger to the base of her throat. 'Me? Friend.' She pointed the finger at him. 'You? Friend. Yes?' She nodded slowly. 'Yes?'

His eyes touched on her then returned to the piece of paper once more. Unsure of exactly what to write, she'd decided not to bother with words. Maybe, she thought, the simple picture I drew has just saved my life.

He adjusted his grip on the knife, freeing a forefinger so he could hook out a roll of insulation tape from his back pocket. Using his teeth, he pulled a length free then gestured at her hands.

He wants to tie me, she thought, pressing the insides of her wrists together. She lifted her hands up to him. He attached tape across the backs of her wrists then looped it round several times. Ripping more tape free, he repeated the process. Then he waved the knife towards the room at the corridor's end.

As she struggled to her feet, she thought something made a bumping noise from beyond the closed door he was standing in front of.

Edging carefully past him, she walked slowly into a sparsely furnished front room. Typical Uncle Bilal, she thought. Nothing's changed from when he showed me round.

Then, to her surprise, she saw a TV and Xbox in the corner. A broadband router was on the windowsill. When he appeared, he was holding her bag. She waited for him to point at the sofa before she sat. Dumping the hold-all on the coffee table, he lowered himself into the armchair, wincing as he did so. Once he'd undone the zip, he placed the knife on the table, took out a photo and examined it. After a few seconds, he sent her a questioning look.

She tipped her head to show she couldn't see the image. He rotated the frame to reveal her parents. 'That's my – ' She stopped. Nursing kids in the A & E department who spoke no English had taught her a few tricks. 'Mama, Papa.'

A stillness seemed to come over him as he stared at the image. Then he put it to one side and removed the other photo. She was about to say his name when he said, 'Brat?'

'Brother,' she said uncertainly. Is that what he'd just said? Surely, the family resemblance was obvious. She directed her hands at the photo of her parents. 'Mama, Papa.' She pointed at herself. 'Elissa.' Then she pointed at the photo in his hands. 'Tarek.'

He placed the photo on top of the other. After rummaging through her clothing, he studied her for a second. 'Bilal?'

'Bilal?' she sat forward. 'Uncle. He's my uncle.'

His face was blank.

God, she thought. How do I explain this? She looked around. There was a pen on the narrow mantle piece above the gas fire. She nodded at it and mimed writing. 'I get?'

He gave a nod, knife back in his hand.

OK, she thought, getting to her feet. Careful to move slowly, she plucked the biro from where it lay. Paper, she thought. Where's some bloody...the instruction booklet for the Xbox was lying on the floor. She bent down and picked it up. Back in her seat, she turned the booklet so the blank back cover was facing up. I hope he understands a family tree, she thought.

Her hands were starting to throb, veins bulging with trapped blood. Clumsily, she wrote the words, 'Mama, Papa' before joining them with a wobbly line. She intersected that line with two vertical ones and wrote 'Elissa' at the end of one and 'Tarek' at the end of the other. From the word 'Mama', she drew a horizontal line and at the end of that wrote 'Bilal'. Below that, she drew a short vertical line and at the end of it wrote, Feiz Atwi.

She turned the booklet round and slid it towards him.

Cautiously, he lowered his eyes.

'Uncle Bilal' she whispered, watching him trace the tip of the knife down to Feiz Atwi.

The knife moved back across, coming to a stop over her brother's name. He glanced up. 'Tarek. Brat?' Urgency had lifted his voice.

'Brother, yes. My brother.'

'Tarek Yared? Kunduz? Medics Interna...' he wrestled with the word.

'International, yes! Medics International. Doctor.'

'Boom!' he said, bunching a fist then splaying his finger out. 'Boom!'

'Yes. He died.' She bowed her head to wipe a tear from her cheek.

Next moment, the knife appeared inches from her face. She lifted her chin.

He was before her, gesturing at her hands with the blade. Tentatively, she lifted them and, with sharp, decisive movements, he sliced through the tape.

'Thank you,' she said, rubbing at her fingers. 'Thank you.'

He backed away to the armchair and retook his seat. Knife still in his hand, he cupped his left elbow and examined the back of the instruction booklet again.

Her fingers were tingling as she peeled the tape away, fine hairs from her wrists coming away with it. 'Shoulder,' she said and waited for him to look up.

She turned her left shoulder inward then pointed at his. 'Shoulder.' She contorted her fingers, twisted her wrist and made a wrenching noise at the back of her throat.

He stared back, admitting nothing.

'I.' She pointed at herself. 'Medic.'

'Medic?' His dark eyebrows lifted. 'D – doctor?'

She shook her head. 'Medic. Nurse? I fix.' She hunched her left shoulder, gripped it with her right hand and returned her shoulder to its normal position. 'Fix.'

His eyes lit up. 'Postavit na mesto moyo plecho?'

I'm sure he's speaking Russian, she thought. But he doesn't look Russian.

'Vy mozhete eto sdelat?' he added. 'Da?'

Now, she realised, comes the awkward bit. She pinched her collar with a thumb and forefinger, mimed lifting her top over her head and immediately pointed at him.

He gave an eager nod and stood. 'OK.' But his eyes started to roll and a hiss of air escaped from his clenched teeth as he tried desperately to lift his left elbow.

When his legs started to buckle, she touched his arm. He stepped quickly away from her, eyes refocusing. Snipping at the air, she looked at the kitchen doorway. 'Scissors?'

He shook his head, raised the knife to the base of the V neck collar and cut through the material like it was made of tissue. Once through the hem at the bottom, he wriggled his right arm out of the sleeve, slid it off his left arm and cast it aside.

She felt her eyes widen. Beneath a thick layer of black hair, his torso was dotted by scars. Two especially thick welts ran across his right pectoral and down his ribs. The tight skin of his abdomen was puckered in two places. Those are gun-shot wounds, she realised, as her eyes went to his left shoulder.

As she suspected, there was a fullness at the front where the humerus had come forward of the joint. When she gestured for him to try and straighten the limb, it hung down, the dislocation rendering it flail and useless. She wondered how long it had been like that. The injury must have occurred when the car crashed. That was in the early hours of the morning; the shoulder muscles would have been in spasm for a while. It was going to take a heck of a lot of force to put it back in. The pain, she knew, would be excruciating.

CHAPTER 19

Jon knocked once then half-opened the door.

The man sitting at the head of the table didn't look impressed as he stopped speaking. 'Yes?'

'Sorry to interrupt, sir. I think we have a match with the call record of the mobile phone recovered at the RTA on the M60.' His eyes swept the room; she was sitting in the far corner. Like everyone else, her expression was one of curiosity and bemusement. 'Could I borrow Detective Constable Khan, sir? Just for a moment.'

He turned to her. 'Appears you are being summoned elsewhere. And who are you?' His attention was back on Jon.

'Oh, Detective Insp – Constable Spicer, sir.'

'Ah, Spicer. Yes.'

A loaded answer if I ever heard one, thought Jon. 'I just started today.'

'Clearly.' One of his eyebrows was at a slight angle. The sort of look that said, your card is marked.

Iona had made her way round the table and Jon was glad to step back outside. In the other meeting room, he saw Hugh Lambert was back in his seat and staring intently out of the window.

'DC Iona Khan,' Jon announced, holding the door open for her. 'Earlier, we were talking about connections to Bilal Atwi. Iona mentioned the name of a nurse she'd been sent to question.' He turned to Iona, who had failed to step fully through the door. Her hands were clasped tightly in front of her. A stab of unease went through Jon. If I've got this wrong, he realised, the whole unit will be laughing. 'What was the name again?'

Keeping her eyes on Jon, she said, 'Elissa Yared.'

Jon turned to Hugh Lambert. 'Does that...?'

The other officer glanced at his sheet. His reply seemed to take ages. 'It does.'

Relief surged up Jon's spine. 'How many calls to her phone?'

'Seven.'

'Seven?' Iona stepped into the room and the door swung shut behind her.

'And a text, which says, 'We must only talk about this when we meet'.'

Iona's lips were tight with annoyance. 'How long did the calls last?'

Lambert examined the sheet. 'Two minutes seven. Three minutes forty four. One minute twenty eight. Six minutes – '

'She told me she had no direct contact. None.'

DCI Pinner got to his feet. 'Right. We need to bring her in. DC Khan, you have her address?'

'Yes, sir.'

'Good. And DC Spicer? I want you along, too.'

'I'm just saying,' Iona sighed.

Jon tapped the steering wheel with the side of his thumb.

'You didn't notice the awkward atmosphere?' She sneaked a quick glance at him. That ear of his with the top bit missing. Yuk.

'Oh, aye. I noticed the awkward atmosphere. Your boss, he was looking at me like...but, for fuck's sake, it was major. Pinner had only just said in our meeting if there were any – I stress any – links between your team and ours, we were to shout out.'

Iona smiled inwardly: the big guy's attitude was certainly going to shake a few feathers in the CTU. Especially among the ones who peacocked about the place, trying to draw attention to their own achievements. 'Maybe things were done a bit differently where you last worked.'

It was Jon's turn to shoot a sideways look. 'What do you mean by that?'

'What I said. It sounds like you're used to – '

'Have you heard where I used to work?'

'No. Should I?'

Jon looked across the street. It had been about half an hour since they'd banged on Elissa's door. There'd been no reply. Now they were waiting on the go-ahead for a forced entry on the basis she could be in danger as a result of her association with Bilal Atwi. 'Doesn't matter.'

Neither said anything for a few seconds.

'You've got me interested now,' Iona stated. 'Where did you work?'

Jon swivelled his head. She had a cheeky half-smile on her face.

'What?' she protested. 'You raised it. Bet you wanted me to ask, secretly.'

Jon looked back across the street. He wondered whether to say that, during a temporary assignment with the Tactical Aid Unit in the wake of the 2011 riots, they'd crashed in loads of doors, particularly in certain areas of Salford. But now she'd probably take that as him trying to drop clues about his past career. Safer to say nothing.

Her mobile went off. Six rapid notes; first four ascending, last two descending. Efficient and businesslike, he thought. A bit like her.

'Iona here. Lovely. How long? OK, we'll be waiting outside.' She cut the call. 'It's happening. There's a van two minutes away with an Enforcer in the back.' She opened the glove compartment and removed two black baseball caps. White letters spelled out POLICE above the visors. 'Need to have one of these on when we go in.'

As Jon climbed from the car, his mind was back on that glorious summer of the riots. Dawn raids, dragging scrotes, bad-boys and would-be gangsters who'd been out looting from their beds, hauling them down stairs to waiting vans. Some in just their boxers if they'd put up a fight. What fun it had been.

'When you spoke to this lass,' Jon said over his shoulder as he crossed the street, 'what did you say to her?'

Iona had to almost jog just to keep up. 'I tried to warn her that, given a few details connected to the crash, it was likely her aunt would need to be questioned further.'

Jon kept walking. 'You didn't let anything slip?'

'How do you mean?'

He reached the far kerb and stepped onto the pavement. 'About the wider investigation.'

Iona started to say no. Her mouth closed and she glanced at the property. 'You mean like I spooked her?'

'I'm only trying to anticipate what your boss might be asking you. If something's caused her to disappear, just make sure your arse isn't in view.'

'Crap, didn't think about that.' He was looking off down the street and she studied him for a moment. He didn't act like a lowly constable. She started going over exactly what had been said when she had been alone with Elissa in the kitchen.

'Magic key's here,' Jon said a minute later as a police van pulled up. 'Afternoon, boys.'

The driver turned the engine off and reached for some paperwork. 'Number 4a?'

'That's the one,' Iona replied.

It only took one impact for the door to fly open. The uniformed officer stepped aside and Jon, now wearing a baseball cap, thundered up the stairs. 'Elissa Yared! Police!

Elissa!' He moved swiftly into the first room, eyes darting about. 'Hello? Elissa, are you here? Police.'

A doorway at the far end led into a galley kitchen. To his left, another door. He opened it: a short corridor, with a bathroom at the end. A closed door off to each side. Jon stood between them, lifted both hands and rapped loudly on them both. 'Elissa, we're coming in, OK?'

He waited for Iona to reach for the handle of the right one. On his nod, they pushed both doors open. Jon's room lacked soft, feminine colours. There were photos of mountain bikers on the walls. The duvet on the bed was dark blue and he realised the room smelt slightly musty. Unused. Hangers rattled as he checked the wardrobe. Empty. He stepped back out. 'Clear!'

Iona called a reply. 'Clear!'

Jon was already moving towards the bathroom. No one in there, either. 'I presume that's her room,' Jon said. 'I'd say mine belonged to a bloke.'

'You were in her brother's,' Iona responded, looking through the door. 'Still not changed anything in it.'

'What did you say happened to him, again? Killed out in Iraq?'

'Afghanistan. American missile strike on the field hospital he was working in.'

'That was it.'

They walked back into the front room. 'It looks like a lot of her clothes are missing,' Iona said, making her way round. She paused at a small cabinet full of hideous little ornaments. 'Nice.'

Jon was down on one knee before the TV unit. 'Everything's switched off at the wall. Don't suppose she mentioned going on holiday to you?'

'Er, yeah.' Iona lifted a forefinger. 'Now you mention it, she did.'

Jon twisted round, saw her sarcastic grin and relaxed. 'OK, dumb question.'

Iona snapped on a pair of latex gloves and started opening drawers. When Jon wandered back out from the kitchen, he was holding a small photo encased in thick plastic. 'This was stuck to the fridge. I'm thinking brother, not boyfriend.'

Iona had a look. The shot had been taken in a pub's beer garden. They were sitting next to each other at a chunky wooden table. Encroaching at the edge of the frame were two muddy front wheels. 'Mountain biking together. Seems they were close.'

She handed the photo back and opened another drawer. The first thing she saw was a passport. 'That's odd.'

CHAPTER 20

Christ, Elissa thought. How the hell do I explain this?

He was looking at her with a hungry expression. 'Bistryei!' He nodded down at his shoulder. 'Davay dyelai eto!'

'I can't just...you'll need...' She made a cup of her hand, covered her nose and mouth with it and took several deep breaths. She lowered her hand. 'Gas and air, yes? For the pain.'

He was almost on the balls of his feet, his whole body tense. 'Bros! Prosto postav yego na mesto. Bistryei!'

Was it Russian? she wondered again. She spotted the booklet for the Xbox and an idea struck her. She picked it up and flicked past the instructions written in English. Next was Deutsch, then Francais. She kept on turning. Nederlands, Espanol, Portogues, Italiano, Svenska, Dansk, Suomi, Norsk, Russkiy.

'This!' She held a finger to the page. 'Russkiy. You speak Russkiy?'

He glanced at it. 'Da, Russkiy. Bistryei!' He tried to take the booklet from her.

She stepped back, mind now speeding. She turned to the section written in English. There it was: using your Xbox to search the internet. This is how we can talk.

She raised a finger at him then knelt before the telly. As the screen came to life, she turned the Xbox on.

'Chto ti delayesh?' His voice was sharp and impatient. 'Hey!'

'Give me a minute. You'll see.' As she grabbed the controls, the knife appeared before her face.

'Prekrati seichas zhe delai chto ya govoryu.'

She tried not to let her fear show. 'Internet. Russkiy, English. English, Russkiy. Google translate. Yes? We can use – '

He used the heel of the knife's handle to knock the controller from her grip. 'Snachala moyo plecho.'

He was poking the damn knife in her face again and for the first time, she felt a flash of anger. 'Fine! You want me to put your shoulder back in?' She stood up, mimed the action, made the crunching noise at the back of her throat. 'Yes? No drugs, nothing? OK, let's see how long you last. On your back.'

He frowned.

'Get on your back. Lie down. Here.' She brandished a hand at the threadbare carpet. 'You, here. Like this.' She held her arms at her sides and lifted her chin.

'Mnye lyech zdes?' he asked uncertainly.

'That's correct. Right there.'

Suspicion played on his face as he slowly sat. Gingerly, he leaned back on his right elbow. She could see pinpricks of sweat on his forehead as, inch by inch, he lay flat and placed his injured arm by his side. His stomach flexed as he took in quick breaths.

Think that hurt? She kicked off her trainers. Just you wait. 'Now, I'm going to take your left wrist in both of my hands, like this. OK? Now I place my foot in your armpit, like this.' His right hand was gripping the knife's handle so tightly, the veins in his forearm had started to bulge. When the pain really kicks in, she thought, I can see him swinging that knife across and burying it in my leg. 'Now, I'm going to start slowly leaning back. Like this.'

His shallow panting suddenly cut off. Deep in his chest, a groan gathered strength.

Told you, she thought, easing the pressure so she could lower his arm back down.

'Ne ostanavlivaisya, prodolzhay.' His voice was snarly and ragged as he lifted the knife so it was level with her thigh. He glared up at her with crazed eyes. 'Davai delai seychas!'

Flecks of spit flew from his mouth. She felt one hit her cheek. My God, she thought, he wants me to carry on.

Gripping his wrist, she leaned back once again and the groan returned. But rather than turn to a roar, he somehow kept it at the back of his throat. She felt his muscles start to spasm and waited. After a bit they relaxed and she returned the pressure. A sharp tangy smell filled her nostrils and she could see sweat pooled in the hollow of his throat. You cannot bear this for much longer, she thought. You can't. The muscles contracted again and she waited. It took a minute for the spasm to pass. As she started to pull again, his eyes swivelled, fixing her with a look of desperate intensity.

He nodded encouragement. 'Da, da!'

'OK,' she whispered, increasing the backward angle of her body.

He placed the rubberised handle of the knife sideways in his mouth, clamped it in his teeth and started to pound the floor with the flat of his hand. Now all her weight was being transferred through his arm; if she let go of his wrist, she would fall flat on her back. Just when she thought it would need someone heavier than her, she felt and heard a dull thunk. The joint had gone back in. He snatched the knife from his mouth and heaved in mouthfuls of air.

Hardly able to believe it, she lifted her foot from his armpit and gently lowered his arm down so it lay across his stomach. 'A sling,' she mumbled, stepping back. 'You'll need a sling.'

To her astonishment, he sat up and flexed the fingers of his left hand. 'Teper khorosho,' he said, nodding with a grim smile. 'Da, seychas khorosho.'

CHAPTER 21

'So, she's in the wind?' DCI Weir was a dark-haired man with a wide mouth and eyes that were just a fraction too far apart. It gave him a slightly comical look. He sat back and interlinked his fingers. 'Bugger.'

Iona placed some plastic folders on his desk. 'Apart from her passport there were lots of documents lying around. These are copies of her bank statements, utility and credit card bills. One for her mobile phone, too.'

'She won't be using that again,' Weir stated glumly. 'Not if she's got any sense. Did she have a landline?'

'No.'

'Computer?'

Iona shook her head. 'A Tivo box – could be a history on that if she was accessing the internet through her telly.'

Weir reached for his phone. 'Andrea? Pop up, please. We need provider permission to access some customer records.' He replaced the receiver. 'Anything else?'

'We left uniforms knocking on neighbours' doors,' Jon replied. 'That could give us an idea of how long ago she left. Any word on the Porsche Cayenne?'

'Not as yet. It's logged now, so if it strays onto any motorway, ANPR cameras will pick it up soon enough. All divisions have also been given the alert. I know Tameside and Trafford have checked known spots for where stolens get dumped. Nothing from those.' He looked Jon up and down then turned to Iona. 'DCI Pinner likes the look of you two as a pair and I don't have any objections. So I'll let you both get on with typing-up. Oh, DC Spicer? DCI Pinner wanted a word.'

'Who are we actually reporting to now, Sir?' Jon asked. 'Yourself or DCI Pinner?'

Weir raised both hands off the desk. 'Not sure. I'll have a word with him in a bit.'

Back out into the corridor, Jon glanced towards Iona as he stepped towards DCI Pinner's door. She didn't seem to be bursting with enthusiasm about the prospect of working with him. 'See you downstairs?'

'OK.' She was already walking towards the stairwell.

He turned to the door and knocked lightly, head bowed.

'Come in.'

The DCI was standing at a filing cabinet. Sliding the top drawer shut, he turned round. 'Jon. How did it go?'

'Missed her, sir. We were just explaining to DCI Weir it looks like – '

Pinner cut him off with a flick of his fingers. 'I'm meeting him shortly – I'll get everything then. Now,' he leaned a shoulder against the cabinet. 'We've had a complaint. Member of the public.'

'About me?' Jon said, completely taken by surprise.

'Yes. A car driver. His vehicle was at the front of the queue at the M60 crash site.'

Him, thought Jon. He clasped his hands behind his back. Not another complaint for my collection.

'You know the individual I'm talking about?'

'I think so.'

He stepped over to his desk and retrieved a piece of paper. 'You said to him, and I'm quoting from his report,

"Shut up, get back in your car, close the door." Sound about right?'

Jon cringed. First day in the bloody job, too. 'Sir, I think that's somewhat out of context. If I remember rightly, it was more like, 'The best thing you can do is shut up.'

Pinner cocked his head. 'Dancing on the head of a pin here, are we not?'

'The man was behaving in a way that I judged to be – '

Pinner waved a hand. 'It's fine. The person has been assured you'd be suitably reprimanded. So, there: consider yourself suitably reprimanded.'

Jon wasn't sure if he'd heard correctly. 'Sir?'

'But you'll find yourself in far more pressured situations than that, Jon. So bear in mind that, however big a pain in the arse, Joe Public are not the ones you let rip at.'

'Sir.'

'They even come in useful.' He reached for another piece of paper. 'In his incident statement, he described how the mystery man fished a phone from his pocket, snapped its SIM, crushed the handset underfoot and flung the pieces into the grass verge.'

Jon processed the information. 'That was before he fled?'

'Yes – as soon as the officer who'd helped him over to the barrier rushed off to deal with a car fire. Our man sat there with his head drooping forward. After a few seconds, he seemed to come around and immediately reached for his phone. It sounds to me like he was assuming he would be searched – so he got rid. But when he realised no-one was actually paying him any attention, he made off down the slope.'

'So, before doing anything else, he destroys his handset,' Jon mused. 'That's a worry. Have we found it?'

Pinner nodded. 'It's already upstairs. Though they're not hopeful of recovering any data. If we're lucky, there might be a decent fingerprint.'

'Shame. There must have been something worthwhile on it. Any more on his identity?'

'The photo is with foreign office staff stationed out in Moscow. They're liaising with the Russian police.'

'What's your view on it, sir? You reckon we're looking at a planned attack? An active terror cell?'

'What do you think?'

I'm thinking nice deflection, Jon almost blurted, his opinion of the other man immediately plummeting. 'Me? I've not been here long, as you know. But as a police officer? I don't like the feel of it. Not at all.'

'Chief Superintendent Gower spoke very highly of you.'

'Sorry?'

'Gower. When it was being weighed-up whether to bring you on-board.'

So that's how my transfer came about, Jon thought. A nod and a wink from my old boss in the Major Incident Team.

He pictured the silver-haired bear of a man. Jon knew the exact moment he had earned himself a permanent place in the older man's good book. He'd been captaining Greater Manchester Police's rugby team in the final of the Cheshire Cup. During the match, he'd knocked the opposition number eight out. In the club house afterwards, Gower had sought him out to congratulate him on the quality of the punch.

Seems like, Jon reflected, my career's been built on knocking other men over.

'Everything OK with you, so far?'

Jon's focus returned to the DCI. 'Fine, sir. One thing: I gave some cash to one of the working girls – the one who gave me the info on the red Porsche picking up her mate. Is there any way I can get that – '

'See the civilian support worker for your section. He'll give you a form. I'll sign it off, no problem.'

'Thanks. It's been...quite a first day.'

'Certainly has.' Pinner glanced at his watch. 'Not long until your shift's over. I'll let you get on.'

Once Jon had sorted the expenses claim with Peter Collier, he started typing-up his reports and logging everything on the CTU's secure system. As he pecked laboriously away, he could hear Iona at her computer on the next row of desks. Her fingers on the keys sounded like a hoard of rushing ants. He couldn't believe anyone could type so fast. To his dismay, she started shutting her computer down when he was barely half-finished. From the corner of his eye, he watched as she tidied some bits away on her desk. As she started to make her way over, Jon minimised his screen, sat back and looked to his side. 'Are you all done?'

'Yes.' She glanced at his screen then at the mess of paper and old cups. 'You?'

'Just about.'

'Right I'll see you in the morning, then.'

'See you in the morning.'

It took him another forty minutes to complete his report, by which time a new set of detectives had started to appear. The night shift. After logging out, he went downstairs and into the departure lounge.

Kieran Saunders was coming out of the men's locker area. He was in a vest top and baggy shorts. Jon spotted the crest for 1st Battalion, The Royal Welsh on the chest of his top. 'Jon. Not off home, are you?'

'Yeah, I thought it was about time I did.'

'A few of the boys, we're down in the gym. A bit of sparring, like. Come and have a look.'

Jon hitched a thumb at the outer door. 'Maybe another time. I told the missus that – '

'Awww,' the man lifted a hand to one ear. 'All I'm hearing here are excuses.'

Bollocks, Jon thought, not wanting to create any kind of bad impression with the men he'd be shoulder-to-shoulder with out in the field. 'Go on, then.'

The gym, Jon had to admit, was impressive. A little too much of it had been given over to workstations, but its centre was dominated by a long rack of free weights. Exercise mats were spread out on either side of it, with several Swiss Balls and Bosu Balls in the corner. Unusually for a work-place gym, it didn't smell like someone had stuffed several pairs of old socks and pants under the floorboards to fester. He noticed the extractor fans set into the ceiling.

Hanging mid-way down one side of the gym was a row of punch-bags. They stretched away in a long line right to a boxing ring, raised about eighteen inches from the floor. Not full size, Jon guessed, but it couldn't have been far off.

A group of three men were gathered at its edge; inside the ring, two pairs were swinging away at each other's heads. Jon immediately saw their hands were encased in 18 ounce boxing gloves. The padding was so thick, it was like being biffed with a cushion: unless the other person really let rip, there was little chance of walking away with anything worse than a nose-bleed.

'Oh, Tommo's going for it, tonight. Look at him!' Kieran called out as they approached the ring. 'Do him, Tommo, he needs a good pasting.'

Jon couldn't help grinning at the sight of a five-foot-eight man ferociously wind-milling away. His much larger opponent was patiently fending off the blows, waiting for the barrage to weaken.

'Two minute rounds,' Kieran said, eyes glued to the fighting. 'Just keep swopping it round like that. Killer, it is.'

As Jon watched punches being traded, he felt a tightening in his chest and a tingling in his arms. A buzzer went and a couple of the men who'd been fighting gratefully backed towards the ropes. They were swiftly replaced by two who'd been spectating. The buzzer sounded once more and they were off. To Jon's surprise, none of the men seemed like experts. Some had a proper guard up, one or two were on their toes, dancing – but, for the most part, it was a simple lung-busting slug-fest.

'Fancy a little go?' Kieran was looking at him knowingly. 'You do, don't you?'

A smile caught the corner of Jon's mouth. 'I've not come with any kit.'

'Fuck that – go bare-foot, man. T-shirt and jeans is fine. Andy! Chuck me and the new boy here some gloves, we're going in!'

Two pairs of gloves flew through the air.

Jon's trainers came off, and as he tugged at his socks, he sneaked a look at the other man, wondering if this was some king of initiation-test in disguise.

But Kieran's face only showed genuine glee as he said, 'Now, I don't want to be waking up on any hospital ward, big man.'

Jon laughed. 'I reckon it's me needs to watch you.'

'Oh, you'd better watch me. Float like a butterfly, I do. Balletic, it is.'

They'd worked their gloves on when the buzzer sounded again.

Jon climbed through the ropes, the springy canvas of the ring rough against the soles of his feet. Turning round, he saw Kieran before him, capering around like a village idiot.

'Look at the footwork! Just look at it!'

Jon raised his gloves and, with a quick shrug of his shoulders, touched them against his forehead. He'd arrested plenty of people who liked to clown about, shooting-off stupid comments in the build-up to actual physical contact taking place. In his experience, the tactic arose for two reasons: sometimes the person was crafty, using it as a distraction before lashing out with a surprising viciousness. Other times, the person was genuinely unhinged and, because they relished the prospect of violence so much, they just couldn't contain their excitement.

The buzzer sounded.

Kieran bounded forward with a banshee-screech and let rip with a wild flurry of punches. Right, left, left, right, left, right, right. Definitely unhinged, Jon thought. I think I'm going to get on well with this guy. He kept his gloves up and his eyes open. The other man was letting the elbow of his non-punching arm ride far too high. Jon shuffled forward as Kieran skipped about, just out of reach.

'Oh, he didn't even see them coming. I'm just too fast, just too –' He exploded forward again, trying to repeat exactly the same attack.

Jon let him get a rhythm going, dipped a shoulder and drove a glove into the other man's abdomen, just below the ribs.

As Kieran staggered backwards with a look of shock on his face, Jon closed the gap and started with a series of little jabs with his right. As soon as Kieran's focus went to that glove, he hooked him with a left to the head.

The other man was laughing as he fell into the ropes. 'Mother-fucker! Got a punch like a bastard zebra kicking.'

It was now obvious Kieran had no real technique: this was only ever going to be a simple trade-off in punches. Which was fine. Jon lowered his guard and beckoned to him with a grin. 'Come to Daddy.'

'It's the rumble in the jungle!' Kieran said, pulling himself upright. 'Here we go!'

He launched another untidy assault and this time Jon let a couple of blows land before replying with one of his own. Within seconds, they were toe-to-toe, swinging away in time with each other, both suppressing laughter each time a punch connected properly. By the time the buzzer went, Jon's shoulders and biceps were burning.

'Bloody good go, that, cheers!' Kieran's eyes were sparkling, his face bright red.

'Yeah, cheers.' Jon started to pull a glove off.

'Hey!' Kieran said. 'You're up for another now, kiddo.'

Jon's smile dropped. He hadn't realised the two-round-rule would apply to him. He glanced to his side; a few more detectives had appeared while they'd been fighting. Hugh Lambert was climbing swiftly into the ring, Jon the sole focus of his stare.

'Watch this arse-wipe,' Kieran breathed. 'He won some kind of boxing prize in the Paras.'

Jon turned to him. 'And what makes you think he'll want to pair up with me?'

Immediately picking up on the mocking tone in Jon's question, Kieran laughed. 'Well, I don't think it's me who's in his sights.'

Lambert lifted one shoulder, touched an ear against it then did the same on the other side. He bounced on the balls of his feet a few times, all the while drilling Jon with his stare.

Jon gave him a coquettish smile. Just to wind him up a little more.

Lambert removed a gum-shield from his mouth. 'Hear you've been claiming back the cash you've been blowing on whores.' He cast a glance to the side, checking the comment had been heard.

'It's a tough job,' Jon countered. 'But someone had to do it.'

The buzzer went off again.

Lambert slotted his gum-shield back in and put his guard up.

The first thing Jon thought was: feet. He's moving really well. Jon lifted his own arms, trying to ignore the ache in his shoulder muscles.

Lambert tested the water with a jab and Jon immediately knew he was in trouble; the other man had a freakishly long reach. Just as he started to get a sense of Lambert's rhythm, a couple of body shots thudded dangerously close to Jon's liver.

He barely had time to adjust before the punches went back to head height, each one measured for maximum impact. Thank Christ he's wearing 18 ouncers, Jon thought, head reeling.

Knowing he had to do something, Jon feinted with his right, then released his left. A move that rarely let him down. One moment his glove was heading straight at Lambert's face, the next it was extending into empty air. A big impact on his temple and Jon just had time to bring his gloves up either side of his head before two more came in.

Shit, I'm getting leathered here. Ducking from side to side, he peeked through his defence, saw Lambert's feet were flat, planted his front foot as close to them as he could and swung a crook-armed punch at waist height. He felt a good connection and straightened up, knowing he was now inside Lambert's superior reach. Time to pay him back with –

The other man's head clashed with his.

'Woah, woah, woah!' Kieran's voice rang out from the side. 'You can't fucking head-butt.'

Lambert danced back, eyes not leaving Jon. 'Accident. You OK?'

'Yeah, fine.' Jon touched a glove to his right eyebrow. It came away spotted with blood. He could see the other two fighters had stopped to watch. OK, he thought. I'm in a straight scrap, here. Just happens we're wearing pads on our fists.

Wondering how much longer could be left, he moved forward again, knowing his only chance was to get back inside Lambert's defence. But the other man knew exactly what he was doing and kept his distance, punishing Jon all the time with jab after jab. Jon kept going forward, but eventually another blow caught his temple. His lead leg buckled. Desperate not to fall, he threw both arms round Lambert's midriff, happy to see out the rest of the bout by wrapping up the other man.

A stabbing impact at the base of his skull and Kieran's shout of protest was drowned out by a high-pitched humming. Next thing, Lambert's knee started lifting towards his face.

Jon sensed his chance: he tucked his chin in, letting the blow come. As it connected with his forehead, he hooked a fore-arm round the back of Lambert's knee. Then he yanked his elbow back like he was starting a lawnmower. It was a tackle technique he'd used in more rugby matches than he could remember.

Lambert found himself on one foot, arms flailing as he hopped backwards, trying to not go over. Keeping his body low, Jon started to pump his knees. When he felt he had enough momentum, he looked up, saw the side of the ring was a couple of metres away and launched the other man at it. The ropes flexed briefly. Jon planted his feet wide, and as the other man came bouncing back, he swung with all his strength.

Lambert's head snapped to the right, gum-shield flying through the air. He keeled over, arms and legs splayed out.

There was a moment's silence then everyone was jumping into the ring. The two other fighters crouched down at Lambert's side. Kieran grabbed Jon's arm and pulled him towards the far corner. 'Alright? You need some tissue on that. Here.' He took the large blue roll being lifted by one of the other officers. 'Get us one of those ice-packs, too, Ian. From the first-aid kit. Mate? Wonderful punch,' he whispered. 'Bloody wonderful.'

The vision in Jon's eye was now blurring red. 'Did he head-butt me?'

'And the rest! Used his elbow on the back of your head, too, the dirty bastard.'

Jon twisted round to see where Lambert had fallen. Colleagues had sat him up, but his eyes were all over the place.

CHAPTER 22

As the Xbox powered up, Elissa glanced surreptitiously at the man yet again. She still couldn't believe it. He was now sitting on the sofa, left arm supported by the makeshift sling she'd fashioned from a sheet. Every now and again, he'd test the arm by bring his elbow out a few inches. That has to hurt, she thought. Surely.

The home page was now showing on the screen. She scrolled across to the search box and, using the on-screen alphabet, keyed in Internet. Within seconds, she was on Google Translate.

What, she wondered, should I write? The cursor moved with annoying slowness across the onscreen keyboard as, letter by letter, she spelled out four words.

Bilal Atwi is dead.

There was no need to even click enter; the Russian translation appeared automatically in the adjacent field.

The man sat forward, face bathed in the screen's silver glow. He glanced at Iona with suspicion, then gestured for the controller.

By selecting the reverse button, the Latin alphabet was replaced by the Cyrillic one. She handed him the controller.

Gradually, his question appeared. *How do you know?*

She took the controller, switched back to the Latin alphabet, and typed a reply. *His wife is my Aunt. I was at her house when the police came to tell her.*

He sat still, seeming to process this information.

She so desperately wanted to know what the plan was. How they were going to carry it out. She typed another question. *Do you remember what happened?*

He shook his head.

Retrograde amnesia? she wondered. He must have received a concussion when the car crashed. He knew who Uncle Bilal was, but what had happened in the run-up to the accident seemed to have been lost.

She started a new sentence. *The car you were in crashed.*

He looked at her with a frown, clearly not sure whether to believe her.

She typed again. *Uncle Bilal died at the scene. You got away.*

Inviting an answer, she offered him the handset. He ignored it.

She worked the controller again. *How did you get to this house?*

For some reason, he looked towards the window, but said nothing.

The laborious process of selecting each letter was starting to frustrate her. *I am trying to help you.*

He read her words then examined the fingers of his left hand as they curled in and out.

You must tell me. The information Uncle Bilal passed on came from me. She nudged his leg and pointed at what she'd written.

He looked back at her, started to reach for the controller then changed his mind.

Whatever the plan was, it was obvious he needed support to carry it out. Now Uncle Bilal was dead, that support had gone. She typed another comment. *You cannot do this alone. Let me help you.*

The comment caused him to stand. He walked over to the window, paced about before it, looked at her briefly then turned his back.

Jesus, she thought. What can I do to make him trust me? She typed out another message and coughed. *I know you must do it soon. I know because that information came from me!*

He read her words then looked out the window once more.

Ask who sent you here. They will tell you. She coughed to get his attention again.

As he read her latest comment, his face darkened and he rubbed at the back of his head with his good hand.

Something's wrong, she thought. Oh my God. As quick as she could, she typed again. *Do you remember why you are here?*

'Da,' he snarled angrily. He went over to the shelf above the gas fire, picked a piece of paper off it and dropped it on the table. It was the picture she'd drawn. The one she'd pushed through the letter box.

OK, she thought. He knows why he's here. But he can't remember everything. Maybe he can't remember the exact details of the plan. She turned to the screen. *How will you do it?*

He let out a bitter laugh and crossed to the window.

She sighed. Let's start again, she thought. Maybe retracing his steps will help unlock whatever it is he can't recall. His mind was obviously functioning immediately after the accident. After all, he knew to escape, and he knew how to find this address. She guessed he'd fallen asleep after getting here – and that's when his memory had been wiped. Like waking up after a night involving far too much alcohol and having no recollection of how you got home. *Did you walk here after the crash?*

After reading her words, he did nothing for a full minute. Then, hesitantly, he nodded at the window.

She lifted her eyebrows in question.

Sitting down once more, he accepted the controller. *The big red car outside.*

Elissa's eyes widened. The Porsche! He came in that. How the hell did he manage to drive it? Where was it from? She typed again: *I don't understand. Is it Uncle Bilal's?*

His head slowly shook.

Then whose is it?

He shrugged.

You stole it?

He looked away.

He bloody stole it, she thought. Which meant the police could be looking for it. *We must move it. Now!*

He waved a hand at the window, pointing left, right, forwards, backwards.

He doesn't know where to take it, she thought. *Give me the key.*

Yet again, he hesitated.

For Christ's sake, she thought. There isn't time for this. She gestured at her comment on the screen then held a palm out.

With a look that bordered on hatred, he beckoned for the controller. *It is probably in the car.*

She stared at the words, imagining the state he had been in. How he'd done it with a dislocated shoulder, she couldn't imagine. She glanced at her wrist watch. Almost nine, already. She indicated one hour and stood. 'OK?'

He gave a nod and also got to his feet.

At the doorway to the kitchen, she hesitated and then stepped through. The fridge was empty except for a carton of milk. Some packets of flavoured rice were strewn across the work surface beside the kettle. She indicated she would get things to eat.

He nodded.

Out in the corridor, she pointed at the toilet, then herself. With a look of embarrassment, he retreated to the front room. She waited a second behind the closed door, quietly re-opened it and quickly stepped across the corridor to the door that was shut. The one she could tell he'd been shielding earlier.

It opened without a noise.

What she saw caused her to freeze. In a chair beside the bed was a female form. Elissa glanced fearfully towards the front room. No sign of him. She stepped inside and closed the door behind her. The room smelt strongly of urine. The woman's head was hanging forward and her breathing was shallow. She seemed oblivious to Elissa's presence. Tape – the same type he'd used on her wrists – secured the woman's legs, torso and forearms to the chair. More of it covered her mouth.

Elissa leaned down trying to see if she was conscious. With a sickening jolt, she realised the face was one that she recognised.

CHAPTER 23

Jon gazed down at the little lump. The night-light filled the cot with a soft orange. His son looked so snug and warm. He reached down and folded the top of the blanket back so he could see him properly. Brown curls of hair and one chubby cheek pressed against the towelling sheet. His bottom lip was squashed outwards. How, Jon wondered, could something that appeared so serene and placid morph into such a monstrous ball of energy just by opening its eyes?

Affectionately, he trailed his fingertips through the curls. Sweet dreams, he thought, even though they probably involve beating up your big sister.

Two steps took him across the small landing and into her room. A never-ending procession of unicorns, angels and fairies slid silently across the ceiling, down the walls and then over her bed. She was lying on her back, face slightly tilted as if she'd been enjoying the spectacle the bedside lamp made when sleep took hold. One strand of blonde hair was slightly askew, so he lifted it back in place with a finger. Even asleep, she was perfect. Knowing how soundly she slept, he knelt down and pressed a kiss into the smoothness of her cheek.

Alice killed the telly and sat back. There was a bottle of red on the table and he glugged a hefty load into a glass.

'It's pasta bake,' Alice said, with a nod towards the oven. 'I put some on a plate, but you'll probably need to zap it for a couple of minutes: we ate ages ago.'

Jon flipped the oven door open, stooped down and reached inside. Tentatively, he tapped his fingers against the edge of the plate. Still quite hot. 'It'll be fine as it is, cheers.'

He picked the plate out, placed it on the table and took a seat.

'Come on!' she said. 'Stop being all enigmatic, will you?'

He shovelled a forkful of food into his mouth and gave her a frown.

She rolled her eyes. 'The job. You know, the one you started today?'

'Oh.' He chewed for a while and eventually swallowed. 'It's good. Different, but good.'

'Different, but good?' Her legs were stretched across the next chair, ends of her slippers bobbing back and forth as she excitedly wiggled her toes. 'Jon Spicer, you are so crap. How is it different? What are the people like? Does your boss seem OK? Is your desk near a window? Come on.' She clicked her fingers impatiently, like she was summoning a waiter. 'I want the gossip.'

He ate for a bit longer, watching her mounting impatience with amusement. 'Right. People – '

'Hang on.' She leaned forward, breaking eye contact, but only by an inch. 'Is that a cut on your eyebrow?'

'Yes, but only a little one.' He resumed eating.

'Christ. Your first day. They had you out on a job on your first day?'

'No,' he said through bulging cheeks. 'It was in the gym. Downstairs at the base. Sparring.'

'Spar – ' Her face grew serious. 'No. No. You didn't get into a – no. Not with a colleague, please.'

Jon's mind went back to the seconds after Hugh Lambert went down. He'd got to his feet after a minute or so and, helped by a colleague, had climbed slowly out of the ring.

'Fucking prick,' Kieran Saunders had muttered, dabbing at Jon's eyebrow.

Jon was still breathing heavily. 'Will this, you know, will I be – '

'Hey,' Kieran looked him in the eyes, a forefinger raised. 'It stays in here. Any little ring kerfuffles stay in here. He knows that. Everyone knows that.' He threw the tissue aside then scrunched a small plastic pouch of gel-like liquid to start the chemical reaction that would drop its temperature to near freezing. 'Besides, he fucking asked for it with that head butt. Did I mention what a class punch you gave him. Class!'

Jon sucked in breath. 'What was his problem? He's been gunning for me all day. Or is he like that with everyone?'

Kieran held the pouch to Jon's cut. 'He went for DS last year. Missed out. I know he's going for it again. Must have decided you are his competition.'

Jon worked the over-sized gloves off. The knuckles on his left hand were throbbing. 'I've only been here for two minutes. Why the fuck would I be applying for promotion?'

'What can I say? He's a twat.' He handed Jon the ice pack. 'Though something tells me they won't let you stay as a DC for too long.'

Jon pressed his knuckles into the chill surface. 'You what?'

Kieran shrugged. 'You're too good for that, it's obvious.'

Jon lifted more food towards his mouth. 'It's fine. Just one of those things.'

Alice's legs stayed perfectly straight as she angled forward to reach for the bottle. 'I need a drink.' She splashed wine into her glass.

'Honestly, it's fine,' Jon said, slipping his left hand under the table so she couldn't see the inflamed skin of his knuckles. 'This guy bumped heads with me. It's not a problem.'

'Mmm,' she said, not sounding convinced. 'What else, then?'

'Well, I don't have a boss, as such. Not like in the Major Incident Team, anyway. People are put together on a job-by-job basis. So if you need fieldwork guys, surveillance for example, someone with financial training, a couple of SFOs and someone with vehicle pursuit training – they put you all in a group and off you go. Two branch managers run all the ops.'

'And how do they seem?'

'Fine. They seem fine. Quite a few ex-forces, as expected. Funnily enough though, I might have been paired with this female detective. Five feet two, at most. Tiny little thing.'

Alice smirked. 'Beauty and the beast, then?'

'Think you're so funny, don't you?' He smiled.

'How old is she?' Alice asked, eyes on her glass as she rocked the ruby liquid about inside it.

Jon knew his wife well enough to know what that question was about. Threat assessment. 'Babe? She's about twenty-five. I could – literally – be her dad.'

Alice looked up innocently. Wine had tinged her lips purple and she had that mischievous look in her eyes he so loved. 'An older man like you? All big and muscley and powerful?'

He put the fork down so he could lay his hand across hers. 'She'll be sorely disappointed in me, then. Besides, she's dark. And I only like blondes.'

Alice flipped her hand over and gripped his thumb tight. 'Good. Because you know what I'd rip off if you did anything.'

Jon grimaced. 'I do, my sweet little angel, I do.'

She released his thumb with a good-natured grin. 'What's she called, anyway?'

Iona let herself in through the back door of her parents' house. The windowsill of the utility room was lined by glass jars of her dad's green tomato and red chilli chutney.

Below them was a shoe rack fashioned from a recycled pallet. Her old wellies were at one end, next to those of her sister, Fenella. Then came Moira's and Wasim's. On the shelf below was her mum and dad's walking boots. The rich smell of leather mingled with the aroma of food seeping in from the kitchen beyond. Before opening the inner door, she stood still and soaked up the comforting sights and sounds. Was it right, she wondered, that – even after five years in my own flat – this feels more like home?

'Here she is!' Moira announced, looking over her shoulder with delight as the door opened.

Her mum's hair was – for the moment at least – a pale shade of blue. Bangles clinked as she placed a spatula beside a gaping pan. 'Come here, hen.'

Iona dumped her handbag on the wicker stool in the corner. She stepped round the table and hugged the other woman tight. Not for the first time, she thought her mum's back felt more curved and bony. With every visit, Iona seemed to be gaining height; but she hadn't grown since her teenage years.

'How's my favourite youngest daughter?' Moira asked, leaning back to look into her face. 'Beautiful as ever.'

'You've made Puttanesca,' smiled Iona, looking over at the simmering sauce in the pan. 'Thanks, Mum.'

'Well, you've been hard at work all week. How's it been?'

'Fine,' Iona replied, reaching for the fridge door.

'There's a carton of fresh juice at the bottom,' Moira announced.

Iona smiled at their routine. There was always a carton of fresh juice when she came round for tea, no matter how often Iona said she'd be perfectly happy with tap water.

Still facing the fridge, she began to mouth her mum's next comment.

'Or there's a bottle of red wine on the side Wasim opened earlier.'

Iona lifted the carton out. Pineapple, lime and orange. 'I'll pinch some juice, thanks.' She plucked a glass off the rack and sat in her usual seat. 'Dad in his study?'

'He is. So, what's new?'

Iona knew this was Moira's way of asking if she was seeing anyone. She deflected the question easily enough. 'They've got me working with this new guy. Detective Constable. He only arrived today.'

Moira turned the gas on below a large pan of water. 'Older or younger than you?'

'Oh, older. Definitely older.'

'How much?'

'At least a decade-and-a-half. Probably more.'

Moira placed a hand on one hip. 'What rank did you say he was?'

'Detective Constable.'

'And he's about forty? Am I missing something?'

'How do you mean?'

'It sounds like that famous poster with the headline, I never read the Economist. Except it was signed by a management trainee, aged forty-seven or something.'

It was a concern of her parents Iona was well used to. They had never been comfortable with her entering the police, especially not the male-dominated environment of the Counter Terrorism Unit. Once she joined it, they quickly became convinced she was being constantly sidelined, undermined, or both. 'Oh – he knows what he's doing. Well, he does if it doesn't involve photocopiers.'

'So, if he knows what he's doing, how come he's still a detective – '

'He got kicked out of the Major Incident Team.'

Moira lifted a large glass of wine from beside the cooker. 'They've yoked you to someone who's disgraced himself? Brilliant. What did he do?'

'I don't know, exactly. No one's given me the full story. I just heard his transfer from the MIT wasn't voluntary.'

'What does he look like?'

'Well, I'd say he's six-feet-four. Big guy, shoulders out here.' She cupped the air either side of her. 'Half an ear missing.'

'Who has half an ear missing?'

Her dad was standing in the doorway through to the main part of the house. He was wearing a moth-eaten cardigan, a mobile phone in one hand, a glass of wine in the other.

Moira turned to him. 'Wasim, they've paired Iona with this detective who sounds like a right bloody nightmare.'

He turned to Iona.

'Hello, Dad.'

He came over and she lifted a hand to squeeze his arm as he kissed her.

'Chucked out of his last place, turns up at the CTU,' Moira continued. 'So who do they put him with? Iona.'

'Mum,' she protested.

'What? He does sound a nightmare. I don't suppose he's doing anything subtle, not that size.'

Wasim took a seat next to her. 'Another ex-military type, is he?'

This gets worse, Iona thought. Her last boyfriend had been in the army. Iraq had left him mentally unstable and dependent on drink. Wasim, a left-leaning lecturer in Persian studies at The University of Manchester had never approved of him. 'I'm not sure. Physically, yes. But something gives me the impression he's not your usual meat-head.'

'What's his role?' Moira asked. 'You didn't say.'

'Specialist Firearms Officer.'

'Ex-Army,' she stated. 'A fiver says he is.'

Iona decided against taking the bet. 'Have you spoken to Fenella? I saw on Facebook they'd taken the twins for a weekend in the Lake District. It looked lovely.'

'They're all fine,' Moira said. 'Little Archie and Ethan got to feed the animals; it was a proper farm.'

'Nice,' Iona took a sip of her drink. She often suspected that, in her mum's opinion, the chief consequence of her lack of partner was to deprive Moira of more grandkids.

Wasim's phone pinged. He checked the screen then disappeared in the direction of his study.

'His own stupid fault,' Moira said. 'This symposium thing he's organising – he never stops having to sort things out. So,' she leaned forward. 'Is he married, this person?'

'Yes, he's married,' Iona said, rolling her eyes. 'But I don't know any more than that. Don't worry: I'll report in regularly via text.'

Moira beamed. 'Be sure you do. A photo would be good, too.'

'Iona Khan?' Alice sipped her drink. 'Odd name.'

'Yeah,' Jon agreed, shovelling the last of his food into his mouth. He pointed at the ceiling, rapidly chewing.

Alice looked puzzled.

'She's from up there,' he managed to mumble.

'Where? Our loft?'

'She's a wildling.'

'Wildling? What are you on about?'

'Scottish! She's Scottish. Well, half-Scottish.'

'Oh.'

'And half-Pakistani.'

'Wow – that is unusual. I mean, family-wise and being in the Counter Terrorism Unit. Is she surveillance or something?'

Jon thought back to the conversation with Kieran. 'Yeah – analyst stuff, too. She's a smart cookie, they say. Degree in maths.'

Alice's features lifted. 'She can help you out when you get stuck doing The Sun's Sudoku puzzle.'

He raised a middle finger. 'Ho bloody ho. She has a nick-name. The baby-faced assassin.'

'For real?'

'Yeah. She plays striker in hockey. Her dad, apparently, was in Pakistan's national team. She was top scorer for her school and university. She also looks about fourteen. Round little face, big brown eyes.'

'But a killer, beneath. I like the sound of this girl.'

Jon decided not to add in the other snippet Kieran had told him. About Iona's dogged pursuit of a terror suspect through the uncharted warren of tunnels that ran below the city. Squeezing into openings larger detectives were happy to give up on. Refusing to stop until it was only her chasing the man through the pitch blackness.

He finished his wine and reached for the bottle. The last of it only half-filled his glass. 'Been laying into this, you old soak.'

She lifted a finger in response. 'Try being in charge of Duggy for an entire day.'

Jon checked her eyes, gauging the gravity of her comment. 'Has he been...' He paused. 'How much of a pain has he been?'

She ran a hand through her straw-coloured hair. 'He's a boy, that's all. So different to Holly – gorgeous little thing, that he is.'

'Little?' Jon laughed. 'This rate, he'll be bullying me by his tenth birthday.'

'He'll get the hang of things, soon enough.' She smiled. 'Holly just calmly observes him bouncing around. It's hilarious.'

'Until he bounces into her.'

'That we do have to watch,' she agreed, glancing at the clock on the wall. She traced a nail provocatively down the wine bottle before pointing at his glass. 'Anyway, neck that. You're on a five minute warning.'

'Aye, aye, Captain!' He raised his glass and gulped it back.

CHAPTER 24

The Porsche, Elissa thought, wasn't an automatic; he couldn't have driven it. Operating a gear stick wouldn't have been possible with a dislocated shoulder. Not even for him. Which meant he'd got her to drive it. Elissa looked around the plush interior. A car like this cost a fortune. It couldn't be hers. Maybe one of her punters…the thought caused Elissa's head to turn to the window of the room where Kelly was trapped.

Was that how he'd got hold of the vehicle? By creeping up on it while it was parked somewhere quiet? He had a knife. Did he yank open the door, get rid of the owner, maybe by stabbing him? Oh my god, had he murdered the owner? Then made Kelly get behind the wheel and drive him here?

It made sense. Which meant she'd been in that room, tape round her mouth, arms and legs for the entire day. Had he given her any water? What did he plan to do with her?

For the first time, the gravity of the situation hit home. And it had all been set in motion by her. The simple act of passing a snippet of information to Uncle Bilal had led to this. Whoever owned the Porsche could well be dead. He'll probably also kill Kelly. They wouldn't be the last either – the reason he's here is to end more lives. Maybe mine as well, when it suits him.

She also knew things couldn't be stopped. Her part in this was decided. Even if she got out of the car, walked to the nearest police station and revealed everything, her punishment would be severe. Decades in prison. She felt her armpits tingling with sweat. Closing her eyes, she pictured her family.

All dead.

And who, she asked herself, was bothered about them? Who was trying to get justice for Tarek? Certainly not the British government. All those bastards did was brush off her father while actually doing the exact opposite. She shook her head and started the car.

Keeping to side roads and residential streets, she negotiated a path towards the city centre. It felt like she was in a beacon, the car's lurid shade a silent siren, attracting the attention of everyone she passed. Had the police already put out an appeal? Was the incident already a prominent item on the Manchester Evening Chronicle's web site? Main feature on Granada news? She tried to reassure herself: people weren't really looking. Not with any more interest than at any other brightly coloured luxury car. But her sense of anxiety steadily mounted. She reached a main road and, to her horror, realised where she was. Plymouth Grove. The main police station for the city centre was fifty metres to her left. Pulse suddenly thudding, she turned right. The A6. Get off it, Elissa, now. She continued along, desperate to dump the vehicle. Anywhere would do. She took a left, then a right, found herself approaching the Greyhound racing stadium in Belle Vue. To her side was the monumental parking area for the Showcase Cinema. She steered in, drove across swathes of empty spaces to the smattering of vehicles clustered close to the pale building.

Two attendants in fluorescent jackets were leaning on a railing, both watching her approach. Damn it. She circled round, acutely aware the odd manoeuvre had drawn their attention. The exit road led round to the A57. It was one of the main roads out of Manchester, brightly lit and busy with traffic. The last thing she wanted. Faint with fear, she saw an Aldi on her left. That would do. She pulled in and drew up alongside a dark blue van, reasoning it would screen the Porsche from the main road.

The locks pipped, sidelights flashing twice as she walked rapidly away. The shop was still open. Food. She needed food and other stuff. She wandered up and down the aisles, tossing packets and cans in. Did he eat meat? Would he eat pork? Probably not. She found packets of dried beef and grabbed a few. Medicine section: she picked off a few packets of painkillers. That should do.

Outside, she looked around. It was a long walk back to the flat, especially carrying a load of shopping. On the far side of the road, a bus was idling at its stop. The front of it said Didsbury. That would take her in the right direction, at least. But by the time there was a sufficient break in the traffic for her to cross, it had pulled away.

She scanned the timetable on the side of the shelter. In eight minutes, one was due for the Christie Hospital. She studied the route: it went along the A6010, practically past Uncle Bilal's flat. A police car was among the stream of traffic turning onto the A6 from a side road. She stepped back and kept her head bowed as it prowled past.

Knowing she was rid of the Porsche let her think more clearly. She considered the man who spoke Russian once more. What was the plan? All she was certain of was he couldn't do it alone. She was all the help he had. What could she do to convince him to open up? She'd fixed his shoulder, removed the threat posed by the Porsche, bought him supplies. What more was there?

She wanted to stamp a foot in frustration. Instead, she stepped closer to the kerb, unaware of the small CCTV camera set into the underside of the shelter's roof.

He sat on the sofa with the case for the computer game balanced on one knee. Its garish colours and bloated lettering annoyed him. Tilting his head back let him study the ceiling. He followed a thin crack in the white surface. It snaked across to a patch of lighter plaster that was cloud-like in shape. He imagined it was a sky he was looking at. Somewhere peaceful, where the air wasn't stale and warm like here. The craggy pinnacles of rock above the trees. Up past the heavily wooded slopes and the meadows where herds of goats roamed each summer. He thought back to being a child. It was something he rarely did because it seemed so pointless. That world was gone, eradicated by the Russians. They'd arrived and changed everything. New ways to live. New rules. New language. He remembered sitting in the village classroom as the pale-faced teacher with the long face and wisps of brown hair wrote out the new letters they had to learn.

He recalled when the checkpoints first started to appear. The soldiers stopping everyone, poking through the trucks, demanding small bribes before letting them continue to market. The dull noise of their helicopters' engines. How the sound polluted the sky long before the machines actually appeared. The rumble and boom of distant explosions.

It had been around his twelfth birthday when the bus he was on had juddered to a halt. Four men climbed silently down from the storage rack on the roof and strode effortlessly off up the slope. A bend and twist in the road later and they hit a roadblock. The Russian soldiers were more careful than usual. Their faces were tense. Everyone had to get off while they searched the vehicle. Even old women. Two climbed up on the roof and went through the stacked sacks and bundles of produce wrapped in old blankets.

Once they were through, the bus drove on for a few minutes then pulled over once again. After a few minutes, he saw shadows further up the slope. The same four men picked their way back down through the trees. He saw the driver nod at them as they clambered back up the side of the bus. Sticking his head out the narrow window, he glimpsed a Kalashnikov hanging beneath one of their cloaks. It was the first time he really realised: his people were at war.

Slowly, he lifted his head off the sofa. The case with the pictures of dragons came back into view. He'd hoped, by thinking back to childish things, the words he needed to make the game work would reappear. Nothing.

He swept his right arm out, sending the plastic case clattering across the coffee table and on to the floor.

CHAPTER 25

Twenty minutes later, she pressed the bell on the bus. It slowed to a stop and she stepped off: Uncle Bilal's flat was round the next corner.

Within seconds, she was knocking softly on the front door. When she thought there might have been movement on the other side, she bowed her head. 'It's me.'

The lock clicked, the door half-opened and she slipped through the gap. In the dim hallway, he kept his back to the closed bedroom door. Just seeing it made her stomach churn.

'OK?' he asked, dark eyebrows raised. His left hand hung loose from the front of the sling, the knife gripped in his fingers.

'Yes. I have food.' She half-raised an Aldi bag.

He gestured for her to go past, so she stepped round him and went through to the kitchen. Once all the tins and packets were lined up, she looked over her shoulder. He was standing in the doorway, staring at what she'd brought.

'Hungry?' She opened a drawer, took out a fork and pretended to eat. 'Yes?'

'Da.'

'This? Yes?' She lifted a packed of ready-cooked chicken strips. 'With this?' She showed him a family-size sachet of rice and vegetables.

He sent her an approving look then watched as she boiled the kettle and searched for a saucepan and cutting board. Once the rice was simmering, she pointed to the front room. 'We speak? You and me?'

He seemed reluctant, but stepped back to allow her past. She went over to the Xbox, immediately noticing the controller had been moved. And there was a case for a children's game on the floor. He'd been using the machine while she'd been out. Was that how they kept in contact with him? Surely they'd have told him she could be trusted? That he should let her help him carry out the plan?

Once on the internet, she brought up the translation site and started selecting letters. *I got rid of the car.*

She looked for his reaction but only got the slightest of nods.

I paid for the food with my money.

This got her a disinterested stare.

Do you have any cash?

A nod.

How much?

He made a circling motion with his fingers.

Did that, she wondered, mean enough? Or to ask something else? She formed another question. *How will you travel now?*

He immediately lost his disdainful expression, breaking eye contact to adjust a fold in the sling.

Got you, she thought. You don't know. Maybe you don't even know how to drive. And you certainly don't know there's a train that goes all the way to Anglesey. She formed another comment: *I can get us another car.*

He studied the words and looked at her, eyes dark and guarded.

Methodically, she selected new letters. *Let me help you.*

No reaction.

You need my help.

That scornful laugh.

I know where you must go. I gave that information to whoever sent you!

He read her comments and sat back, face like stone.

She typed again. *Ask them!*

She had to tap the controller against the table to get his attention. It was, she thought, like getting a moody child to take his medicine. She held the controller out to him.

Before she could react, it had been knocked from her hand. 'Ya ne mogu sprosit, potomu chto ya ne znayu, kak.' He brought his face to within inches of hers. 'Ti tupaya suka!'

Whatever the words were, he'd dragged them out in a low, menacing voice. It was a threat: a warning. She understood that.

'I'll get the food,' she murmured and rose to her feet.

In the kitchen, she had to lean against the sink and take several breaths. For an insane instant, when he'd closed down the space between them, she wasn't sure whether he was about to strike her or kiss her. His eyes had been brimming with such intense emotion.

She saw now there was only one way to prove herself to him. Shaking off her shoulders, she turned round.

He was in the doorway, watching her.

Ignoring him, she opened the packet of chicken then took a long sharp knife from the wooden rack beside the toaster. Once she'd cut the strips into small pieces, she checked the rice. Most of the liquid had been absorbed. She placed the cutting board on the edge of the pan and used the long blade to push the chicken into the bubbling rice. A couple of stirs and it was ready. She gestured at the small table in the corner.

Without replying, he crossed the room and took a seat.

She spooned his plate high and showed it to him. 'Enough?'

He beckoned for the plate.

As soon as it was before him, he started digging away at the mound of food. Bits fell from his mouth, and as she placed the dirty cutting board and knife in the sink, she thought he'd have been better off with a spoon. With her hands hidden from sight, she slid the knife up into the sleeve of her sweat-top. The elasticated cuff kept it from falling back out. 'Toilet,' she announced, pointing to the door.

He didn't look pleased at having to break off from his food. Not waiting for his permission, she strode across the front room. At the toilet door, she glanced back. As she suspected, he had shadowed her – but only as far as the kitchen doorway.

She closed and locked the toilet door, counted to five, reopened it and peeped out. She heard the chink of his fork; he was back at the table. Quickly, she crossed the corridor and let herself into the bedroom.

Kelly was now slumped so far forward, her chin rested on her chest. Her shallow breathing was turning erratic. The number of times the woman had been brought into the Accident and Emergency department, Elissa thought. Sometimes it was for injuries she'd received on the streets. Almost always, alcohol was involved. Often, she was so drunk, the paramedics had to wheel her in on a trolley. In the parlance of the A & E doctors, she was CTD. Circling The Drain. Every time she reappeared, staff couldn't believe she was still alive.

Elissa examined the woman's skin. Even in the half-light, she could see its yellow tinge. Hepatitis C and B. So advanced, the doctors thought that, if her liver wasn't already riddled with cancer, it soon would be. There was no doubt she had chronic cirrhosis. It was a matter of speculation whether she was also HIV-positive. She always refused the test.

Elissa knew, if she slid the woman's sleeves up, her forearms would be stained with rivulets of black dots.

Needle marks. It had been, Elissa guessed, about twenty hours since she'd have had access to Sofosbuvir, the liver medication she depended on. Even if she got to hospital, it would be touch and go if she'd survive.

'Kelly?' Elissa whispered. 'Kelly?' She lifted the woman's chin. Her face was slack, eyes closed.

She let the head sag back to where it was. I needed to know, Elissa thought as she removed the knife from her sleeve. I needed to know that she wasn't conscious.

Moving quickly, trying not to think about what she was doing, Elissa positioned the tip of the blade in line with the base of Kelly's heart. Grasping the handle in a firm double grip, she closed her eyes and shoved hard. Please don't hit a rib. The blade passed cleanly into the woman's chest cavity and Elissa leaned forward, pressing it in right up to the handle.

Kelly's torso twitched and stiffened. Her legs kicked a couple of times, but the tape prevented her from moving too much. Elissa kept the blade in position, knowing if she withdrew it too early, blood would spurt all over her. Bit by bit, the other woman's body relaxed. She waited another half minute, stepped aside and withdrew the knife. It was covered in blood. Some was on her hands and a large patch had spread down to the top of Kelly's skirt. The seat was dripping.

Elissa walked quickly from the room and along the short corridor. It was like someone else was moving her. It was like she wasn't there. She was just an observer, watching herself entering the kitchen, using a hand wet with red to place the slickened blade on the table before him. That woman then stepped back, arms at her sides and stared at him with a defiance Elissa didn't recognise.

He saw the knife and looked up, mouth full of food. She didn't blink. At her sides, her bloodstained fingers had started to stick together. His eyes swept the rest of her, then suddenly widened with realisation. He stood up so fast, the chair toppled over. Two, three steps back, then he turned towards the door, eyes still locked on hers.

'Me and you,' she said hoarsely as, finally, he hurried out of the room. 'Me and you!'

CHAPTER 26

Jon jogged down the ginnel separating his row of houses from the one behind. The ticking of Wiper's claws slowed as they came to a stop at the gate into Jon's tiny backyard. Once inside, his dog made straight for a stainless steel bowl of water. Jon's hand was turning the handle of the kitchen door when he heard Alice's voice beyond it.

'Duggy, no!'

Family's up, then. He pushed the door open.

'Daddy!' Holly rushed across the room, drawing short when she got within arm's reach. 'Euw, you're all wet.'

He held out his arms and gave her a beseeching look.

She hesitated, wanting to hug her dad, but not wanting to get covered in sweat. Finally, she worked out a compromise and hugged the sleeve of his upper arm. Briefly.

'I wouldn't touch him, either,' Alice said. 'Stinky Daddy!'

Duggy let out an excited cry, claggy lumps of Weetabix clinging to his face and hands. The infant's legs were a mass of sharp little movements. Jon had to grin. 'You are such a little monster, aren't you?'

Alice used his toothless smile as an opportunity to pop the last spoonful of food in. His lips closed round it. She withdrew the spoon to a point just below his chin and waited. His delighted eyes hadn't left Jon as his mouth re-opened and it came tumbling back out.

'He's had enough,' Alice stated, removing the plastic bowl from the reach of his chubby little fingers. She then used his cloth bib to remove the food from his face and hands. As soon as she stood, Jon moved in and lifted him from the high seat. Like hoisting up a sack of gravel, he thought. 'Now little man, no yacking all over your Daddy!'

Duggy started trying to jam his fingers into Jon's mouth. He angled his head back, laughing at his son's persistence. On the shelf above the radiator, his phone started to ring.

Alice checked the screen. 'Private number.'

'If it's a bloody sales call...can you do the honours?'

Alice pressed green. 'Hello? No, he's busy. Listen, if you're selling PPI or something, we're...oh. Right. Hang on a second.' She pressed the mouthpiece to her chest. 'It's Iona Khan,' she said in a low voice. 'Swap?'

Jon glanced at the clock; seven twenty in the morning, and on a Sunday. She was keen. He nodded.

Alice raised the phone. 'Hang on, Iona.'

He transferred Duggy into Alice's arms then plucked the phone from her fingers. 'Iona, hi.'

'Morning, Jon – sorry to ring so early, but did you get the group text?'

'Text? No.'

'I thought not. A text went out half an hour ago. I don't think you've been added to the central list, yet: I had to call Nick Hutcher to get your number.'

'What was this text?'

'The Porsche has appeared.'

'Really?' Immediately, he headed for the corridor. 'Where?'

'There's an Aldi on the Hyde Road; the A57.'

'I know it.'

'The manager found it there this morning, when he arrived to open up.'

'So where are you?'

'Stood looking at it. Someone's had a bit of fun. Kids.'

'It's been joy-ridden?'

'No, they've just wrecked the paintwork. Interior's intact, by the look of it.'

'OK, I'll be there in fifteen.' He cut the call and turned to the stairs.

As Jon neared the Showcase cinema and its vast car park, he looked at the grassy area and small playground on the opposite side of the road. He remembered the woman's body lying there, naked except for a pair of knickers, the skin of her face skilfully removed. One of several partially skinned victims The Butcher of Bellevue had scattered about here a few years before. Jon still had trouble in the meat section of the supermarket if he caught sight of raw pork; it was just too damn similar.

The Aldi was a bit further along, parking area deserted except for five vehicles: two liveried police cars, a Crime Scene Investigation van, a black VW Polo and, set apart from the group, a bright red Porsche.

Jon couldn't decide if the vehicle looked like it had been rejected by the group or if it was stalking the other cars.

Iona looked so small among the cluster of people, her dark hair shifting about as she spoke. He parked his Mondeo beside her Polo and walked quickly across. She saw him coming and met him halfway. 'Morning. What happened to your face?'

'This?' Jon touched the small cut above his eyebrow. 'Bumped heads, sparring down in the gym.'

'Back at base?'

'Yeah.'

'Who with?'

Jon wasn't sure if she meant who he'd bumped heads with or who had been sparring. 'There were loads down there. Not sure of half their names. Anyway, thanks for the heads-up.'

'No problem.'

'And Alice says sorry. For being short with you when you rang.'

'Alice is your wife?'

'She is.'

'She sounded nice.'

'Cheers. What's this looking like?'

'It was the first thing the store manager – Justin – saw on arriving this morning. The store closed at ten last night and he remembered it was one of only a few cars still here at that point. Overnight, local kids seem to have been practising their handwriting skills on it, but they didn't actually break in.'

'So the interior's intact?'

'Seems so.'

'Win.'

'Yes – and so is the situation with cameras.' She gestured to the pole in the centre of the car park. A cluster of cameras formed a crown at its top.

'Fingers crossed for a nice mug shot of our Mystery Man as he drives in.'

'My thoughts exactly. The manager's already inside bringing up the security footage. You coming?' She stepped towards the single story building. At one corner, a panel of the security shutters had been raised. Jon could see lights on through the plate glass door.

As they crossed the asphalt, he glanced over at the Porsche.

Nob-head. Jaz sux dix. Splifta. Crozzer and Dan. Red Scum.

Mr Iwobi would have a re-spray bill when he eventually got his car back, Jon thought. He checked whether it was Nikki that was crouched at the side of the car, twirling a zephyr brush across its door handles. It was a bloke. He spoke to Iona's back. 'This is me being over-cautious, but we should get the boot checked. Just to be safe.'

Iona turned round. 'Just to be...'

He watched as her look of realisation was instantly replaced by one of annoyance. 'I'm such an idiot: tunnel-vision of getting an image of the driver.'

'Easily done. I'm sure it'll be empty, but...' He approached the CSI. 'Got one of those thingummy-jiggies for forcing boots by any chance?'

The man had to tip his head right back to make eye contact. 'In the van, why?'

Jon peered into the vehicle's main compartment: no droplets of blood on the cream seats, or any other signs of a struggle. 'We just want to check inside the boot.'

'It'll trigger the alarm, you realise?'

'So will getting it on a low-loader. You can't delay the inevitable.'

'Back at the depot, we can spring all the doors for you.'

'More urgent than that. Sorry.' Jon headed across to the CSI van's rear doors. As he knew it would be, the slim-line tool with a hooked-end was secured to the floor by two elasticated loops. He popped their fasteners and carried the short length of metal back to the Porsche. 'Ready for a racket?'

The CSI looked seriously pissed-off as Jon positioned the curved end beside the mid-point of the boot door. Bracing his arms, he jerked it sharply down. No alarm. Jon jammed it in further, buckling the body work. 'Kids must have drained the battery last night,' he grunted, working it up and down, 'when they were doing their graffiti.'

With a final wrench, he ripped the lock apart. Readying himself for the sight of a lifeless female body, he lifted it fully open. Thank God, he thought, seeing just three Nike boot bags inside. He handed the implement to the CSI with a sheepish smile. 'Panic over.'

As they stepped into the supermarket, he glanced about. 'First empty Aldi I've ever set foot in.'

Iona cast an eye over the produce in the area before the aisles began. 'Disposable barbecues. Might grab a couple on the way out.'

'You've been bitten by the Aldi bug, then?'

She started along the aisle. 'His office is at the back. I shopped in Aldi for years; I was a student not that long ago.'

'Of course, didn't occur to me it would be popular with students.'

'God, I lived on their packets of flavoured rice, I did.'

They were now passing the cereals section. 'The luxury muesli's very good, if you haven't tried it. The orange one with dried fruit.'

'Prefer the purple.'

'Purple? No way. All those curvy bits of white stuff. Like chewing on giant's toenail clippings.'

She gave him a look. 'The dried coconut, you mean?'

He shrugged. 'Whatever it is, it shouldn't be allowed.'

The door at the end of the aisle read Staff Only. There was a security pad below the handle. Iona knocked and it was swiftly opened by a thin man with thick glasses. Smile ready on his face, he looked out at Iona. Then his gaze lifted to Jon. 'Oh.'

'This is my colleague, DC Spicer,' Iona announced.

'Morning,' Jon said cheerily, extending a hand.

'Yes, morning.' He quickly shook then stepped back. 'This way.'

Jon could see the man was slightly flustered as he turned and bustled along a short passage to the office at the end. They passed a noticeboard with green names on a red grid. Times filled the boxes. The staff area was drab and basic. Like they all are, Jon thought. Inside the cramped office he saw two cups of tea ready beside a boxy television.

'Um...' The manager pushed his glasses back up his nose with a forefinger. 'Did you want a drink?'

'No, you're all right,' Jon replied. 'I've just had one.'

'OK.' The manager gestured for Iona to sit then took the seat beside her. 'Tea with no sugar?'

'Thanks,' Iona replied, sliding the cup out the way.

Jon moved slightly to the side so he was just in her line of vision. Smirking, he looked at the back of Justin's head and gave her a wink.

Studiously, she ignored him. 'So, any luck, Justin?'

'I think this is it,' he said proudly. 'Time: nine-thirty-four.' He took the VCR player off pause and they all watched the red Porsche Cayenne as it swung into the car park. 'You can see the indicator's flashing,' Justin added. 'So it came from the direction of the city centre.'

Good spot, thought Jon.

The car ignored several places closer to the doors to pull up alongside a dark blue van. Reflections meant the windows were impossible to see through, but after a few seconds, the door began to open.

'Here we go,' murmured Jon.

A young female climbed out.

'That's – ' Iona stopped short of saying the name. She twisted round to look at Jon. 'It's her.'

'Well, well, well.'

They watched as she made her way into the store.

'Now,' Justin said, pressing pause. 'I've retrieved the in store footage – it's stored digitally, direct to this computer.' He reached for a mouse and the monitor on his desk lit up. 'Here she is.'

The footage was of inferior quality, but there was no doubt it was her. She came in through the doors, picked up a basket and disappeared from the camera's view.

'Given time, we could follow her entire visit,' Justin stated.

'Right through to the till,' Jon said. 'Including how she paid.'

He saw Iona nod eagerly; if she'd used a card, they should be able to track her movements with every subsequent use. 'Could you get that for us, Justin? Along with what she actually bought?'

'Absolutely.'

'Great. And could we go back to the car park footage, to see what she does on leaving?'

He spun his chair round. 'I'll go to four times speed. Average visit's duration is thirty-five to forty minutes, less with basket.'

For the next few minutes, they watched a procession of people scurrying in and out. Justin pressed play and normal speed resumed. She soon appeared, now carrying two bulging plastic bags. Without even a hint of a glance at the Porsche, she walked across the front of the building, past the chains of trolleys and through the pedestrian access point.

Jon exchanged a puzzled glance with Iona. Did that mean her location was within walking distance of the store? But then why drive to it?

'Bus,' Justin said, as if reading their thoughts. 'There's a stop on the far side of the road. Loads continue on into the city centre from there.'

Iona gave him a smile and the man's face instantly flushed.

CHAPTER 27

Elissa walked along the quiet street. Early Sunday morning and the world was still asleep. She had the same feeling of detachment as when she'd clamped both hands round the knife's handle and...she winced at the thought. The windows of the houses to her side were made grey by pale curtain linings beyond the glass. She pictured what was on the other side of those drawn curtains. Sleeping bodies stretched out in silent rooms. She thought of Kelly. How she was also in a quiet room with the curtains drawn. Sitting cold and stiff in that chair.

The Elissa Yared I was, she thought, is gone. When the man had reappeared in the kitchen doorway, he'd found her at the sink, hands a mass of bubbles as she removed the blood that, on drying, had tightened like a thin membrane of glue on her skin. Methodically, she rubbed a thumb at the creases and grooves, just like she was at work. Once the routine was complete, she carefully checked for any grazes or nicks. There were none. She was fine. She hadn't contracted Hepatitis B or C or HIV. Not that it really mattered: life, as she knew it, had ended with news of Tarek's death. All this? It was tying up a few loose ends before she got to see her family once more.

He returned to his seat and started to finish off the rest of his food. But when she glanced across, his expression was different. More thoughtful. Seeing his meal was almost eaten, she went into the front room and knelt before the TV.

When he came through, her message was ready on the screen. *We could not let her live.*

He beckoned for the controller. *That is true.*

She took it back. *What is your name?*

Doku Zakayev

Thank you. What is next, Doku?

Another place.

She wondered if that included her. It had to include her. What else had she left but this? As she selected the letters, she felt sick with dread. *How will you get to the other place?*

She couldn't bear to look at the screen as he formed his reply. Eventually, he said her name. 'Elissa?'

She dragged her eyes up from the floor. His reply was waiting on the screen. *In the car you will get for us.*

Elissa rotated her hips slightly as she continued walking along. The sofa had been too soft; now she felt stiff. He had offered her the empty bedroom, but his shoulder needed to be properly supported.

After another ten minutes, she got to the A & E department. It was less busy than expected and she was able to slip in through the doors reserved for ambulance arrivals, then continue to the staff room without anyone stopping her for a chat. Inside, a group of four nurses were on their break. As Elissa hoped, Linda was among them. On seeing her, Linda glanced at the big whiteboard where all the shifts were laid out. 'Hello there. You're not on, are you?'

'No. Actually, I was – good morning, by the way.'

'Morning.'

'I popped in hoping to ask a bit of a favour...'

'OK. You need to borrow my car again?'

Elissa smiled. A rosy-faced woman in her fifties, Linda was one of the few people at work who had shown more than a cursory concern over the fact Elissa had lost her entire family in such a short space of time. When arrangements for her father's funeral needed to be made, Elissa's car was off the road. Linda had insisted that Elissa borrow hers, and then offered to help out in any other way that was needed. 'Got it in one. I'm really sorry to ask – but Aunty Furat needs to visit her sister in Rochdale. It's – '

Linda held up a hand. 'Forget the details. It's fine.'

'Thanks, Linda. You know…Sunday trains…'

'I certainly do. Honestly, it's not a problem. I'm on until eight all this week; I won't even touch the thing before Friday.' She went over to her locker and undid a little padlock. 'It's parked right outside my place. Just let me know where you leave it if there's no space there when you get back.' She produced a set of keys from her handbag, slid the one off with a Toyota logo on the fob and held it up with a flourish. 'Ta-da! The pocket rocket.'

'Thanks so much, Linda. Let me give you some money for this.'

'Rochdale and back? Don't be silly. Go on, off you go.'

'Really?'

'Of course.'

Elissa started for the doors. 'Wine, then? A bottle of SB.'

The fingers of Linda's right hand fluttered theatrically at her throat. 'Well, if you insist.'

'It's a deal,' Elissa replied, pocketing the key.

CHAPTER 28

'So, who are we actually reporting to?' Jon asked as they walked from the car park to the CTU building.

'DCI Weir,' Iona replied. 'Since, at the start of this, I had been tasked with looking into Elissa Yared. And, you're the new boy – so you get bounced between teams, not me.' She gave him an innocent smile.

'Fine with me,' Jon answered. He'd already reasoned that Weir might have made him feel unwelcome, but the man seemed like he'd be straightforward to deal with. Pinner, on the other hand, had appeared more friendly – but the way he'd deflected Jon's question about the potential gravity of the case was a worry. It had been evasive. Slippery. And, in Jon's experience, that indicated a man more concerned with his own success than that of his team. He'd take Weir's hostility any day.

They found the DCI in his office, mulling over paperwork.

'Spicer and Khan.' He waved them to the seats opposite his desk and addressed Iona. 'What did you find?'

'The Porsche was being driven by Elissa.' She removed the previous evening's security tape that had been requisitioned from the Aldi store. 'Got her on this, clear as day.'

Weir seemed to take the revelation in his stride. 'She's working with the Mystery Man.'

'Seems so,' Iona responded. 'She also bought a load of food items and some painkillers. Paid with cash.'

'Painkillers?'

'We know he damaged his shoulder in the collision on the M60.'

'She bought this stuff from the same location where she dumped the car? What's that: arrogant or naive?'

'Naive, judging from what she may have done next.'

'That being?'

'Well, she drove to the store from the direction of the city centre. When she left, she had two bags of shopping. We're hoping she crossed the road and got a bus from the stop directly opposite – back to where she came from. While at the scene, we put a call in to Transport for Greater Manchester. They control the CCTV system across the network.'

'There's a camera in the bus shelter,' Jon added. 'Six different services stop there over each half-hour period. We know that, if she did hop on one, it would have been at about ten in the evening.'

His eyes shifted between them, before settling on Iona. 'Good work. How long before they get back to you?'

'They said it should be later this morning,' she replied.

'And the Porsche?'

'It's gone for forensics. They'll go over it properly at their facility.'

'Right. Obviously, you missed the eight a.m. briefing, so I'll fill you in on overnight developments. Russian security services have yet to respond to our request on the fingerprints removed from the mobile phone. I don't think we're top of their Christmas card list these days. Anyway, a more senior member of our consular team is trying to inject a bit of urgency.' His eyes went to the report on his desk and he gave a sigh. 'Aside from that, we no longer have sole control of the case.'

Jon had been wondering how long before the potential hostage situation with Kelly caught the attention of the wider force.

'There's still no sign of the working girl who's missing. And now the vehicle she was taken in has shown up, minus her. It looks very likely that aspect of how the operation runs won't be decided by us.' He held up a hand as Iona started to say something. 'I know – but it's just the way it is. I'll make sure you still play a part in things, don't worry. OK, let me know what happens with the Transport people.' He interlinked his fingers to signal that was it.

'Will do, Sir,' Iona replied, rising to her feet.

'Oh, Iona? Two more seconds of your time.'

As Jon stood, Weir gave him the slightest of nods. He left the room sensing a faint thaw in the DCI's attitude. On the floor below, he made for the canteen area and selected a cup of black coffee from the machine. Of the few officers in there, he recognised a couple from down in the gym. Their heads were down in conversation and he couldn't tell if they'd clocked him or not. No sign of Lambert.

He carried on to the main operations room and did a quick check for any sign of the other officer. The only familiar thing he spotted was the ginger of Kieran Saunders' hair. 'Morning.'

The Welshman glanced round. 'Spicer! All good with you?'

'Yeah, fine.' He perched on the edge of the other man's desk and lowered his voice. 'Lambert's not called in sick or anything, has he?'

Kieran chuckled. 'No – he was here, acting like nothing happened.' He play-coughed into his hand. 'Though we know different, don't we? Your face isn't too bad, I see.'

'And you're sure nothing will get to the grown-ups?'

'It might do, but they'll do fuck all about it. Unless Lambert lodges something official – which he'll never do if he wants anyone to speak to him in this place ever again.' He grinned for a second then craned his neck to see past Jon. Lifting his voice, he announced, 'So, they got you working with the Baby-Faced Assassin, hey?'

Jon looked towards the doors. Iona was heading towards her desk. She raised a hand to Kieran. 'I'll try to be gentle with him.'

He laughed delightedly. 'You do that, Iona. A sensitive flower, he is.'

Jon stood up, took one look at the crap still covering his workspace and decided to join Iona. As he pulled up a chair beside her, she glanced at his coffee. 'Welcome to planet Selfish, population one.'

'I didn't know how long you'd be. What do you want? I'll get it.'

She shook her head. 'Just joking. I'm fine.'

'You're sure? I don't mind.'

'No – really.' She turned on her computer then ran her fingers down her throat and coughed, dryly.

'Fuck's sake.' Jon got up with a smile. He thought back to the Aldi manager's office. 'Tea, no sugar?'

'Yeah, thanks. By the way, you were right.' She bounced a glance off the ceiling. 'Weir wanted to know exactly what I'd said to Elissa Yared, when we crossed paths at her Aunt's.'

Jon turned back to look at her properly. 'And?'

She adopted a formal tone. 'I was able to give him a very succinct and accurate account of my exemplary conduct.' Her shoulders relaxed. 'Thanks for the advance warning on that one.'

'My pleasure. Now, you're sure you want this tea?'

She frowned. 'Yeah...'

He started walking away. 'No, that's fine. You know, I just thought, maybe you weren't really thirsty. Not after the brew the lovely manager at Aldi was so keen to make you.' Glancing back, he fluttered his eyelashes at her.

Kieran's head came up. 'What's that?'

'Nothing to do with you,' Iona said quickly, cheeks starting to flush.

Jon chuckled to himself as he headed out the door.

When he got back with her drink, she was in the middle of her emails. She looked up at him. 'Transport for Greater Manchester are on the ball: they've replied already.'

Jon retook his seat.

'A female matching the description we gave them boarded the 183 to the Christie Hospital at two minutes past ten. Onboard footage shows her disembarking at a stop on the A6010, just before it crosses the A34. They even ask if we want copies of the footage.' She looked at him, her bright blue eyes sparking with excitement.

As Jon lifted a palm so they could slap hands, Weir came through the doors. 'Everyone on Operation Stinger? Word's just back from our security forces out in Afghanistan. Last night's strike on the warehouse facility was called off. It was just about to happen when the gates were opened up and a lorry departed.'

Someone on the next row of desks spoke up. 'They have eyes on the vehicle?'

'They do. It drove to a private residence with a secure compound in the east of the city. They're working out the best way in, as it's a very crowded neighbourhood.'

'And us?' someone else asked. 'We carry on?'

Weir nodded. 'It's all we can do. Primary objective now is to lay hands on the Mystery Man.'

Iona raised a hand. 'Sir? We have something that should help with that.'

CHAPTER 29

Doku Zakayev was squatting on his haunches before the television, knees forming a fulcrum beneath the elbows of his outstretched arms. On the screen was the start-up page for the dragon game. As cartoonish creatures flapped silently about in the background, the cursor blinked patiently in the field that read username.

Down the corridor, the toilet flushed.

He immediately rocked forward so he could eject the disc.

By the time Elissa came into the room, the game was back in its case and he was in his previous position on the sofa.

She looked at her watch. Just after nine. He'd been sitting there for so long. The sling had been discarded and the controller for the Xbox was beside him. We need to go, she thought. Aldi opened at ten on a Sunday. But staff must arrive earlier to get the store ready. She now regretted leaving the Porsche there; she hadn't been thinking clearly. Catching a bus from so close to the store had probably been stupid, too. Which meant they should get going. Now.

Her holdall and his rucksack were on the floor by the door, alongside a single Aldi bag crammed with all the food. She decided to do another check of the flat. The room he'd slept in was stripped bare: discoloured mattress exposed to view. The chest of drawers and wardrobe contained only bits of fluff and a single hairpin. Probably had been there when Uncle Bilal had bought it at some cheap second-hand furniture place on Hyde Road.

Unable to even look at the door to the other bedroom, she went straight into the bathroom. White walls and an empty shelf above the sink. The left hand tap released a single drip. She was about to try and tighten it when she registered the elongated yellow watermark stretching down the porcelain. The thing had obviously been leaking for weeks. Months.

She strode through to the kitchen. Everything was cleared away and back in its place, including the knife. She could see its black handle, hovering in the corner of her eye.

In the front room, she looked out on to the road. A man was raising the awning of the mini-supermarket opposite. The world was stirring, starting to get busy. They needed to go. Linda's car was parked on the drive, three-quarters of a tank of petrol. 'Doku?' She pointed at the window and gripped an imaginary steering wheel in her hands.

He got up, went to the corner of the room and unscrewed the lead for the router. Placing it to one side, he then peeled the carpet and underlay back. Resting against the wooden floorboards was an A4 size sleeve with a piece of paper inside. He lifted it up, walked back over and placed it on the coffee table.

Tentatively, she approached. It was a property profile from an estate agent, Morgan Lettings. 'We're going here?' She pointed at it. 'You and me?'

He nodded.

She sat down and opened the sleeve. A panel of small photos. The cottage boasted its own boat house, sea views and a private jetty that stretched about fifteen metres out from the shore. The place looked lovely: two dormer windows set into the steeply-angled roof. Elaborate white gables. A porch. Separate garage, almost a bungalow in itself. There were no other properties visible beyond the generous garden.

She searched for a location. Somewhere called Burwen, north Anglesey.

At the doorway to the corridor, she surveyed the front room once more. Something nagged at her. What was it? The router was in the top of his bag. The Xbox had been unplugged and returned to its box. They had everything. The only thing she'd written on was the back of the game console's user manual; that was already in the box with the dragon game that had come with it.

She carried her bag down to the front door. Best thing, she'd decided earlier, was for her to pack the car. By leaving a rear-door open, he could slip out the flat and into the back seat of the vehicle when no one was passing.

She turned and saw him standing with the Xbox in his arms. It was amazing how his shoulder didn't seem to bother him. Most people needed a sling for days. Sometimes weeks.

Her hand was almost on the latch when the sight of the letterbox triggered a thought. The note! The note she'd pushed through it. What had happened to it? 'Oh my God.'

She hurried back into the front room and looked frantically about. What the hell had... She dropped to her knees and bent forward to see beneath the sofa. A slither of white was just visible. She reached into the gap and pressed her fingertips down. The carpet made a faint rasping noise as she dragged it out. Temples throbbing, she straightened up.

He saw what she'd found and his mouth opened slightly. Holding it before her, she went into the kitchen, lit a gas ring and touched a corner of paper to the bluish flicker.

As yellow flame took hold, she held the note above the sink and watched her crude image of a helicopter, piloted by a man who wore a crown, start to blacken and buckle and turn to ash.

CHAPTER 30

'I'm still not convinced there was a better way,' Jon said, following the police van out of the station on Plymouth Grove. As the vehicle turned left, he could see the rows of uniformed officers inside.

The decision to flood the area had caused mutterings among his new colleagues. The CTU liked to operate below the radar: surveillance, covert tracking, research quietly conducted in the virtual world. Not dozens of bodies tramping up and down streets, banging on doors and thrusting mug-shots in everyone's faces.

'Well,' Iona said from the passenger seat, 'it guarantees one thing: they'll know we're on to them.'

'I think they were aware of that anyway,' Jon replied. 'And I can't see any quicker way than this.'

'There's a team of geeks back at base,' Iona protested. 'Going through all of Bilal Atwi's financial arrangements. They could uncover something at any moment that cracks the whole thing open.'

'Could,' Jon stressed. 'Meanwhile, Kelly is still missing and the pair of them are free to move on to their next safe house whenever they feel like it.'

'We've got surveillance outside all the family homes. We've got people making discreet enquiries at her workplace. Her bank accounts and phone: they're being monitored. This,' she flicked a hand at the van, 'is as subtle as a flying brick.'

Jon thought back to the meeting at the CTU facility. Once Iona had declared they had a possible location, a map of that part of the city was swiftly laid out across the meeting room table.

First, bus stops for the 183 were marked out on it: if Elissa had disembarked at the top of Hawthorn Street, the chances were she was heading to a property in a radius within the next and previous stops on the route. Those two places were the A34 on one side and the A6 on the other. The two roads were used to define the side boundaries of the search area. Between them was a cramped mass of residential streets. Going north, Weir went as far as the police station on Plymouth Grove.

'Bed sit city,' someone announced glumly. 'A cousin looked for digs there when she got a place at The University of Manchester. It's grim, to say the least.'

With basic parameters established, attention had turned to possible targets.

'Shops – of the variety that sell food.'

'She stocked up in Aldi. Could be local places are being deliberately avoided.'

'Take-away places, possibly?'

'Worth trying.'

'Garages and car rentals. Assuming they need a vehicle.'

'The train station.'

'How about the coach station in Manchester while we're at it?'

'Houses with a garage? For keeping that Porsche out of sight.'

'Chemists – Mystery Man could be needing more than Ibuprofen.'

'OK,' Weir said. 'We need a grid.' He placed a ruler over the defined area and starting scoring off blocks of streets with a black pen.

The car park behind a disused church had been commandeered as the rendezvous point. As they followed the van in, Iona was studying the enlarged map section that covered their portion of streets. It only stretched for about one-hundred-and-twenty metres in each direction, but within that area were seventeen different roads.

Two police vans were already in the car park, along with six marked cars. A gaggle of uniformed officers had gathered in the middle of the asphalt. Overwhelmingly males, white and under thirty, they reminded Jon of a sports team about to go on tour. He parked on the opposite side, next to the unmarked vehicles from the CTU.

Within minutes of locking his car, they'd been allocated four uniformed officers and were off.

'How long before the local press gets a whiff of this?' Jon asked, eyeing another pod of officers heading off in the direction of the A6.

'I imagine they've had words already,' Iona said, leading the way towards the turn-off into their area. 'Come to an arrangement to keep the cameras away.'

As they tramped along the A6010, Jon's gaze took in the tall Georgian houses fronting the street. Judging from their size, it had obviously been a well-to-do neighbourhood. An area for wealthy cloth merchants, from when Manchester was the industrial capital of the world.

How times changed.

The officer who'd made the comment about bed-sit city had been right: untidy clusters of wheelie bins clogged every front garden. Most bore untidy paint-strokes on their sides: Flat 1, Flat 2, Flat 3. Where any lawn still existed, long grass fringed the bins' bases. Concrete was the more common choice of surface. He saw old sofas, a mattress, unidentified bags of rubbish, a pale red kids' scooter with a wheel missing. A mangled carousel washing line. Many of the windows still had their curtains drawn. Brown cables trailed like lianas down the walls. He doubted any of the landlords lived close by – most had probably moved out to the countryside to count their pennies in peace.

On the opposite side of the road, the ground floors of the houses had been converted into commercial premises.

Clear Cut Accountancy.

Accident Specialists. Workplace. Slip, trip or Fall. Finance Guaranteed.

Ahmad and Co. Solicitors.

MWA Immigration Advisers.

M Lazeera, Financial Adviser.

'This is us.' Iona turned to the group shadowing them and pointed down the side street. 'We've got the right-hand side. Down to that shop half-way along.'

'The one with the green awnings?' A young officer in a stab-proof vest asked, eyes flitting between Iona and Jon, even though Iona held the map.

Jon looked at her for confirmation.

'Correct,' she replied. 'You've all got copies of the two sheets? Photos of the Porsche Cayenne and the female called Elissa Yared, plus a written description of the woman known as Kelly.'

All the officers nodded.

'OK. Any male fitting the description you were given back at the station, you do not engage with. Instead, move on as normal and shout for me or DC Spicer first opportunity you get. Both our mobiles are on the back of your second sheet. If no one answers, make a note of the number of that property. Let's get started.'

The group fanned out, each pair heading towards a front door. The first Iona and Jon reached was sheltered by a cavernous front arch. Greying shades of sodden newspaper lay crumpled in one corner. On the wall beside the front door was a panel of twelve buttons. Six were just blank numbers, six had a name.

Mrs J Lato
Sidi Moallim
Mr L McNair
Shwan Khesro
Mr Kuklys
Igors Ikaunieks

'Any preference?' Jon asked, lifting a forefinger.

'Eleven.'

The number she plays in her hockey team, Jon thought. He pressed the button and waited. No reply. 'And your second choice?'

'Your turn, I insist,' Iona replied.

He tried seven. The number for openside flanker: his position from when he played rugby.

'Hello?' A male voice, sounding surprised.

Jon bent nearer the intercom. 'Good morning. I'm an officer with Greater Manchester Police. Could I have a brief word?'

'Why?'

'We're making enquiries in this area.'

'Enquiries.'

'Yes.'

'About what?'

He gave Iona a look that caused her to smirk. 'That's what I'd like to have a word with you about. Sir.'

'Now?'

'Yes please.'

'I don't want a new phone.'

'I see.'

'I don't want to buy anything.'

'Well, that's fine. I'm a policeman, not a salesman.'

'You're a policeman?'

'Yes. Detective Constable Spicer. I can show you my identification.'

'Press the door. You'll see me on the first floor.' The buzzer sounded.

They stepped into a dim hallway with an elaborately tiled floor. Closed doors and the smell of old food. The dark green stair carpet added to the gloom. Looking up, Jon could see a pale face looking over the banister.

'Where is your police force badge?' the person called down.

Jon reached for his ID as he began trudging up the stairs. This, he thought, is going to be a long morning.

They made it back out almost fifteen minutes later. There had been no response from four of the flats. The other eight had all drawn blank looks from the occupants.

On the front path, Jon raised his face to the sky and breathed deeply. 'One down.'

A pair of uniformed officers appeared from the neighbouring house. One met Jon's enquiring glance with a shake of the head. He sent a grim-faced smile in return. Further down the road, three officers from a separate group were gathered at the intersection with the first side street. As Jon tried to work out why they were standing about doing nothing, a fourth officer came hurrying out of the corner shop with the green awning. He began conferring excitedly with them. 'Something's up,' Jon announced.

Iona turned round. One officer who, to Jon, looked nearly old enough to be a Premiership footballer, started speaking into his handset. A colleague stepped to the edge of the pavement and looked up and down the road.

Jon started in their direction. 'Lads?'

They turned to him with a look of excitement and relief. The officer who'd been in the shop used a thumb to point back at it. 'The owner of this place.'

Jon glanced at the awning.

Mega-Mart. Cash & Carry. Grocery. Halal Meat. Fish and Poultry.

He guessed the loose piles of fresh fruit and vegetable in crates at the front would be a damn sight cheaper than what he was used to paying in Asda. 'What about him?'

'He says, for all of yesterday, there was a bright red Porsche parked outside the house across the road.'

CHAPTER 31

Half an hour of driving and the silence in the car had grown oppressive. Every so often, Elissa stole a glance at him in the rear view mirror. Head bowed, arms crossed, he stared down at his feet. Several times, she was tempted to try and find out what was bothering him. But what was the point? She'd ask, OK? He'd reply Da or Net and, from that point on, further communication was impossible.

She switched the radio on but, after a matter of seconds, she could see his posture tensing. She tried changing stations, searching for something that didn't fill the car with thudding bass or breathless vocals. The fourth station the tuner settled on was, initially, silent. She was about to press again when faint piano notes tentatively drifted from the speakers. He lifted a hand. Do nothing.

The notes began to build, forming into something delicate and beautiful.

'You like?' She asked. 'Good?'

'Good,' he replied, closing his eyes.

Thank Christ for that, she thought, now also able to relax. As the hypnotic music played on, she surveyed the land on her side of the M56. A flame wavered like a yellow flag against the pale blue sky. She spotted a second, trapped deeper within the metallic snarl of pipes that writhed and twisted along the horizon. Stanlow Oil Refinery. In less than two hours, they should be at the property.

Then what? She still had no idea of how the plan would be carried out. She wondered how much Doku knew. Probably only fragments, as well. That's what it was like, being a soldier – if he could be called that. You didn't question orders, you followed them, trusting that those giving them knew what they were doing.

She so hoped they did. The information she'd given Uncle Bilal all those weeks ago was only relevant for September. And tomorrow would be the final day of the month. They were almost out of time. There wouldn't be another chance. Not now she'd left her job, abandoned her flat, revealed herself to the authorities.

The music faded into silence. Doku took a sudden intake of breath, like he had been jerked from sleep. His eyes snapped open. 'Phone,' he announced, word heavily accented. He repeated it more loudly. 'Phone.'

His voice had an emphatic tone. He looked at her eyes in the mirror and lifted his right hand to his ear. 'Phone.'

Something was starting up on the radio that involved violins and a flute. She turned it off. 'Phone call? You need to make a call?' Had he remembered a contact number? What was so urgent? 'You need to phone someone?'

He was about to speak, hand cupping the air before his mouth as if trying to pull the words out. Grunting with frustration, he scanned the road before them. After a few seconds, he directed a finger at something in front. She tried to work out where he was pointing. They were passing some kind of tanker in the slow lane. A bright yellow triangular sticker with an exclamation mark was on its rear. Did he mean that? But the vehicle fell behind them and he was still pointing. Further off, all she could see was countryside. A line of trees. A distant plane in the sky. 'What?'

He jabbed his finger, hand now drifting across so it stayed pointing in the right direction. Something they were passing. She looked to the side window and saw a fenced-off grey pole with antennae at the top. A mobile phone mast.

'Google,' he said, returning his hand to his ear. 'Phone. Google. You and me.'

She suddenly understood. Google translate. A mobile phone! 'Yes, yes – I see. We can talk using the internet. Yes.'

His rested his hand on the back of the front passenger seat.

'OK, we need services. A shop, to buy one.' She thought back to the last time she'd driven out this way. It had been to visit Cheshire Oaks, a retail park with dozens of designer outlets selling off old stock. It had been with Tarek. They'd left with loads of outdoor gear from The North Face. She recalled that, adjoining it, was a normal shopping centre. It was bound to have a mobile phone store.

CHAPTER 32

Once Iona put the call in, Jon was amazed at how fast the nearest houses in the street were quietly cleared of their occupants. Next, a plainclothes officer parked an old Ford Ka outside 17a. Before he got out of the vehicle, he briefly fiddled about, as if looking for something. As he checked under an empty BurgerKing container on the dashboard, instructions were coming to him through his earpiece. The cardboard container needed to be angled slightly more anti-clockwise so the camera hidden inside it was pointing directly at the property. He did as asked, climbed out of the vehicle, locked it and sauntered off.

Back at the church car park, they now had a live feed on the target property.

Gathered outside the van were a dozen CTU officers, none of them small. With no intelligence to directly suggest firearms or explosives, they knew any request for bursting into the property with an armed unit would be refused. That left the Effective Unarmed Entry option. Trained to Level One in Public Order, Jon had immediately volunteered. Among the other members of the squad, Jon recognised five from the basement gym, including Hugh Lambert. To his relief, Kieran Saunders had also put his name forward; that was his raid-partner sorted.

Using a neighbouring ground-floor flat that had been cleared of the people living there as a template, a plan of 17a had been drawn up. The eight man raid team were put in pairs, and each one allocated a room. They would use flood tactics, pouring into the property at high speed, the first pair taking the first room, second pair the second room, and so on. The sight of anyone inside the flat overrode that system: the nearest officers would simply rush the person, using whatever force was needed to restrain him.

As Jon zipped up his turnout suit, what looked like a rigid grey suitcase was being taken out of the van.

'Hey, Jon – seen one of these before?' Kieran asked him.

'Got no idea what it is,' Jon replied, strapping a shin protector that incorporated a knee-pad to his leg.

'Show him, Ian.'

'Not much to see,' the detective replied, holding it up. He opened the lid to reveal a piece of equipment that seemed more suited to a hospital ward. 'Thermal imager,' he announced. 'I slip into the flat next door and sweep this across the adjoining walls. Anyone in the flat shows up as a big glowing blob.'

'Even in rooms on the far side?' Jon asked.

'Even them,' he confirmed. 'Though the reading will be a lot less clear.'

'Got all the best toys in the CTU,' Kieran said proudly.

'We have,' Jon slid his hand into a forearm protector. 'Though my guess is it will still come down to just snotting some bastard.'

'Bloody lovely,' Kieran grinned, lacing up a steel-toe-capped boot.

Ten minutes later, they were all kitted up. Helmets with visors and leather neckguards, full limb protection, reinforced gloves, attack vests, tasers, batons and handcuffs. Jon knew the gear added a few inches of bulk to them all; they were a fearsome sight.

Hugh Lambert squared up to his raid partner and announced in a low voice, 'I feel epic.'

'You, Mr Lambert,' the other man replied, 'are so Money Supermarket.'

Pockets of laughter around the group.

'Any movement in the target property?' the search co-ordinator, an inspector Jon hadn't met before, asked.

Iona was over by the monitor showing the live feed from the camera car. 'Nothing, Sir.'

'OK, no sound now, lads.' He lifted a radio and spoke more quietly. 'Ian, have you swept it yet?' He listened for a few seconds before replying. 'Roger that.' He turned to the group. 'Listen up, a faint reading in the room across the corridor; that's first door on the right. The one with a window out onto the street. Who's Raid One?'

Hugh Lambert and his partner raised their hands.

'Right. It's your room. Could be a cat, could be someone in a sleeping bag, could be electrical equipment: just be aware. Shall we get this done?'

Their van came to halt thirty metres from 17a. Because curtains in the property were all drawn, they didn't need a covert approach. Instead, they jogged along the pavement, the two officers at the front carrying a Double Wam. Larger than an Enforcer, the Double Wam needed two officers to swing it and delivered something closer to fifteen tons of energy to any surface it connected with.

The raid team started to line up in their pairs. Seeing the battering ram being readied, Jon stepped forward. It was the first rule of a forced entry and one pumped-up officers frequently forgot: try the door handle. Locked. 'Worth a go,' he whispered and stepped back alongside Kieran.

The Wam officers raised the battering ram again. They looked at each other and gave a simultaneous nod. A signal to the rest of the team. Jon's mouth felt dry. Adrenaline had made his eyes feel too big for their sockets. Knees slightly flexed, he rocked back and forth on the balls of his feet, just like the rest of the group. If anyone was unfortunate enough to be in the corridor beyond the door, they were getting it. Big time.

The Double Wam was swung slowly back and then rapidly forward. The door flew in with a huge crash. 'Breach! Stand clear!' the Wam officers screamed, jumping out the way.

Lambert and his partner piled through the doorway. 'Police! Stand still! Police! Stand still!'

Also roaring, the next two pairs set off directly behind, followed by Jon and Kieran. By the time they started down the corridor, Raid One were in the first room. As he rushed past, he heard Lambert shouting 'Body, body, body!'

Raid Two barged into the second room and Jon had to slow up as Raid Three collided in the doorway to the bathroom. He squeezed round the rearmost officer and charged into the living area, yelling as loud as he could. 'Police! Stand still!'

Armchair. A sofa. No one behind it. Coffee table. Kieran was next to him screeching the word Police like a banshee. Curtains drawn, gap at the bottom. No feet showing. TV in corner. Desk. No one beneath. The pair who'd wielded the Double Wam barrelled past them and into the kitchen, also shouting.

Now Jon could hear cries of Clear from up the corridor. He looked at Kieran and got a nod. 'Clear!'

They both turned towards the kitchen and, a second later, got the same call from there. Containment officers at the rear of the property would be checking the yard, including any wheelie bins. It had been known.

Chest still hammering, he pushed the visor of his helmet up. Everyone else was doing the same thing. Up the corridor he could hear muffled voices. What had been the shout as they went in? Body. It had to be Kelly, he thought sadly. Wrong place, wrong time: a life could end that easily. It was Lambert who'd been yelling it.

The other officers were trooping back towards the front door, their part in the process now over. Next would be a thorough search of the place, right back to timbers and brickwork if necessary. The merest scrap of evidence could be crucial.

He couldn't resist a quick look about. Nothing of note in the kitchen. In fact, it looked like someone had given it a thorough wipe down. Toaster in the corner, block of sharp knives next to it. Everything in its place. Turning to go, he looked into the sink.

The remains of a tear-shaped ring of ash, its narrow end merging with the plughole. A piece of paper had been set alight and dropped in, then a burst of water had spread the debris outwards, but not washed all of it away. He wondered what had been on it. Something important, that was for sure.

The rest were filing out the front door into bright sunlight. 'Anyone recognise her?' Jon called.

Lambert looked back. 'Who says it's a her?'

'Well, is it?'

'Yeah.'

Jon was nearly at the bedroom door. 'And?'

'One of your lady friends, by the look of it.'

He peered in. She was practically a silhouette in the half-light. Her posture was lifeless, yet she was oddly erect in the chair. Eyes adjusting to the gloom, he began to make out sections of pale grey covering her forearms and midriff. Tape. She'd been taped into the chair.

Now he was able to make out the blondness of her hair. She was wearing black boots that rose almost to her knees. The padded jacket was yellow. Kelly. He thought about the other girls and how they wanted to know if they should be worried. If a psycho was out there.

'Is it her?'

He looked round to see Iona beside him. 'Yeah, looks it. She's been restrained by tape.'

Iona stared at the lonely figure. 'Nasty: doing it while she couldn't even move.'

'Yup,' Jon replied. 'Wonder whether he took his time. To get some enjoyment from it.'

'We'll find him.' She placed a hand on his arm. 'We will.'

'I bloody hope so,' Jon replied dejectedly.

Outside, he contemplated driving over to the street where Kelly had been touting for business. He wanted to let the others know that, although she was dead, it wasn't a Ripper-style killing: the start of a brutal, random spree that might involve them. But he couldn't. Not until all the formalities had taken place.

Beside them, the front door of the neighbouring ground-floor flat opened. The officer who'd been scanning through the walls with the thermal imager stepped out. The equipment was now back in its carry case. He plonked it down on the pathway and checked the door behind him. 'Is the number of this place 17a or 18a?'

'You were in 18a,' Iona replied. '17a was the target flat.'

'Thought so.' He held up a magazine, sealed tight in its polybag. 'This had been put through the letterbox – but it was meant for 17a. A Mr H Omari.'

Iona stepped closer. 'What is it?'

'A magazine. The postie put it through the wrong door.'

'What kind of magazine?'

'Speed boats. Bloody great things, by the look of it. The sort for taking out to sea.'

CHAPTER 33

The signs for Cheshire Oaks started to appear just before the stretch of M56 came to a finish. At that point, traffic could continue straight on to the A55 and into Wales – or it could branch right on to the M53 which led north, into the stubby finger of land called the Wirral. The signs for the shopping centre took Elissa right.

A few minutes later, they turned off the M53. After negotiating a confusing series of roundabouts, she saw a parking area beside the retail outlet. It was packed. Elissa had to circle about for almost five minutes before a space became free. All the while Doku's eyes roved from side to side, taking in the ranks of gleaming vehicles on either side. She wondered what the cars were like where he came from. Probably some obscure make you couldn't buy in Europe.

She drew to a halt and looked at the shops. The walkways teemed with people, most laden with large bags. 'OK.' She pointed to herself then the shops. 'Me, go. You,' she patted the dashboard, 'here. OK?'

'Da.' He reached into his rucksack and took the router from the top of it. After pointing to the nearby bin, he handed it over.

'OK.' She stepped out into a treacly fug. Donuts or crepes. The aroma brought back memories of fairgrounds. After dumping the router, she walked over to a notice board that gave the layout of the place: not far away was a phone retailer. As she weaved her way through the slow-moving throng, she checked the logos on the bags hanging from people's hands.

Fossil. Levis. Superdry. Diesel. Timberland. Nike. Jack Wills.

Once, not long ago, she would have cared. She would have wondered what deals she could have found for herself. None of it mattered now.

The sales assistant tried to engage her in a process she soon realised was funnelling her towards a monthly contract. One that lasted eighteen months. She stayed firm: pay-as-you-go, ready charged, on a deal that gave maximum internet access. Calls and texts were irrelevant. She withdrew her bundle of notes when he tried, once again, to convince her of the advantages of what he was offering. 'Listen, I'm in a hurry. If you can't help me, fine. There's a Tesco not far away. They do phones.'

'No, no – it's not a problem,' he said, lifting both hands. 'Let's head over to the till and get you up and running.'

She stepped back out of the shop and couldn't help feeling slightly elevated. A plastic bag hung from her fingers. It was always the same when she acquired something new. She could see the same emotion reflected in the faces of those passing by; a shine in their eyes, flecks in their cheeks.

A rapidly-speaking voice drew nearer. Someone on their phone discussing options for a forthcoming holiday. Not Tunisia. Not Turkey. Declan, I don't care how cheap the flights are. I'm not going. Those places aren't safe, you seen the news. No, we want somewhere safe. All inclusive. Why not the Canary Islands, like last time? Why? I told you, you are not listening!

Elissa saw the woman as she stepped round a stationary couple. She was gaunt, with an angular face and slashes of smoky blue above her eyes. Hair too big for her head and too blonde to be natural. The hand holding the phone was covered by a garland of flowers. The tattoo stretched down her forearm. Elissa thought of Kelly, of pressing the blade into her chest cavity. Nausea surged through her. The woman went past, no pause in her stream of words. Elissa's gaze moved to other people. Two teenagers, college age. Three lads, all carrying bags from Under Armour. A middle-aged man checking his phone as what was probably his wife and friend discussed lunch venues. Wagamama's or YO! Sushi.

Elissa pictured them all dropping to the ground, their bodies twisted, blood pumping from rips in their flesh. The scything throb of blades in the sky as the helicopter gunship brought its racks of cannon to bear on the wooden shack doling out scoops of caramelised peanuts. The queue of people started jerking, limbs being flung out by the impact of rounds. People screamed with terror as wood splintered and jars of peanuts blew apart. The block paving felt like it was undulating as she tottered over to a bench and sat. The vision of carnage faded. Normality gradually returned. People like these, she thought, will die like my brother did. It might not be a helicopter that kills them. It might not be when they're out shopping. But their deaths are what the people I'm helping want. It's what they're trying to make happen, anyway they can.

'Are you all right, my dear?'

She looked up to see the woman who wanted Wagamama's.

'Do you need any help? Can I call someone for you?'

'No, thanks.' She used the sides of her forefingers to wipe the tears away. 'I'm fine.'

'Well...if you're sure?' The friend was next to her, also looking on sympathetically.

'It was…just…a silly thing.' Elissa smiled. 'Thanks, anyway.'

She watched the trio wander away. Concern caused the woman to look back one more time. Elissa gave her a nod. I'm not part of those plans, she said to herself. To maim and kill indiscriminately. All I want is for the people who helped cause my pain to know what it feels like. That is all.

Doku was now in the front seat. His dark eyes tracked her approach to the car. She sat back in the driver's seat and took the phone out of the bag. 'Got it,' she said, sliding the outer-sleeve off the box.

As they waited for it to start up, Doku hardly moved. Every so often, he brushed a finger against the side of his nose. The third time he did it, she realised he was nervous.

'Here we go.' She scrolled through the menu to the web browser icon. When Google Translate appeared, she immediately noticed the little microphone symbol. Even better, she thought. No need to type anymore. She selected English to Russian and touched the screen. The phone emitted a beep. She asked, 'Am I doing this correctly?'

Bringing the handset away from her face, she looked at the screen. It gave a double-beep and, a second later, a robot-voice said, 'Ya pravilno delayu?'

He accepted the phone, tapped the screen and opened his mouth. But he then lowered it, seeming to change his mind. Head bowed once more, he thought for a while. With another glance at her, he lifted the phone back up and spoke.

Two beeps and the robot voice said, 'I cannot remember.'

Unsure what he meant, she waited for more.

He made another comment. 'From before the car crash my memory is not there.' Then, 'I cannot remember how to make contact. I don't know what I am meant to do.'

She leaned across and spoke at the screen. 'The Xbox is how you make contact?'

'Yes. My password is gone. It is not possible without that.'

Retrograde amnesia, she thought. It wasn't necessarily permanent. Especially for information that had been mentally stored some time before the incident that had caused it. 'How long did you know this password before the crash?'

'A few days. It was sent to me on the phone that I destroyed.'

'It will be in your head. You can still remember it.'

'How? I have tried many times.'

'I'm not sure. But do not worry.'

'Because you're a nurse, you know this?'

'Yes.' She decided to lie. 'I have seen it happen many times.'

'Memories arriving back?'

'Yes.'

The troubled look on his face eased slightly. He cleared his throat and spoke once again. 'After it is done, come with me.'

She looked at him, unsure if the comment had been translated properly. Lifting his hand, she spoke into the phone. 'Come with you?'

'Yes.'

'To where?'

He leaned forward, hand still gripped in hers. 'France. I have a boat. People are waiting.'

CHAPTER 34

The message left on Iona's phone asked that they go straight to briefing room two. When she opened the door they found it jammed with officers.

DCI Weir waved them forward to where a couple of chairs had been kept free. 'Let's hear it, then,' he said as soon as they were seated.

Iona looked at Jon, who tipped his head in reply. You go. She gave a light cough. 'The owner of the shop facing flat 17a on Fairbourne Road says, when he went to open up on Saturday morning, the Porsche was already on the drive. It wasn't there when he had cleared stuff away at eight o'clock on Friday evening.'

'Any sightings of who was actually in the flat?'

'Yes – a female. Dark haired, about five-feet-three.'

'When?'

'She drove the Porsche away at about nine fifteen on the Saturday night.'

'So it had to have been Elissa Yared.'

'Yes – we showed him the photo of her. It tallied,' Iona responded. 'She was also loading up a different vehicle at about eight forty this morning. A white hatchback. Micra or similar. He didn't see when it actually left.'

'So we don't know if Mystery Man was with her.'

'She put several items in. A rucksack and a cardboard box. Plus a holdall and a bag of shopping from Aldi. I reckon, his gear was amongst it. Maybe he just missed him getting in.'

'OK. Ed – this tallies with what you were saying: carry on.'

A droopy-faced detective with a flop of brown hair spoke. 'Elissa returned to the MRI this morning. She got in through an entrance that wasn't being watched and went into the staff rest area. There, she asked to borrow a car from a colleague – something she'd previously done when her own car had been off the road. She left with the keys for it at about seven thirty. The car is a white Toyota Yaris.'

Weir addressed the room. 'We ran the registration through the ANPR system. Cameras along the M56 clocked it. Unfortunately, the last camera is where the motorway merges into the A55. However, they didn't carry on at that point. Instead, they took the M53 north.' He glanced at his watch. 'That was twenty-eight minutes ago. Traffic police have been alerted along with local units.' He turned back to Iona. 'You mentioned a magazine earlier?'

Iona placed it on the table, poly wrapper still intact. 'The manufacturer – XiC – specialises in larger sea-going vessels. Twenty-thousand quid and more, just for the boat. They're all built to handle powerful motors, which add a few thousand more to the cost. The smaller end of the range you'd use for towing water skiers, the bigger ones are good for going further out to sea: fishing trips, that kind of thing.'

'And this was in the empty flat next door?'

'Yes, among a whole pile of junk mail. This was the only item that had been delivered through the wrong door, though. Addressed to a Mr H Omari.'

'The flat is registered to a Mr Hassan Omari,' Weir said. 'Which appears to be an alias of Bilal Atwi. When was this magazine sent?'

'Eight days ago. The way we reasoned it is this: the uncle makes a purchase. He has to give valid details to pass their credit checks, so he gives the Fairbourne Road address. Those details were then automatically fed to the company's marketing department. He probably missed the microscopic box on the form that said, "Do not mercilessly bombard me with crap for the rest of my life". Either way, this magazine gets spewed into the post.'

Weir swivelled round to the only other female in the room. 'Mary, see how many places in the north west deal in this particular make of boats. I'm thinking not many. We need to know if a Bilal Atwi or a Hassan Omari have visited any – and if they bought one. This is definitely looking to me like something very naughty is being planned.'

'The Wirral peninsular, sir – where they've headed: it'll have loads of places for launching boats.'

Weir glanced at the officer who'd spoken. 'Marinas, docks, boat clubs – anything like that. We need to know of any new members who've turned up with one of these things in the last few weeks.' He tapped the magazine then consulted his notes briefly before looking at Jon. 'How long had this Kelly girl been dead for?'

'They thought twelve hours, or thereabouts. Single stab wound to the heart.'

'Unlucky there, Jon: you did well working out as much as you did. An earlier spotting of the Porsche and things could have been very different.'

'Sir.'

Weir roused himself. 'OK. A few other things you all need to know. Computer guys have been going over Bilal Atwi's financial arrangements. The flat on Fairbourne Road doesn't feature in any of his existing records and, as mentioned, had been registered under a false name. If a twenty grand powerboat has been purchased, where did that money come from? Same for the drone and other equipment. Someone's funding all this, and I want to know who.'

Iona considered her senior officer's comment. From her training she knew many clandestine groups moved money about the world by means of an informal banking system known as Hawallah. And if Bilal Atwi was using it to receive payments from an overseas source, they stood little chance of ever discovering who was involved.

Weir was consulting his file once again. 'We've now got a Cross Border Policy in place, so we can send Armed Response Vehicles into Merseyside and North Wales. Gold command stays with us, here. Officers for the field: Evans and Coe, Mitchell and Green, Spicer and Khan. You lot head over to the Wirral. While you're en route, we'll draw up a list of places where this boat might be. Any which need a face-to-face visit, that's you. Everyone else, back to your desks and keep at it.' He slapped his file shut and the room started to empty.

Jon turned to Iona and muttered, 'The Wirral doesn't feel right.'

'How come,' she said, lips barely moving.

Checking Weir's back was to them, he said, 'Have you ever been out there?'

'No. Only Liverpool.'

'The Wirral's where Scousers move to when they've got enough money to escape from Liverpool.' To his surprise, she started jotting his words down. Didn't she know this stuff? He wondered how sheltered – or studious – her upbringing had been. 'Apart from a load of posh houses, there's not a lot there. A couple of decent rugby clubs; heard of New Brighton?'

She shook her head, pen bobbing across the page.

'And the other thing: it's taking you in the wrong direction for Anglesey and that power station. The drone footage? That was taken not far along the coast from Wylfa. Wirral's bloody miles away from it.'

'You two hatching a plan?'

Jon looked round to see, apart from their senior officer, they were now the last two in the room. How much had Weir overheard? Deciding not to try and fob him off with some kind of non-comment, he took a breath in. 'I was just wondering, sir, if we shouldn't have someone on or around Anglesey. Closer to where the last bit of drone footage was shot.'

'Even though we know they drove into the Wirral?'

'It could have been a diversion – or even a tactic, if they're aware of the ANPR cameras.'

He assessed them both. 'And you'd like to cover Anglesey off yourselves?'

Jon picked up the distinctly prickly edge to Weir's voice and responded quickly. 'First off, sir, this is my reasoning here – I was just running it past Iona. But if someone needed to do it, then yes, I'd like it to be us.'

His attention swung to Iona. 'DC Khan. Your thoughts?'

Crap, Jon thought. If she doesn't back me up, I'll be left high and dry. He avoided looking at her.

After a moment, she said, 'I agree with Jon.'

Weir cocked his head. 'Why?'

'The drone footage suggests there's a good chance Anglesey is their ultimate destination.'

The other man sucked in air through his nose and, eventually, shrugged. 'We need to cross off the Wirral first. Let's see exactly what that will entail. If it looks like the other two teams can cover the face-to-face stuff, you can do the follow-up on Anglesey. Deal?'

Jon shot a glance at Iona who raised her eyebrows in encouragement. He turned back to Weir. 'Definitely. Thanks, Sir.'

'Good.' Weir turned to the door, the start of a smile on his face. 'You two. You make me laugh.'

Once he was gone, Jon looked at Iona. 'Was that good? That we make him laugh?'

There was a puzzled expression on her face as she considered the door he'd gone through. 'I think so.'

CHAPTER 35

As Elissa negotiated the succession of roundabouts bordering Cheshire Oaks, she took a wrong turn and ended up threading her way along a minor A road. Eventually, it brought them out on the A55, a few miles past the final junction of the M56.

The onward journey to Anglesey took another ninety minutes. Once over the Menai Bridge and on the island, he jabbed a finger as soon as the turn-off for the A5025 came into view. The road took them north towards the top end of the island. The countryside was largely agricultural; beyond the thin hedges bordering the road, waist-high drystone walls criss-crossed the fields. They'd almost reached a small coastal village when Doku began to look about. Sensing they were close, Elissa slowed the car down. The road dipped then rose to a small crest at which point he pointed to the right. All she could see was a gnarled pine tree off to the side.

A small lane came into view and Doku gestured with his entire arm. 'Tam!'

She turned down it, aware the sea now couldn't be far off. A small humpback bridge came into view. On the other side of it some kind of work had been taking place: a digger and a dumper truck were parked just beyond a gate that gave access to a narrow field. An ugly trench had been carved into the grass. She glimpsed a stack of green pipes beside the digger.

Doku waved a hand for her to stop. He was out of the car before it came to a halt. Moving cautiously, he skirted round the work vehicles. Then he approached the truck, climbed up to the cab and peered in through the side window. After a few seconds, he jumped down and returned to the car.

'OK?' Elissa asked as he got back in.

He regarded the vehicles for another second, gave an uncertain nod and pointed to a driveway further up on the left. She pulled in, and as she came to a halt on the gravel, the first thing she saw was a generously-sized garage.

Immediately to its right was the stone cottage. It had a huge chimney at one end and Elissa could only imagine the size of the hearth inside. It would probably be large enough for roasting a cow in. She wondered how long her uncle had hired it for. Maybe a long-term let to guarantee no disturbances.

She took the phone out of the cup-holder and checked the signal. Three bars. 'How do we get in?' The Russian words sounded a moment later.

For a few moments it seemed like he didn't know. Then his head turned towards the front door and he narrowed his eyes. 'Tam...' Gently, he twisted her hand so the screen pointed towards him before he spoke. She waited for the translation. 'The keys are above the door.' He seemed surprised. 'I did not remember that, then I did.'

'See? Your memories are not all lost.'

Over at the porch, he reached up to a hook at the side of a rafter in the roof. There was only one old-fashioned door key among the Yales. He inserted it and opened the solid-looking wooden door. The kitchen was modern and in perfect condition. On the wall by the door was a laminated sheet of various instructions.

Doku crossed the kitchen, stepped through the door on the other side and turned right. She trailed behind, finding herself in a corridor that stretched down the entire side of the property. Doorways to her right led into a utility room, a store room and a study. A narrow set of stairs rose to the first floor. Three en-suite bedrooms, if she remembered the print-out rightly. After the stairs was a downstairs bedroom. The end room was a living area, complete with local interest books, board games and a few packs of cards. The hearth was as huge as she suspected, though within it sat a relatively small wood-burning stove, with neat piles of chopped wood on either side.

Doku had knelt before the TV in the corner. Using his right hand, he dragged the cabinet out from the wall so he could disconnect an ancient DVD player. He got back to his feet and retraced his steps out of the room.

She moved to the main window and saw they really were beside the ocean. The tide was out, exposing the green and furry legs of the wooden jetty she'd seen in the photo. Brightly coloured buoys dotted the smooth expanse of sand. The walkway led back to a structure which she guessed housed the motorboat.

Not far across the water, she could see heavily-wooded land and she realised they were on some kind of inlet. To see the actual ocean, she had to look through the window of the adjacent wall. The view consisted of two elements: dolphin grey sea and an eggshell sky.

The sound of a car engine drifted to her. She walked back to the kitchen and looked out. He'd opened the garage's double doors and was parking the Yaris inside. Next to it was a large trailer. For towing the boat, she guessed. Back in the front room, she went to the window and stared nervously out towards the open sea.

He reappeared with the Xbox and laid it like an offering before the TV. Rather than plug it in, he pointed to the boat house and beckoned. A flagstone path led round the cottage to a short flight of steps. He had the set of keys with him and selected a bronze Yale to open the side door of the boathouse. Inside held the faintly sulphurous smell of rotting mud.

The boat was massive; she guessed about thirty feet in length. It was some type of inflatable: tubular rubbery sides narrowing to a blunt point. Crouching down, she felt the material. Rock hard.

At the front were two padded seats that looked more suited to being in a racing car. A steering wheel was before the one on the right. Behind them were two rows of bench seats, each wide enough for three or four people. The rear of the vessel was more open – for bags and other luggage, she guessed. Diving gear, maybe. Mounted at the very back was a large black engine. Lettering on the side of it said, Mariner 200. She imagined the thing could go ridiculously fast.

Doku had leaned in to remove a thick vinyl bag from the passenger seat. Opening the heavy zip, he started to remove items. A rubber torch. A coil of rope. A green pack that said Crewmedic First Aid Kit. A compass and whistles. A packet of four red tubes with bright yellow handgrips near the base. Each was about a foot long and she leaned down to examine one. Block-like text down the side read, "Hand-held rocket propelled flare distress signal. Caution! Stand with back to wind and point away when igniting."

She looked up to see Doku had removed a booklet. He handed it to her and she had to tilt the cover to the light in order to read it.

Operating manual. XiC 700 Rib.

Surely, she thought, he doesn't expect me to...drive this thing, if that was even the right word. She realised it was the first time she'd ever seen him smile. Strong teeth in his tanned face. He fished the phone out, touched the screen a couple of times and spoke. The voice sounded after the usual delay. 'You look worried.'

'Correct,' she replied, trying to hand the manual back.

He thought for a moment. 'That big truck on the road, it is easier to drive than that.'

'You could drive that truck?'

He waited for the Russian words and gave a knowing nod. 'Of course. I can drive many things. This boat, it is very simple.'

'But how will I kn – ' She snatched the phone from his grasp and spoke into it properly. 'Where will we go?'

From the bag, he produced a device that looked a bit like a mobile phone, only chunkier. Its narrow screen was blank. Taking the handset from her, he spoke again. She waited for the robot voice. 'When we know where they want us to go, we use this to guide us.' With a straight arm, he gestured towards the open sea, curving his wrist as if reaching beyond the horizon.

A long way out, then, she thought, eyes straying nervously to the lifejackets in the rear. I hate the sea. Even on a thousand-ton cross-channel ferry, I hate the bloody sea.

'But,' he added. 'The co-ordinates will be sent through the Xbox.'

Of course, she thought. Without that, nothing happens.

'You will be content to drive this ship?' He kept looking at her, concern shadowing his eyes. 'Yes?'

'I think so.' She stepped back out into the daylight, as if to see the booklet properly. Staring down at the cover, she tried to make sense of it all. It must have been Uncle Bilal's job then, to drive the boat. He had been ready and willing to play a far more active role than she had guessed. Now she would be taking his place, following Doku's instructions so they arrived at a pre-arranged point. They had to be meeting another vessel.

CHAPTER 36

Every now and again, Jon sought out the reflection of the ledge that stretched behind the passenger seats. He pictured the weapons boot just inches below it. Second day taking an ARV out, and it still seemed utterly surreal. As soon as they passed the turn-off for Manchester Airport, the flow of traffic thinned. Jon relaxed back in the driver's seat, wondering whether to put the radio on and, if he did, which station to choose. He couldn't stomach Radio 1, which would probably be the one Iona would want.

Beside him, she continued studying the page of a road atlas that covered the Wirral. 'Could they be aiming for Liverpool?' she mused, almost to herself. 'Drive to the tip of the Wirral and take a ferry across the mouth of the Mersey into Liverpool itself?'

'Weird way to do it. Why not just stick to the motorways? More direct, much faster.'

'You're right,' she sighed, head still bowed over the page. 'There can't be that many boatyards and other places to check. Did you say you've been there before?'

'I did. Just to play rugby.'

'Played quite a lot, did you?'

Jon contemplated the years he'd spent in the first team for Cheadle Ironsides. For much of that time, he'd also been representing, and eventually captaining, Greater Manchester Police's rugby team. Everyone seemed to relish taking on a load of police officers; some of the games he'd played towards Liverpool had been among the most violent he ever experienced. 'Yeah, I played a fair bit.'

'Is that how you lost that bit of your ear?'

His eyes cut sharply to hers. He detected nothing other than curiosity in them.

'Sorry, if you'd rather not say...'

'No,' he replied. 'It's fine. I lost that over in Ireland. Not that long ago, actually.'

'How do you lose part of an ear? In Ireland?'

He glanced at her again, searching for anything to suggest her innocent tone was an act. 'No one's said anything to you?'

'No. Why?'

'I wasn't sure if it was common knowledge, or not. The WIO knew all about it before I met him yesterday morning.'

'Well, if it is, no-one's let me in on it. Wouldn't be the first time, either.'

He let the implications of her comment settle. 'People don't involve you with all that's happening?'

She injected regret into her voice. 'I guess if you're not male, down in that gym, getting punched in the face, you miss out on all the good gossip.'

'Come on, it's not that bad, is it?'

'How many females have you counted in the unit? One's that aren't just there to fetch and carry.'

'Well…not many.'

'I rest my case. Anyway, don't try changing the subject; you haven't explained your ear yet.'

He smiled briefly. 'Someone tore the top of it with a pair of pliers.'

'Pliers?' She looked horrified. 'Pliers? That's gross. Why did they do that to you?'

'I'd been pissing his boss off. Deliberately.'

'Were you over there – no, you wouldn't have been.'

'What?'

'Over there on a job.'

'No. I was trying to find someone. A relative, of sorts. I'd been told she'd been working at a business owned by this boss I mentioned. When I couldn't find her, I started acting the maggot, as they explained to me.'

'Acting the maggot?'

'Being a general pain-in-the-arse.'

'So they assaulted you?'

'They planned to do a lot more than that. I wasn't meant to leave the country alive.' He turned to look properly at her for a second. 'That's why I moved to the CTU. I was a DI in the Major Incident Team. Had been for years. But what happened in Ireland – the way I lied to my bosses about where I was, what I was doing, the trouble all that caused – they kicked me out.'

'I heard you were made to leave the MIT. But I didn't know why.'

'Well, now you do. And you got it direct from me.'

'Was the person who did that to your ear, was he arrested?'

'No.'

'And the boss who ordered it?'

'He vanished shortly after. I can't say what really happened...I'm not totally sure myself. But the person I went over to find, she's fine.'

'A happy ending, then. Sort of.'

'Sort of.'

She turned her head to look out the side window. What a weird story. One that raised more questions than answers. It must be so hard for him, she thought. Dropping two ranks and having to take orders from people younger and less experienced. He was handling it all very well.

'So you feel left out of some stuff that goes on in the CTU?' he asked.

She looked across at him now, checking for any hint she was being mocked. 'Does that surprise you?'

'No, not really.' He kept his eyes on the car in front. 'A few in the unit seem stuck at the Neanderthal stage. Someone said your nickname's The Baby Faced Assassin.'

'That's right. What's yours?'

'I don't really have one. Some people call me Slicer. As in Spicer the Slicer – a tackling thing.'

'You'd slice people? What, with your studs?'

'My shoulder. Hit them really hard in the tackle; slice them in half. Baby Faced Assassin came from you playing hockey, didn't it?'

'Yes. How do you know?'

'One of the lads – I asked someone I get on with. When it looked like we were being paired up. I asked him then.'

'Who?'

'Kieran Saunders.'

She smiled. 'He's all right, Kieran. Not sure he's all there, in the head.'

'No, me neither.'

'When were you talking to him?'

'Funnily enough, after that sparring session down in the gym.'

'There you go; my point proved. It's where all the good gossip takes place.'

'Kieran seems straight-up. Friendly. Not everyone is.'

'No. Too many alpha males. Or people who think they're alpha males.'

'I agree. Baby Faced Assassin: because of your impressive scoring ability?'

She spoke as if reciting from a script. 'Paired with a deceptively innocent appearance that lulls defences into a false sense of security, is how the name works – I believe.'

'And you're OK with it being used in the office, too?'

'Most people have a nick name of one sort or another.' She lowered her voice to a bloke-ish level. 'Stevo. Dano. Wellsy. It goes with the territory.'

'And you're OK with yours?'

Second time you've asked that, she thought. Her eyes flickered across the side of his face. 'Come on, Jon. Spit it out.'

'It's...it's just the sort of name that can work two-ways, isn't it? Or the Baby Faced bit of it, anyway. I can imagine some in the unit using it, you know, they could turn it into a negative thing.'

She leaned her head against the rest, partly to move out of his peripheral vision. This person, she thought, is a lot more perceptive than he looks. Her mind went back to a headline – taken from an old local newspaper report – which someone pinned to her monitor when she'd first joined the unit. It read: The Baby-Faced Assassin. But it hadn't taken long before the other words were snipped away to just leave Baby.

She sneaked a look at the wedding band on his finger. 'Have you got kids?'

His face immediately brightened. 'Two. Holly and Doug.'

That'll be it, then, she thought. A wife who's trained him well. 'It did get shortened by someone. Like I was the mascot of the unit or something.'

'How did you put a stop to that?'

'By earning their respect, I suppose. Doing something that took some bollocks, is probably how they'd describe it.'

'What was that?'

'Remember the thing to do with the Labour Party Conference the other year? All that kerfuffle?'

'The bomb plot? The group trying to get into the tunnels?'

'They weren't trying. They were in. They found a tunnel not on the council plans; it had got them very close to the politicians. It was almost a total disaster for us.'

'Almost?'

'Minutes away from mass fatalities.'

'Jesus. And – of course – that never made the papers.'

'Of course.'

'So you were on that op?'

She wondered how much to tell him. How it was only because she'd pieced together the jigsaw of clues that the plan was disrupted. Like bats flitting across a dusk sky, brief snatches of the final chase through the dark tunnels played across her mind. She didn't want them coming back. Didn't want to remember that sensation of being trapped, unable to free her arms, as rough fingers yanked her head back, exposing her throat to the dull blade...

'Iona?'

She looked at him, eyes refocusing. 'Yes, I was on it.'

After a moment, Jon turned back to the road. 'You still play hockey?'

'Not at a serious level. This job, I can never make it to training.'

'But you turn out every now and again?'

'Yeah – I play for the second or third team. Firsts if they're really short. But it's a nightmare keeping up.'

'I know that feeling.'

'You still play?'

He shook his head regretfully. 'Not for a while, now. I was waking up on Sundays and I could hardly peel myself off the mattress. Like I had rigor mortis. It was getting stupid.'

'You didn't want to carry on, but in a lower team?'

'No. There's a time to stop. I reached it.' His gaze lifted to the overhead signs. 'Here we go, exit for the M53.'

She studied the roadside notices as they neared the turn-off. 'Cheshire Oaks. That designer outlet place. I wonder if they went there?'

Jon snapped the indicator down. 'Worth a punt, I reckon.'

CHAPTER 37

Cheshire Oaks had the air of a seaside town in winter. Closed-up shops and abandoned areas of seating. Jon looked at a nearby wooden shack with padlocked shutters. An A-board beside it announced caramelised peanuts. Litter bins were being emptied into the rear of a small lorry by three lads in brown tops while an older man sat at the wheel of the idling vehicle, listening to the radio.

Two seagulls padded officiously along the edge of a planted border, cruel orange eyes scanning between the plants.

Iona studied the layout of shops on the display at the edge of the empty car park. 'Could have swung in here for any number of these places. If they even did.'

'Anything stand out as worth a detour?'

'Honestly, Jon, the possibilities are endless.' She realised he had his back to her. Hands in pockets, he was surveying the promenade of unlit shops. 'Why don't you have a look for yourself?'

With an air of reluctance, he half-turned and gave the map a cursory glance. 'What about outdoor gear? Camping or something?'

She realised he wasn't going to trawl through the shop listings himself. 'I take it that shopping is a favourite hobby of yours?'

'Oh, yeah – love it me. Places like this? Heaven.'

Typical bloke, she thought. 'The closest to camping is a North Face or Timberland, but they're more for trendy outdoor gear. More your fashion-conscious camper, I'd say.'

'Fashion-conscious camper,' he muttered. 'Ready-prepared yurts and electric hook-ups, you mean?'

Hearing his disdainful tone, she smiled. He was obviously more primer-stove and enamel mugs. Cutlery that folded up. Definitely no inflatable mattresses allowed.

One of the seagulls darted at something. Instantly changing from companion to competitor, the other bird raced over to see what it was. They began shrieking in each other's faces, wings half-raised. 'Last tussle before the real shoppers return tomorrow,' Jon remarked. He stepped back towards the car.

'Are we not going to check over there?' Iona gestured to the deserted shopping centre over the road.

'Nah,' Jon replied. 'I can't see us getting anything worthwhile.'

Back in the vehicle, he slid the key into the ignition but didn't start the engine. 'The further we drive into the Wirral, the more I feel we're going in the wrong direction.'

'Annoying, isn't it?'

'Very.' He checked the rear view mirror. 'Five o'clock already and we haven't even started checking places.'

'I'll call in and see if they've got our hit list sorted.' She brought a number up and held the phone to her ear. The instructions came back: drive to Birkenhead and wait in the car park of the McDonald's at The Rock Retail Park.

As they rejoined the M53, Jon pointed to the radio. 'Music? It'll have to be the radio.'

'OK.' She reached for the on button. 'Any particular station?'

'I'm not fussed. Smooth FM or something like that?'

'Nothing loud, you mean?' She turned it on and something thrashy filled the car. They looked at each other and she pressed the scanner without saying a word. Next was a choir singing. 'Something spiritual for your Sunday?'

'Had enough of that as a kid. Next.'

The third station was playing Marvin Gaye.

'This is all right with me,' Jon said straight away.

She sat back. 'You like a bit of soul?'

'You can't not like this stuff, surely?'

Iona thought of her initial conversation with Elissa. How their taste in music seemed so aligned. Had that coloured her judgement? Made her less alert to the woman's subterfuge? 'She was very good.'

'Say again?' Jon replied, one finger tapping lightly on the steering wheel.

'Elissa Yared. The way she hid her anger. It was very good.'

'You reckon she's angry?'

'Absolutely. She's full of rage – about her family. Her brother. I certainly don't think she's motivated by any religious conviction.'

'So you think she's a willing party to all this?'

'Yes. You don't?'

'I'm not sure. What if they have something on her? Something that means she has no choice but help the Mystery Man.'

'Like what?'

'Usually, it would be a threat to the welfare of her existing family.'

'But she's lost them – unless you mean the Atwi lot.'

'Doesn't she have relatives on the dad's side of the family back in Lebanon? Maybe some of them are being held.'

Iona considered the comment. 'No. I think she's perfectly willing to help the Mystery Man.'

'Would that include killing the working girl, Kelly?'

'Who knows.'

Jon glanced across. 'I can't see her being happy with that. She's a nurse for a start.'

'Did you have a religious upbringing?'

'My mum tried her best. Irish Catholic. But she didn't have much luck.'

'Your dad?'

'British and a total atheist. They met when she came over to do her nurse's training in Manchester. He was never into all the church stuff. You sniff it out as a kid, don't you? Any chinks in your parents' united front. I soon learned that mini rugby with dad on a Sunday morning got me out of having to go to mum's church. Dad was relieved, I know he was.' He caught the knowing smile on her face. 'How about your family?'

'Scottish mum, Pakistani dad.'

'Either of them religious?'

'Dad's side of the family – back in Pakistan – they all are. He's not though. In fact, he moved to Britain to escape from it all. There isn't much contact now. They kind off cut him off.'

'What does he do for a living?'

'He's an academic. Lectures in Persian Studies at The University of Manchester. He met my mum when working at Glasgow University. She was in the support office.'

'And she's not religious?'

'Completely not.'

'Kieran mentioned your dad was a top hockey player.'

'You two were discussing me.'

'No, well – not much. It was brief. Kieran was explaining your nickname and mentioned your old man.'

'Yeah – he played for Pakistan. Won gold at the 1982 hockey World Cup and at the Olympics two years later.'

'That's bloody impressive. And he taught you as well?'

'For hours. Up and down, up and down. Practise, practise, practise.'

'Until the stick was an extension of your arm?'

'Basically.' Her phone gave a chirrup. 'Here we go,' she said, examining the screen. 'Thurstaston Boat Club.' She sent an acknowledgement back then consulted the map. 'Come off at junction four and follow the A5137. It's not far at all.'

The string of cub scouts walked in pairs, green jumpers adorned with badges of various shapes. Flanking them at regular intervals were adult helpers and a few parent volunteers.

The boys were having trouble keeping their alignment; a transport plane was being wheeled out of a hangar to their left. Heads were twisting round, heels were being trodden on, bodies were colliding.

'Come on lads, stop dawdling.'

'Harry, look where you're going!'

At the head of the column was a man in a crisply pressed shirt. His stride was a little too fast for a group of eight-year-old boys, but neither Akela or any of his assistants seemed prepared to point that out.

The low buildings they were aiming for were positioned at one corner of the airfield. As they drew closer, the area beyond them came into view. Out on the tarmac was a bright yellow helicopter, its long rotor blades drooping slightly. A squat dragonfly taking a nap.

'Sea King!' one of the boys exclaimed, arm, wrist, hand and forefinger stiff as a lance. 'Sea King!'

Excitement radiated back along the column. Boys started to hop and jump. One placed his hands on the shoulders of the cub in front to pogo above his companions. 'Awesome!'

'Boys! Keep in line! Stop bunching at the front, you'll all get a look.'

The painted pathway led to the main entrance of the building. The RAF officer halted at a knee-high notice board on the neat grass verge by the doors. He waited as the group gathered round, hawk-like eyes locking on any boy who wasn't being quiet. Once he had silence, he tapped the white wooden frame. 'Who can read this?'

Arms shot up.

He nodded at a taller boy towards the back. 'Go ahead.'

'C Flight, twenty-two squadron, RAF Search and Rescue.'

'Very good. Britain's search and rescue capability is made up of twelve detached flights. Of these, the RAF provides six, including the one here on Anglesey.'

Akela surveyed his group uneasily: every single one of the boys was staring across at the helicopter. Not one was listening to the talk.

The RAF officer pressed on, oblivious. 'Each detached flight has a very particular type of helicopter, which you may have spotted behind me. Who knows what type – '

'Sea King!' Eighteen voices simultaneously shouted.

The officer smiled. 'That's correct. In the building behind me is the First Standby Crew. If a SAROP comes in, they can respond. How long do you think they need to respond?'

'What's a SAROP?' A small boy with curly black hair asked.

'A search and rescue operation. How long?'

'Two minutes.'

'An hour.'

'Quarter of an hour.'

'Ten seconds.'

'Thirty two minutes.'

'Whoever yelled quarter of an hour was correct. If a call comes in at night, it's a little longer: forty-five minutes. That's because the crew would have been asleep.'

'So they live there?' the same boy asked.

'For their shift, they do. Each shift lasts twenty-four hours, commencing at nineteen hundred hours. All detached flights are self-supporting. In the building behind me are offices for flight planning, medical stores, specialist equipment stores, bedrooms and a rest lounge with basic cooking facilities – though the crew here get their meals delivered from the main canteen in hotlock containers.' He paused. 'Now, before we go inside, were you told about the well-known person who is currently working on this airbase?'

Heads eagerly nodded.

'Right. I have a feeling he may well be inside.' He dropped his voice down. 'Shall we go and see?'

The boys edged into the building like they were entering a shrine. No one was in sight. At the far end of the corridor came the massed rumble of voices. As they got nearer, the rumble grew louder. Shouted words started breaking through the general din.

'Jammy wanker!'

'Unbe-fucking-lievable!'

'Bastard!'

The RAF officer signalled for the group to stop, then hurried ahead. He leaned his head through the doorway and spoke quickly. The noise subsided. A few people laughed. He looked back down the corridor and beckoned to the boys. 'This is the rest lounge where the crews can relax. In you come.'

Goggle-eyed, the boys shuffled in from the corridor. The first had to be pushed forward by the ones behind. Dotted in the soft seats were several crew. Most had books in their hands: Wilbur Smith, Tom Clancy, Michael Crichton. One of the books was the wrong way up. They grinned amiably at their visitors.

'As you can see,' the guide announced. 'There's a TV and games console and an upturned bin with a red spot on the bottom.' He bent down and righted it. 'But the crew generally prefer to read in their free time, don't you lads?'

A chorus of agreement.

'Although sometimes, they also like to play with this.' He crossed to the central table and picked up a miniature helicopter. 'Mmmm, still warm. Strange. Any of you got this type of toy at home?' He held it up to the cubs.

A few hands tentatively lifted.

'Yes, I think it's very popular with people who are under ten.' He sent a mocking glance at the crew. Using his book as a screen, one lifted his middle finger. 'The boys here were hoping to meet the resident member of the Royal Family.'

'Ops room,' came a reply.

The cubs were led across the corridor and into a large open-plan room. On the far side, a tall man was seated at a computer screen.

'This person,' the guide announced, 'is known around here as Howie. You're probably all used to his other title: The Duke of Cambridge.'

The man swivelled his chair round and stood. 'Hello there.' He smiled at the mass of awestruck faces. 'Which group are you from?'

Once again, Akela had to speak. 'Conwy County District.'

'Ah, I can see a fine collection of badges on your jumpers. You are all obviously very committed. How are you enjoying your visit to our airbase?'

A few of them dared to move their heads.

'And are any of you thinking of becoming a pilot when you're older?'

The boy with the curly hair croaked a reply. 'Yes.'

'You are? Excellent. And what would you like to fly?'

'Sea Kings.'

He clapped his hands softly. 'A superb choice. Has anyone explained to you what's involved with a search and rescue operation?'

Silence.

'Would you like to know?'

Heads nodded with comical speed.

'Well, we always have a crew ready to respond to an emergency call. That crew is known as First Standby. If you look at the roster board on the wall over there, you'll see the fourth name down is Howie. That's my nickname here. Something to do with House of Windsor, I believe. The red line indicates if you're on a shift: as you can see, I start tonight at seven o'clock and I'm on duty until seven o'clock tomorrow evening. How many other red lines can people see for tonight?'

Eventually, someone floated an answer. 'Three.'

'That's right. Each search and rescue crew is made up of four people. I'm First Pilot and Operational Aircraft Captain for the coming shift. That means I'm in charge. There's a second pilot and there's a radar and winch operator, or Rad-Op. He or she has a really good job because, while we're flying to the incident, they operate the Searchwater radar and the thermal camera so we can find whoever needs rescuing fast. Once we've located them, the Rad-Op leaves the radar shack and goes to the rear cargo door to operate the winch. The last member of the crew is the winchman, who may be female. In fact, we have two female winchmen serving here at the moment. They're the ones you see dangling beneath the helicopter. Almost all winchmen are registered paramedics because, on board, we carry a lot of first aid items. Things like neck braces, limb splints and special little tanks of oxygen for pain relief.'

His fascinated audience watched him move closer to the white board. 'Tonight is my last shift, then I'm off for three nights. Which means, tomorrow, I can see my two sons again – and sleep at home in my own bed.'

'Do you live here on the airbase?' a small voice asked.

'No, there are family quarters, but we rent a house not too far away.' He looked at the group. 'Any other questions?'

'Does your younger brother also fly helicopters?'

'Harry? He does. But he's in the army, so he trained to fly helicopters known as gunships. That's what he's doing at the moment over in Afghanistan.'

'Do you speak to him much?'

'We Skype a bit. Sometimes he even reads my children their bedtime story.'

The guide gave a cough. 'Thank you for that, Howie. We'll let you get back to preparing for your shift. What do you say, boys?'

A chorus of thankyous filled the room.

'My pleasure. And, if you're still on the island later and spot a Sea King taking off, give it a wave: I'll be flying it!'

CHAPTER 38

When they arrived at Thurstaston the sun was still well clear of the horizon, but fast-losing strength. Dozens of boats on trailers lined the road, shadows from their masts laddering the long strip of asphalt leading to the clubhouse. They pulled up in a cramped car park, the corner of which formed a slipway down to the water's edge.

Three boats were moored at the jetty as the owners tossed kitbags, lifejackets and other items onto the sun-bleached boards. There was a contented looseness to how they moved. One woman paused to sip from a bottle of beer and Jon watched her carefree state with envy. To their right a piece of paper stuck to the door of the clubhouse reminded members that mooring fees were now due. The door opened and a bronzed man of about sixty wearing shorts and a baggy polo shirt looked them up and down with a faintly amused expression.

For the first time, Jon got a sense of how odd they must look standing side-by-side. He reached for his badge.

As club secretary, it only took the man a moment's thought to confirm that no new members with a Rib had recently joined. Iona asked if he checked the type of vessel each new member claimed to own was the one they actually brought on site. He did, to ensure they were being charged the correct amount.

'And about how many of these Ribs do you have here?'

'Five. But they all belong to long-term members.'

'If I had one of these boats,' Iona said, 'and I wanted to launch it somewhere here on the Wirral, where might I keep it?'

'Well, presuming it's on a trailer, take your pick: a friendly farmer's field, a large driveway, a garage if it's big enough. Just tow it to a slipway and you're off.'

'How many people would you need to do that?'

'One could manage, but two is ideal. You reverse down the slipway, preferably at high tide, until the trailer is submerged. The boat then floats free; it's really not difficult.'

After thanking him and leaving their contact details, they made to go. 'By the way,' Jon said, turning round but continuing to walk backwards. 'The phone line in the clubhouse is out. Colleagues back at our unit couldn't get through.'

The man pointed up. 'Local idiots. They climbed up during the week and took the satellite dish. Ripped down the cabling while they were at it.'

They were almost at the car when Weir's name appeared on the screen of Iona's phone. 'Sir, we've just seen – '

She stopped talking, eyes losing their focus as she listened intently. 'This was when? OK.' She listened for another minute. 'Yes, understood. I will, yes.' She cut the call but continued looking at the screen. 'Shit.'

'Tell me in the car,' Jon said, pipping the lock and climbing swiftly in. The interior was stuffy and hot, so he left the door partly open.

Iona sank into the seat beside him, both hands clasped protectively around her phone. 'It wasn't there. The surface-to-air missile. Not at the private residence or the storage facility.'

'They struck both places?'

'Yes – joint operation with the Afghan security forces. Now they're not sure it was even there in the first place.'

'Why do they think that?'

'Our people put out an appeal. The Egyptian intelligence services came back with something almost immediately. It's almost a fortnight old and since then, nothing more relating to it has come up.'

'What did they say?'

'An informant linked to a group in Libya reported them receiving payment for the safe passage of a small group who had some sort of cargo. This group had originally come by boat from a port in Syria. The Libyan group were accompanying them to the border with Algeria.'

'That's sounding bloody vague.'

'Yes, but the sum of money the group in Libya were paid suggests it was of significance. How much do you remember of geography from school?'

'Not a lot, why?'

'The country that borders Algeria is...' She looked at him with eyebrows half-raised.

He didn't even bother trying to search him mind for the answer. 'Put me out of my misery, please.'

'Morocco. And from Morocco, you're a stone's throw from the southern tip of Spain – and Europe.'

It suddenly felt too hot in the car. Jon pushed the door fully open. 'Timings-wise, if that information is a fortnight old...'

'Exactly, it could be anywhere by now. What's more worrying is how it tallies with a separate report our embassy staff in Athens filed nine days ago.'

'What the hell was that?'

'An asylum-seeker brought ashore on the Greek coast who'd crossed from Libya. The boat that brought him over originally set off from a port in Syria – but rather than aim for Turkey, it went East. They eventually landed in Libya hundreds of kilometres away. Not what was promised.'

Even though he knew it was stupid, Jon had to check his mirrors to make sure no one was in earshot. 'Libya? What did he say?'

'He claimed the detour was made to deliver a cargo. Something wrapped in oiled sheets. This object wasn't large: one guy lifted it out from the boat. But it was a big deal to the people involved. They were all heavily armed and immediately rode off in Toyota Land Cruisers. This guy took the information to our consular staff in Athens hoping it would assist in his application for asylum here.'

'And did it?'

'They told him to hop it. But they put his story on the system anyway.'

'So what are we meant to do now?'

'The other teams will cover here; we proceed to Anglesey. We'll be sent a list of places that need double-checking. He said to grab a couple of rooms somewhere cheap and cheerful then crack on first thing in the morning.'

'Was there anything about the dealers for that boat – the XiC?'

'Only that they're hoping for more progress Monday morning when places are open again.'

'Christ.' He glanced at his watch. Just after seven. 'I'd better let Alice know I won't be back.'

'We'll need a hotel that sells toothbrushes; I haven't packed a thing.'

'Me neither,' Jon replied, climbing back out while bringing up his home number. Holly got to the phone on the second ring. 'What are you still doing up, my little treasure?'

'Daddy! Where are you?'

'At the seaside,' he answered, ambling towards the jetty. 'Have you had an ice-cream?'

'No, the shops are all closed.'

'That's because it's Sunday.'

'It is. How's Duggy?'

'Asleep.'

'I thought it sounded quiet. And where's mummy?'

'Right here. We're reading Stickman.'

'Again?' He suspected Alice knew the story off-by-heart. 'That's nice.'

'Hello you.' Alice's voice.

'Hi babe. All OK?'

'Yeah, done bath time. Nearly wine time!'

'I'm not going to make it back tonight, Aly. This op is growing bigger.'

She sighed. 'OK. Are you anywhere near?'

'Not far from Liverpool. On the coast.'

'With Iona?'

'Yeah, and a couple of other teams.'

'All in a hotel together?'

He decided not to say that wasn't the case. No point in her worrying any more than necessary. 'I just hope they have a family room big enough.'

'And one with good air-con; we all know about your farts.'

'Says Mrs Windy-Arse herself.' He savoured the sound of her chuckle coming down the line.

'Well...you be careful out there, won't you?'

He could hear the tension in her voice. 'Of course I will.'

Silence.

'Ali, are you there?'

'I know you will be. It's just...this new job. I didn't think you'd be away from home so soon.'

'Me neither. I don't think it happens much.'

'Let's hope.'

'I'll see you tomorrow, OK?'

'OK.'

'Kiss them both from me.'

'Will do.'

Jon pocketed his phone and leaned against the wooden handrail. Now barely above the horizon, the burning sun had cast a layer of copper across the ocean. From somewhere behind him came a distant throaty hum. He craned his neck and saw a passenger plane, its nose tilted as it scaled the cloudless sky. It was low enough so that, when it started banking north, he could almost count each window wink in the sun. Liverpool Airport, he realised, was just the other side of the narrow stretch of water that separating the Wirral from the mainland.

When he climbed back into the car, Iona's attention was on her phone, one finger brushing steadily at the screen. Assuming she was going over an important communication from work, he leaned across a bit further than necessary while reaching for his seatbelt. The screen was full of slowly falling, brightly-coloured shapes: Candy Crush.

CHAPTER 39

He tipped an admiring nod at the plate of food. 'Mmm, vkusno.'

'Spasibo,' she replied.

His face, usually so impassive, broke into a smile. 'Ty govorish po Russkiy!'

'Njet.' She dusted her plate of spaghetti with pepper then replaced the pot between them on the table. 'Only the odd word.'

Silence returned, but it was one she didn't feel that she had to fill. They understood each other better now. She suspected he had the same low level of adrenaline humming about his body. A continual sense that something was about to happen. From beyond the kitchen's dark windows came an owl's haunting cry. He reacted instantly to the sound, shoulders stiffening, eyes lifting.

The phone was never out of reach and she picked it up, spoke and waited for the translation. 'It is an owl.'

The noise came again and she gave him a nonchalant shrug. It's nothing. He looked over at the window for a while, head cocked for anything else. After a few seconds he turned back to his food and started to eat again.

She thought about how they were almost out of time. It had been seven weeks ago when Frank the Delivery Man had sat next to her in the staff area at the MRI and quietly shared his morsel of gossip.

He'd been replenishing the supplies of oxygen tanks in the medical store at the Search and Rescue facility over on Anglesey. You know: the one where the older of the two Princes was currently stationed as a Sea King pilot. Frank was a familiar face to the crews there. Security clearance and everything. Pretty much came and went as he pleased. They were a friendly bunch, the crews there. Happy to let him sit in the Operations Room and chat, if things were quiet. No, he'd not seen the Prince in person that day, but he had seen something to do with him.

Flight rotas for the coming month. They were being written on this big whiteboard on the wall of the operations office. Prince William? He's known as Howie. House of Windsor? Get it? He had eight shifts coming up as First Standby crew over September. Almost seven but he'd got the very last day of the month. Unlucky. It's good though, that they don't treat him any differently. Does the same twenty-four shift as all the other pilots, seven in the evening through to seven the next evening.

In fact, the only real difference between him and the other crew was the fact he didn't drive himself. That was done by a special armed police officer. A bit like a chauffeur, the officer had to sit for hours in the dark blue Jaguar.

Iona had rung her Uncle Bilal that afternoon asking to meet.

She picked at her food. What was that definition of a secret she'd read? A piece of information told only to one person at a time. She stared at the unfamiliar pattern on the plate. The table. The kitchen. The fact she was sitting here, on the Welsh coast, the rest of her life a huge unknown. The sense of staring down into a black chasm started to grip her. Before she could blink it away, her shoulders suddenly shook. She checked to see if he'd noticed: and found him studying her face.

'OK?' he asked.

'Yes. No.' She fluttered a hand and smiled. 'Nervous.'

He shook his head to show his confusion.

'Nervous,' she repeated, lifting her fingers and pretending to chew her nails. 'Nervous.'

'Ah,' he replied.

She picked up her fork again, but her appetite had vanished. It rattled slightly as she laid it back on her plate. His hand moved across the table, sliding over the top of hers. She looked at it for a moment then up at him.

'Ne nervnichay. Ty silneye chem ty dumayesh.'

His voice was warm and low. 'I...I don't understand you.'

His hand left hers and he picked up the phone. The screen washed his face with a faint blue. He repeated his words and she waited for the double beep. 'Do not be nervous. You are stronger than you think.'

She tried to smile. 'Thank you.'

Silence returned, but this time she couldn't let it continue. Taking the phone from him, she said, 'I am scared. We don't have much time left.'

As the translation sounded, he picked up his glass and raised it to his lips.

'I feel weak,' she added. 'Because I do not know what is happening.'

Now he looked away. As he lowered the glass, his forefinger moved back and forth along its rim. Small movements. He reached for the phone. 'I will tell you what I know. It is not everything, but it is all I know, OK?'

She dipped her head, eyes staying on his. 'Yes.'

He pushed his plate aside. 'There is a boat coming across the sea. It is coming now. On this boat is a special weapon. A missile. It can destroy a helicopter.'

She saw then how it would work.

For some reason, she'd been imagining an ambush. Only one road led from the air base. She knew the type of car the Prince would be in. A stalled vehicle, forcing the Prince's to stop. Doku waiting at the side of the road with a gun. The rendezvous at sea was, she assumed, to take delivery of that gun. This was far more clever.

'We will meet this boat,' Doku continued, 'and then call on the radio to say it is sinking. The Prince will come in the helicopter. And I will be ready, like this.' The way he positioned his arms reminded her of a photo from her geography classroom: a lumberjack balancing a log on his shoulder. The drone. The camcorder. It all made sense. They wanted to capture it on film. A spectacular in every sense. Even as the flaming wreckage sank beneath the waves, they would be racing across the sea to safety.

A fresh wave of nervous energy surged through her. This was it. This was how they would be made to feel her pain. The one over in Afghanistan who joked about playing at soldiers while holding the controls of an Xbox. Now he would experience the same reality as her: losing a brother. His family would experience the loss of a son. They would all taste her world, the bitterness that could not be washed away.

'Now you know,' he announced quietly, lowering his arms.

'Are you OK?' she asked, noticing how his lips had tightened in pain.

He touched a finger to his neck in explanation.

Of course, she thought. The muscles in his shoulder would be trying to compensate for his injured shoulder. It was likely they'd lock if he wasn't careful. 'Let me see.'

She circled the table and stood behind him. Gently, she probed at the top of his shoulder, feeling the rigidity of his trapezius, right the way up to the base of his skull. Moving her hands across his shoulders, she tracked rock-hard muscle all the way to the deltoids. If he'd kept the sling on, he could have avoided most of this. Using slow, circular movements, she began to massage the back of his neck, employing her thumbs to get at the muscle closer to his spine. His head began to sag forward. Once those muscles felt looser, she ran her palms across his shoulder, using her fingertips to ease the tension trapped there.

His right hand suddenly came up, fingers enveloping her wrist. She thought she must have hurt him: jarred the shoulder joint, perhaps. Anxiously, she leaned forward, and as he turned to her, she had that same flutter of confusion. Whether he was going to strike her, or kiss her.

CHAPTER 40

They spotted a twenty-four-hour supermarket on the approach to the ferry terminal in Holyhead, Anglesey's main town. Jon waited in the car park as Iona nipped inside to grab overnight supplies for them both. It was slightly odd, he'd reflected while sitting there, to have someone you'd worked with for one day buying you boxer shorts, socks, deodorant and toothpaste.

A little further along was a motel with plenty of spaces in the car park. Jon considered leaving the car there overnight, but drove back out in search of the police station. 'I'd crap myself,' he'd explained to Iona. 'Imagine if it got nicked with that lot in the boot.'

'Who's going to get round the vehicle's immobiliser? And the weapons box itself can stand up to an acetylene torch. Then there are the GPS trackers.'

'I'll just sleep better knowing it's properly secure.'

'Suit yourself.'

As it happened, the police station was only a couple of minutes' drive further into town. His badge got them through the gate and, after leaving the car in the compound, they walked back to the motel. The receptionist allocated them a couple of rooms before letting them know dinner was served for another hour. They could also add breakfast to the deal for just seven pounds ninety-nine extra.

'Is it continental or the full spread?' Jon asked.

'Both. There's a counter with cereals, fresh fruit, yoghurt and croissants, plus a hot buffet of sausages, bacon, black pudd – '

'I'll take it,' Jon cut in. 'Iona?'

'Why not?'

He clocked her ambivalent tone. 'Not partial to a good dose of trans-fats in the morning?'

'Funnily enough, no.'

'Not even when work are paying?'

She shook her head.

'Well, there's always the fresh fruit.' He looked at his watch. 'Shall we meet back here in twenty? I could do with grabbing a bite to eat before they stop serving.'

'So,' Jon placed his half-drunk pint of fresh orange and lemonade on the table. 'This is nice.'

Iona assessed their sterile surroundings. A vending machine was beside the door leading to the stairs. Below the flat screen TV mounted at the opposite end of the room were three men. Lorry drivers, she guessed. Half the tables had already been set for breakfast by the staff member who now stood behind a pokey bar. 'Isn't it?'

'Ever been out in Holyhead?'

'Can't say I have.'

'It's...interesting.'

'What was it, a rugby tour?'

'No, work as per. A bit further on there's a massive set of cliffs. You get thousands of seabirds nesting on them.'

'It feels like the back of beyond, here,' Iona whispered.

'It kind of is, if you think about it. Far corner of an island off the coast of Wales, on the edge of Britain. Except for the truckers coming off the ferries from Ireland, I think the gene pool's a bit limited.'

Iona surveyed the three TV watchers. Two bald heads and a shock of ginger hair. 'Spoilt for talent.'

Jon grinned. 'When are we going to get a break, then? This pair's luck is lasting far too long.'

'I can't see it being us who finds them. They'll get snagged further down the line: trying to leave the country, or Elissa will use a cashpoint card. Something silly.'

Jon removed the plastic stirrer from his glass. 'Or she'll get an opportunity to escape and raise the alarm.'

Iona sat back. 'You still think she's an unwilling participant in this?'

'I think there's a good chance of it. We have no idea who the man she's with is. Maybe she misjudged what she was getting into.'

Iona shook her head. 'She knows exactly what she's doing. They're scopers, is my guess. Gathering information for possible targets.'

'Hence the drone? Reconnaissance on Wylfa, Stanlow, maybe Liverpool Airport...'

Iona looked past Jon. 'Food's here.'

The waitress had a plate in each hand. 'Steak, mushroom, chips and peas, plus a small tuna salad?'

Jon patted the table.

The woman didn't even check whose dish was whose.

It was almost three in the morning when something caused Jon to wake. Sitting up in bed, blinking stupidly at the darkness, his first reaction was to find his phone. He was still fumbling for the switch for the bedside light when a light knocking sounded on his door. Was that what had woken him? Someone at his door? He swung his feet to the floor. 'Yes?'

'Jon, it's Iona.' Her voice was an urgent whisper. 'Put some clothes on, I need to come in.'

He hauled his jeans on and pulled the door open. She was fully dressed, bag on the floor between her feet, phone in hand.

'What's up?'

'A call from Weir.'

He stepped aside, scratching at his ribs as she crossed to the armchair in the corner. 'That sounds ominous.'

'It is.'

He lifted his t-shirt off the end of the bed and slipped it over his head. 'What did he say?'

'The Russians got an identity from those prints. The ones lifted from the mobile phone.'

'In the early hours of Sunday bloody morning?'

'What I said. Weir reckons it's their little joke: they probably have had the information a while, but thought it would be fun to call it through now.'

Jon filled the kettle from the tap in the toilet. 'Have we time for coffee?'

'Yeah.'

'So: these prints?'

She flipped her phone around. 'Most is in this email. Shall I read it out while you do the drinks?'

'Deal.'

'OK, starting at the top. His name is Doku Zakayev and he's a thirty-four-year old veteran of the Chechen War. That's fighting against the Russians, not with them. He's from the mountainous region in the south of the country – which certainly fits with the words on the map found in the crashed car.'

'Veteran of the Chechen War? Jesus, that involved some brutal fighting.'

'Precisely.'

Her forefinger played across the screen, then she turned the phone round so he could see it. 'This is the best picture they've got. It was taken in 2008, by local Chechen police. They'd detained him but then let him go before the Russian military were aware he was in custody.'

The photo was typical of law enforcement agencies the world over: an eye-level shot against a plain background, subject looking direct to camera. He had a thick mop of black hair and an unruly beard. Dark eyes were directed slightly off to the side, as if something more interesting was taking place there. Jon recognised the closed-down, impassive look – it was the type of expression people adopted when making it clear they'd been unjustly taken in. I've done nothing, it said. And I resent being here.

'The reason this guy is of interest to the Russians is because they believe he fired a surface-to-air missile that downed a transport helicopter in south Chechnya in 2000. All fifteen Russian military personnel on board were killed.'

Jon took the phone from her and studied his face more closely.

'It gets worse. You know how the Russians are active in the conflict over in Syria? They picked up some chatter recently: it was about a surface-to-air missile that had been transported into North Africa and then up into Spain. They intercepted that information six days ago.'

Jon gave the phone back. His head was bowed as he stirred the two cups. 'Are we now treating all of this as connected?'

'There's a top-floor meeting first thing in the morning, but Weir's already making contingency plans. He's bringing everything under Operation Stinger.'

Jon placed her cup on the desk. 'What are your thoughts?'

'This guy – Zakayev – is in the UK, we know that much. We don't know how long he's been here. But the car involved in the RTA was stolen one week ago, so it seems reasonable he's been here from around that point.'

Jon sat on the end of the bed. 'If we're working on the assumption the cargo spirited into Libya was that missile, it got there – what – around two weeks ago?'

'Which means, potentially, it reached mainland Europe a few days after that.'

'Southern Spain to northern France. You can drive that in three days, I should think. Iona: it could be here already.

Brought across the channel on that bloody great Rib. Or on a private yacht. Anything.'

'They've discussed that. A highest priority alert has gone out to security services across Europe. Wylfa is not being regarded as under threat. The SBS boys said a strike is highly unlikely to have much effect because the nasty stuff is stored mostly below ground. They're staying on site though, and keeping up patrols off the coast.'

'So what are the priorities now?'

'Airports. We know they took the M53 into the Wirral. The easterly shoreline looks directly across the Mersey estuary – '

Jon clicked a finger. 'John Lennon Airport. Earlier on, I watched this plane flying over. I could almost see the passengers' faces, it was that low.'

'As international airports go, it's not nearly as busy as Manchester. But there are still plenty of flights leaving from it: New York, Orlando, and one each day direct to Tel Aviv.'

'Jesus. I was wrong. I thought this was where they'd be.'

'I wouldn't say you were wrong. There's footage taken not far from a nuclear power station. That's not something to ignore.'

He put his cup on the carpet so he could stretch both arms above his head. 'The airports are where it's at,' he said, fingers reaching towards the ceiling. 'Has to be.'

'Now it is – but only given the information the Russians finally sent.'

Jon's arms dropped like someone had cut his strings. He rotated his shoulders and leaned his head from side-to-side. 'It's all right. I can take being wrong.'

She shrugged. 'There's still the question of where they've put that boat. Find that thing and we find them, surely.'

'So we're going back to the Wirral?'

'Not yet. For the moment, we stay here.'

'Really?'

'He said other teams are being deployed there.'

Jon stared down at the carpet. So the Wirral looked like where all the action was going to be. And they were almost two hours' away, on a warty outgrowth off the far edge of Wales. Shit. 'What's he want us to do here?'

'We're to get a map of the island and start marking down where that boat could be.'

'What happened to the support from the office?'

'Everything's being focused on the Wirral.'

'Does he realise how far it is to go right round the coast of Anglesey?'

'Probably not. Mind you, I couldn't say either.'

'My old man fancied walking the ring path when they opened it a few years back. He changed his mind when he realised it's over 124 miles long.'

CHAPTER 41

Sudden movement stirred Elissa from the depths of sleep. For a heart-wrenching instant, she had no idea where she was. It wasn't her own bed; she sensed that. Beside her, she could hear breathless words being spoken. By a man. Her entire body went tense. And, when a hand came down on the bare flesh of her shoulder, she nearly leapt to her feet.

'Mne nuzhna ruchka!'

Everything came back to her. Oh my God. I'm naked. She turned her head. He's naked. Sitting bolt upright, looking down at her with a look of... astonishment. They hadn't even drawn the curtains. Pre-dawn grey lay like a sheen on his skin.

'Mne nuzhna ruchka.' He wrote across his palm, as if requesting a bill in a restaurant. Then he swung his legs over the side of the bed and hurried for the door. She watched his buttock muscles bunching alternately with each step and remembered running her hands across them.

Her clothes were nowhere to be seen. Probably on the floor of the kitchen, mingled in with his. The memory of leading him by the hand along the corridor to the ground-floor bedroom. His face, made boy-like with an expression that was at once thrilled and apprehensive. She'd soon got the feeling it was something he'd never done before. Knowing his shoulder was vulnerable, she'd lain him on his back and taken the lead.

There was a bath towel on the rack in the en-suite, so she wrapped it about herself and stepped into the corridor. The kitchen light was on and she found him sitting at the table, a red biro in his hand. He'd ripped the sleeve of a cookery book and had folded it over to expose a blank area.

On it, he'd scrawled a single word and was adding another. He stood, unconcerned, or oblivious, to the fact he had nothing on. 'Ya vspomnil! Xbox.'

What he so needed has re-surfaced in his memory, she thought. Now he could find out when and where the boat that was coming from the continent would be. She also knew that, as from seven o'clock the previous evening, the prince had been on shift. Any distress call that came in until seven o'clock that evening would be responded to by him.

The mission was on.

Brushing past her, he hurried toward the living-room and a part of her registered disappointment at his lack of affection. She glanced at the kitchen wall clock. Almost five in the morning.

The TV was already on when she caught him up. He was kneeling before it, controller from the console in his hands. The computer game was up on the screen and he was busily selecting the letters he needed.

'I vsyo eto vryemya oni poyavilis vo snye.' He looked back at her, face full of delight. 'Neveroyatno.'

Smiling, she ran a hand down the back of his head, leaving it resting lightly on his neck.

'U nas yeshche yest vremya,' he said, dragging letters into the upper field. She decided to get the phone, otherwise she'd just be nodding at him like an imbecile. It was still on the kitchen table. The sight of all their clothes strewn on the floor caused a brief smirk as she grabbed the handset.

The dragon had the eyes of a deer, liquid brown and beautiful. It lowered its heavy lashes every now and again as Doku searched through a map in a panel at the bottom of the screen. 'Tam ona.' He moved the cursor back to the dragon and, by manipulating the controller's buttons, it launched itself off the mountain ledge and into the endless blue sky. Each beat of its wings made a swooshing sound as it hovered in the air. Doku pressed the front of the cross-shaped button down and it began to fly forward. Other dragons of varying sizes and colours were also flapping languidly about. Whenever one came close, he'd veer round it. Sometimes, speech bubbles appeared beside these other dragon's heads, but he didn't respond. Every now and again, the layer of fluffy cloud beneath was punctuated by a mountaintop. Smoke rose from some and occasionally a flaming rock would arc up as if fired from a catapult deep within the crater. The smoke trails they left slowly dwindled to nothing. She presumed the floating text boxes contained the name of each of these peaks.

From the compass in the mid-point of the screen's base, she could see he wasn't straying from a bearing of north by north-east.

Eventually, another peak came into view below them. 'Crolobin,' he announced quietly, taking the dragon into a gentle dive. The top of the mountain drew closer and, once at eye-level, Doku circled round it until he caught sight of a dark opening. As he made for it, the beat of the dragon's wings slowed to a stop. Gliding silently in, it alighted on the ledge before a cave. The wings folded in and, stubby tail sweeping from side-to-side, the creature moved forward.

Now it was at the threshold of the opening, Elissa could see a pair of wooden doors set deep into the rock. The dragon got to within touching distance of them but could go no closer, even though its feet continued to move.

Doku brought up another panel and selected an envelope icon from the menu. In the text box, he copied out the first word he'd written on the cookery book's inner cover. The little envelope sealed itself and flew through a crack between the two doors. Doku stared at the screen. Nothing was happening. After a minute, he turned to Elissa with a confused expression. 'Ih nikogo net doma.'

She held the phone out to him so he could speak into it. The double beep. 'They're not at home.'

CHAPTER 42

'Never got to have the hotel breakfast,' Jon muttered as he drove out of the police station's car park. The biscuits from his hotel room had been a very poor substitute.

'Is it always on your mind?' Iona replied. 'Where your next meal is coming from?'

'It's not my fault I have a high metabolism,' he protested. 'I'm like a mouse, really.'

'Yeah,' she laughed, 'a hippopota-mouse.'

'Oh! That's bullying, that is. I might take that to Weir and get you done.'

Iona pushed her feet as far into the foot-well as they would go. There was just enough room to fully straighten her legs. She tensed her thighs and felt her hamstrings stretch. Too much sitting in a car. It was beginning to feel like a cage.

The sky had lightened but the streetlights were still on. There were a few people up and about; workers trudging in the direction of the ferry terminal, some in fluorescent jackets. Sitting motionless in the harbour was an enormous vessel, glowing lights strung out along its decks. The trail of smoke rising slowly from its tower-like chimney was white against the lead-coloured sky. 'I don't suppose a surface-to-air missile would have much effect on one of those things,' Jon observed while negotiating a roundabout.

Iona looked across at the ferry. The neat lines of waiting lorries and cars were dwarfed by it. 'Not so it would sink.' She checked her phone against the map of the island which they'd borrowed from Holyhead's police station. 'Nearest marina, then, is straight along this road.'

Jon scowled. 'This is such a long shot. I mean, say you were planning to hold-up a cash-delivery van, would you park the car you were going to use in the local multi-storey?'

'Could be hiding in plain-view. And don't forget, they're unaware we even know about this boat. If it wasn't for that junk-mail, we wouldn't have a clue.'

'True. Though my money's on a lock-up or something similar. Somewhere safely out of sight until it's needed.'

'Need a bloody big lock-up. Some of those things are nearer the length of a bus.' She pointed. 'Take a left at that junction.'

The road took them alongside the sea. Thin waves ruffled against the edge of the empty beach. As the road curved inland, Iona focused on her phone. 'They've put the intelligence on this Zakayev into the shared file.'

'Go on then, what else has he done?'

'This bit is interesting: his parents were among the fatalities when a Russian missile hit a crowd queuing outside a building in Shali, a town in the mountainous region in Chechnya's south. At the time, it had been declared a safe area for civilians.'

'For real?'

'That's what it says. Nine days later, the Russian army transport helicopter was brought down by a surface-to-air missile. Guess what type of missile.'

'Stinger?'

'Yup. They think he fired it.'

'So revenge, then?'

'Maybe.'

A large driveway appeared on the left. Penrhos Wharf Marina.

Jon turned in and followed the smooth asphalt to a two-storey building. A wide balcony ran along the side of it that faced the ocean. 'Spoilt for choice,' he said, taking one of the empty parking spaces near to the building's side door. A single light was on in the foyer but, apart from that, the building was entirely dark.

They followed the path that led to the water. At regular intervals, walkways sloped down to narrow jetties. Lined up on either side of each one were dozens of vessels.

'There's some money in these places,' Jon stated, gaze settling on some of the larger boats on the far side.

'Seven jetties, about eighteen boats along each side. That's about two-hundred and fifty boats,' Iona replied.

Jon nodded knowingly, wondering how the hell she'd worked that out so fast. 'My calculation, exactly.'

'Anything with a mast, we can forget – that's about half, at least.'

'And that far jetty, looks like it's reserved for your floating gin palaces.' He pointed to a line of larger yachts, many with jet skies attached to their rears.

'Shall we start on the right, then? I do one side of the jetty, you do the other?'

'Sounds good.'

Their feet made hollow thuds as they made their way down the walkway. Many of the motorboats had covers stretched over them. Judging by the volume of seagull droppings they'd collected, some hadn't been touched in months. By the time they'd checked four of the jetties, they'd counted eight Ribs, but only three of those appeared new. Iona carefully noted the berth number of each one.

'Hey up,' Jon said, as they made their way towards the fifth walkway. 'There are people in that end one.'

Iona looked up. 'Oh yeah.'

A head and shoulders had appeared at the rear of the single mast yacht moored at the very end of the jetty. Looking more closely, Jon could see cracks of light in the row of windows running down the vessel's side. The aroma of fresh coffee wafted to them on the breeze. 'Jesus, that smells good.'

'Doesn't it?' Iona murmured.

By the time they reached the jetty's end, the person had been joined by another. Jon could tell they were a couple, both into their sixties. 'Morning.'

The man was wearing a faded red baseball cap. He glanced round slowly and intelligent eyes swiftly assessed Jon. 'Hi there.'

The twang in the man's voice was unmistakeably Australian. His partner was casually raking fingers through her short hair. What is it about boats? Jon thought. Everyone seems so damned relaxed. The man's t-shirt read, Waratahs, a rugby team based in New South Wales.

'You've not sailed here all the way from Australia, have you?' Jon tapped his chest and pointed at the man's top.

He glanced down, realised what he was wearing and gave an easy smile. 'No, just up from Almeria. Originally, we sailed from Greece. Been making our way round since Spring.'

'Some holiday.'

'Retired, mate. Life's one big holiday now. I'm Mike, this is my wife, Sue.'

'Jon and Iona.'

The woman rose to her feet, toes flexing in her flip-flops. 'Can I get you two some coffee?'

Jon glanced at Iona and imagined the craving in her eyes matched his. 'No, don't go to any trouble – '

'There's a pot just brewed, it's no trouble. Milk and sugar?'

Iona spoke up. 'One plain black, one with milk, thanks.'

'On its way.' She stooped down and disappeared below deck.

The man gestured to his side. 'It's a bit cramped, but you're welcome to come aboard.'

Seeing they'd be almost on each other's laps, Jon raised a hand. 'No, you're fine, thanks.' He looked back along the jetty. 'We shouldn't stop too long: we're working.'

'Something told me you didn't own a boat. What kind of work?'

'Police,' Jon replied.

The man tipped his head in response.

Something about the gesture prompted Jon to ask, 'Were you in the job?'

'Australian navy, thirty-five years.'

The woman reappeared, an enamel mug in each hand. 'Here you go.'

Once they all had a cup, the man said, 'Can we be of any help?'

'Well, we're looking for a particular type of Rib. How long have you been moored here?'

'Arrived Saturday, we carry on today. Heading north.'

'How does it work, sailing between one country and another?' Iona asked, glancing back at the closed building. 'Do you have to report in somewhere?'

'We did on first arriving in British waters,' he replied. 'We sailed into Dartmouth and got our passports stamped there. You're expected to show your faces at the harbour master's office as soon as it's practical. This place, we phoned ahead to see if they had any spare berths. We paid in advance for two nights.'

'What's to stop someone just sailing into a larger harbour, mooring up among other boats, then sneaking off without paying?'

He looked at her for a moment. 'Well, nothing in theory. But other boat owners might not be happy. These berths are all numbered.' He nodded to their feet. 'This is forty eight.'

Jon looked down: a small brass disc had the number engraved on it.

'It's like an office car park. Rock up in someone else's berth and the owner won't be happy. These things don't come cheap. Then there's the harbour master. It's that guy's job to keep an eye on things. You'd be surprised at how good they are at it, too.'

'Even in busy harbours?'

'Oh yes. His office will be somewhere with a good view. Big pair of bino's to hand. They develop a mental map. Any boat appears that they don't know about, they pick up on pretty damn fast.'

'Soon, they'd be round to politely ask how you intend paying for your stay,' his wife added with a laugh.

Jon stepped back to look along the length of their boat. Its name was painted on the side: McNoon. 'Lovely looking yacht you have. So this is what you do now?'

'Only for the summers,' Sue replied. 'Mike would keep going through the winter, but I get too cold. We fly back to Australia when it starts to turn.'

'And the boat?'

'Dry dock it somewhere,' Mike answered. 'Probably in Spain. Your prices in the UK are way too high.'

'That doesn't surprise me,' Jon said. 'What a superb way to spend the year.'

They smiled modestly.

'Say you were on Anglesey,' Jon said, swilling his coffee round. 'You had a Rib that you needed to launch at some point, but you don't want to draw any attention to it. Where might you keep it?'

He thought for a moment. 'Depends how long I was here for.'

'Why?'

'If it's a while, I wouldn't keep it in the water. It rots stuff. Me? I'd keep it on its trailer, tow it inland and chuck a tarp over it.'

'Let's assume it needs to be launched pretty fast,' Jon said.

'So a barn or inland storage facility would be out. What are we talking about here, smugglers?'

'Something like that.'

'Somewhere private?'

'Yes.'

'And I'm not bothered about cost?'

'No.'

'Then I'd rent a place with its own mooring, assuming it's not a flying visit. A holiday home at the water's edge.'

Jon glanced at Iona. 'Holiday home. Now there's a thought.'

She nodded her agreement and finished her drink. 'Sue, that was just what I needed, thanks so much.'

'Yup – I feel human again,' Jon stated, handing his cup over, too. 'Thanks for your help.'

Iona waited until they were out of earshot before saying in an American accent, 'I think we're gonna need a bigger boat.'

Jon looked at her appreciatively. 'Jaws. Aren't you a bit young to be quoting from that?'

'I love all those old classics. Jaws, Alien, Taxi driver: they're brilliant.'

'Old classics? I wouldn't say – ' Jon stopped himself. To her, he realised, films like that were old classics. They'd been made before she was born. He felt old. 'You're right, we can never cover this on our own. Surely Weir needs to start involving the local police? Unless he wants us to do a long-term booking at that motel and spend the next few months here.' He glanced at his watch. They'd be serving breakfast there soon, and they had already paid –

Iona's phone went off.

Seeing the caller identification, she raised an eyebrow. 'Speak of the devil. Morning, sir. We're just leaving the first location on our list. Thing is, sir, we think that, given the scale of the area, it – ' She stopped speaking. Then she stopped walking. Jon came to a halt. Her eyes went to him, the start of a smile tickling the corners of her mouth. 'Really? That's confirmed? Beyond all doubt?' Her entire face lit up. Elation, relief, incredulity. 'I don't know what to say... that's...oh my God.' She looked at Jon properly. 'Yes, I'll let him know. Jon, the French coastguard boarded a vessel at the edge of their territorial waters. They got it.'

'Got what?'

'The Stinger.'

CHAPTER 43

'That's bordering on obscene.'

'Most important meal of the day, breakfast.'

'Should be your only meal of the day, eating that much.'

Jon slid in at the opposite side of the table. He picked up his napkin and theatrically shook it out. A magician preparing a trick. 'Now, behold as I make it vanish.'

She shook her head. 'If you piled all that between two slices of bread, Scooby-Doo couldn't open his jaws wide enough.'

Jon regarded his plate. Maybe he had gone a bit silly at the self-service buffet. But he'd only had the hotel biscuits and a cup of coffee – and it was way past his usual breakfast time. Anyway, things called for a celebration. 'Edge of international waters and heading this way. Close one.'

'And only because they left the marina near Cherbourg without informing the harbour master.'

'Just like that guy from the Australian navy said,' Jon responded.

Iona draped an arm across the back of the chair next to her. The bowl before her still held a few cubes of melon and sliced grapes. On her side plate was a single croissant. With her coffee-coloured skin, Jon thought she belonged outside a street cafe in Europe. Barcelona. Venice. Monaco. Somewhere drenched in sun, anyway.

He began sawing through his stack of bacon. 'Three men on board?'

She took a sip of tea and nodded. 'That's what Weir said. No paperwork, nothing. North African in appearance. That'll be French security speak for Algerian or Moroccan.'

'And the charts they had out were for the Irish Sea. How long did they think it would be before they reached this part of the coast?'

'Mid to late afternoon.'

'It must have been a rendezvous. Our man meeting them somewhere out at sea for the transfer. Question is, where would be the best place to set out from? The Wirral or here?'

'If the target was a flight leaving from Liverpool airport, does it matter? Once the missile was ashore, they could pick any number of places to launch it.'

Jon chewed for a while. 'This place has more secluded spots to access the sea, in my opinion. Isolated coves, little inlets, tiny beaches. You've seen the map.'

Iona brushed crumbs from the tablecloth. 'I'd be interested to know what the thinking is for their escape plan.'

'Manchester airport?'

'No. If a passenger plane was brought down, all flights would be suspended. They wouldn't be leaving by air.'

'Ferry over to Ireland?'

'Same, I imagine. The entire country would go into lock-down.' She lifted a finger. 'But they have the Rib. It's fast. Larger ones can handle the open sea. That could be how they were going to do it.'

'Over to Ireland?'

'Maybe further? France. Even Spain?'

'The bastard boat. Locate that and we locate them.'

Iona pulled her croissant in half. 'Another thing: what if word about the missile being intercepted gets back to our two? Once they know it's all off, they'll go straight to a contingency plan.' As her fingers flicked out, a flake of croissant dropped through the air. 'They'll be gone.'

Jon's eyes narrowed. 'Don't say that.'

'It's true.'

He sighed. 'What else did Weir say?'

'He didn't. They're liaising with the French. We're to stay put until then.'

'I'm not happy sitting on my arse doing nothing. How about we carry on looking?'

'That's not what Weir's instructions were.'

'You know, the Australian navy guy had a point,' Jon said quietly. 'A secluded spot inland and you cover the boat with a tarpaulin. Or a holiday home with a private mooring – which would make it far easier to come and go as you please.'

'You're suggesting we go off script?'

There was a mischievous glint in Jon's eye. 'I might be.'

'Officially, we're to await further instructions.'

'Officially. He didn't specify what, exactly, we do in the meantime.'

She propped her chin on a hand and studied him. 'Remind me: how was it you got thrown out of the Major Incident Team?'

Jon dipped his head to stuff some sausage into his mouth. 'You think we should stay put?'

'If that's what we were asked to do, yes.'

One cheek now bulged with food as he looked back up at her. 'You could argue we're using our initiative. Don't they like you using your initiative in the CTU?'

'They do.'

'Well?'

She sighed. 'What do you suggest?'

'Well, it's either check inland holiday homes for any boats and trailers, or check ones on the coast with private moorings. We haven't time to do both.'

Iona weighed it up. 'Which one will there be less of?'

'Private moorings, I should think. You know, there was a holiday lettings place near the supermarket. They could direct us to any of that type of property they have on their books. Ones that are currently occupied.'

'Are you sure you didn't have this planned out already?'

Jon laid his cutlery down. 'How could I?'

'I don't know,' she murmured, checking her watch. 'And you want to start now?'

'May as well. But if we're going to do this, let's go about it properly.'

'How do you mean?'

He nodded at her phone. 'Can you go on the system and get us the file of that bit of drone footage they filmed on the island?'

CHAPTER 44

She tried to keep her mind off things by flicking through a book. Something from the shelf in the corner of the room about Snowdonia. Lots of nice photographs of sheep-dotted valleys, golden beaches and tumbling streams.

Doku simply couldn't sit still. Hearing him pace around the cottage brought back memories of a visit to Chester Zoo. Some kind of rare desert creature that had restlessly patrolled its enclosure with a desperate intensity, as if puzzling over how it had been trapped. Watching the miserable animal had made her sad and she had often wondered since how long it had kept moving before succumbing to the lethargy of its neighbours.

'Pochemu ih net? Pochemu oni ne otvechayut?' Doku would mutter each time he checked the cave doors and found them still closed.

The digger's engine coughed to life shortly after nine. The instant it started, he dropped to all fours and crawled over to the window. He bobbed his head above the sill for a second. The rapid juddering of a drill joined it. Unpleasant, harsh sounds that shattered all sense of peace. Sometimes a raised voice calling truncated instructions. More. Enough. Stop.

From the sofa, she observed him. 'It's OK,' she whispered, reaching for the phone. 'Only workmen.'

The Russian translation did little to calm him. After watching through the windows for a while, he stood up and extended his pacing to the entire cottage. The ceiling creaked as he moved about above her, then his foot on the stairs before he entered the room once more. There was now no point in lifting her gaze as he came in; his attention was fixed on the TV as he crossed the room, checked the screen then turned away in disappointment.

Shortly before eleven, the gravel on the drive began to crunch. She was off the sofa and at the window in an instant. Through the net curtain, the approaching workman appeared insubstantial. But his footsteps were solid and heavy.

She moved out into the corridor and looked up the stairs. He was crouching at the top, one hand loosening the evil-looking blade from his ankle. The bell rang as she raised her hands to him. 'Stay there, stay!'

Not waiting for a reply, she went through to the kitchen, quickly checking the room as she crossed to the door. Plates on the table. Two cups. A carton of orange juice. Everything looked normal. She opened the door to a heavy-set man with long brown hair tied back in a ponytail. Stubble covered his lower face and his blue overalls were speckled with mud.

'Morning love, sorry to disturb.'

Not opening the door any further than necessary, she smiled at him. 'That's fine.'

He tried to see past her, interest apparently piqued by a lone young woman coming to the door. 'Here on holiday then?'

'Yes.'

'That's lovely.' He gestured back to the road. 'Wasn't sure if anyone was here. No car on the drive.'

'I put it in the garage.'

'Oh, right. So...' His glance went to her hand.

She knew what he was checking for: a wedding ring.

He hitched the waist of his overalls up a bit. 'Enjoying your stay?'

It was like being in a pub. Some married saddo about to try his luck. 'Could you keep your voice down. My partner? He's in bed recuperating from a recent operation. How can I help?'

He stepped back, voice now matter-of-fact. 'We need to cut the water off; you might want to fill the kettle and a few pans.'

'The water?'

'Only for a few hours.'

'What are you doing out there?'

'Improving the drainage to keep that road from flooding.'

'Right – I will do. Thanks for letting me know.'

He was already walking away.

'When will it come back on?

'Three at the latest.'

She swung the door shut and almost jumped backwards. Doku was there, knife in his hand. Part of her was thrilled. No one was going to touch her, not with him around.

CHAPTER 45

Iona popped her phone on the dashboard and hit play. A buzzing noise filled the car and, on screen, the field started to fall away.

'There's the tortured pine tree that techie guy, Carl, mentioned,' Iona remarked. 'Left hand side.'

'Got it. Does look bent over in pain, doesn't it?'

'He didn't think they were in a garden when they shot this. More like open countryside.'

Jon could see Carl was right. The camera was pointing straight down at scrubby grassland dotted by gorse bushes and a stone outcrop. As the drone lifted higher, the land at the top of the screen dropped abruptly away. There followed an apron of rippling rock and then the sea. The water had a greenish hue, and as it grew deeper, the rock soon vanished beneath its murky depths. The drone rose higher; whoever was controlling the camera must have directed it to look forwards, not directly down. Ocean filled the screen, as far as the eye could see.

'Right, he said at about forty seconds, the view swings to the left,' Iona said. 'Not that I can tell what's happening anymore, all I can see is water.'

Distant land encroaching at the bottom left-hand corner of the screen allowed them to get their bearings. Iona waited until the view improved before she pressed pause. 'That's it.'

Grey and squat, the power station dominated a bulbous head of land that extended a short way out to sea. 'That's a distance, he estimated, of six to eight miles. Which means it was filmed somewhere to the west of Amlwch.'

'Still a long way off for a recce, don't you think?'

'Yes. Shall we carry on?'

Jon nodded.

The view rotated back to the open sea and, for the next half a minute, they listened to the annoying whirr of the drone's engine. At one point, it changed pitch, but until the coastline suddenly crept into the bottom of the screen, it had been impossible to tell the thing had been descending. It continued to drop smoothly then, at head height, swept to the side, thick grass suddenly jumping up to envelope the lens. The footage cut.

Iona slid the map of Anglesey across her lap. 'From here, Amlwch is about fifteen miles away. We just stick to the A5025.' Her finger followed the red line as it jerked its way north then west as the coast curved round. If the island was a clock, Amlwch sat at a point just before one.

As they drove along, the amount of space seemed strange. Rolling fields with little in them. An occasional half-collapsed farm building. A few strings of meagre trees where the land dipped too sharply for a farmer to use for cultivation. And always an awareness that, just beyond view, the sea lurked silent and still.

Earlier, when they'd called in at the lettings agency, the owner had calculated there were fourteen properties with coastal access on their books. Of those, eleven currently had people in them.

Describing the actual location of each property was far from easy: aside from the A5025, most of the roads on the top end of the island had no designated number. The owner of the lettings agency explained that using a satellite navigation was pretty much useless; post codes were only a rough guide and frequently led down tracks only negotiable in a Land Rover. Far better was to use the old way of navigating: landmarks. The turn after the white cottage with roses at the front, the lane immediately after the old windmill, the hidden drive half-way along the approach road to Hen Borth Beach. Jon had slid a look at Iona. This was going to be a nightmare.

The owner had also pointed out that Holyhead had a second, smaller, lettings company: Menai Cottages and Caravans. It also had some coastal properties in north Anglesey: probably about four. Then there were a smattering of properties let privately and at least two that belonged to the National Trust that the public were free to book.

It was more than they could ever hope to cover in one day.

'What do you reckon?' Iona asked, holding up the sheet for each property once they were outside the office. 'Concentrate on these?'

'May as well,' Jon replied.

By lunch time, they'd only located two. Driving slowly past the first, they saw a line of small wet suits draped over the garden fence. The sounds of children playing in the back garden carried in through Iona's open window.

The other appeared empty.

'You'll need to take a closer look,' Iona stated. 'Elissa Yared? She knows me.'

'Good point,' Jon replied. He parked further down the lane then wandered back on foot. As he neared the front drive, he readied the property descriptions the owner of the lettings agency had printed off. If anyone asked, he was a holidaymaker, scouting potential holiday spots.

There was a salmon pink bungalow next door with an old lady sitting out front. Jon held up a hand in greeting. 'Hello.'

She watched him warily.

'I'm camping with my family, but my wife is interested in renting a cottage for next year. The place next door looks nice. Does it get busy?'

'This time of year, it does. You'll need to book early.'

He had to lift a hand to shield his eyes from the sun as he surveyed the cottage. 'Anyone in it at the moment?'

'Divers.'

'Divers?'

'Yes, they have a boat. They load it up each morning with their things then disappear out to sea.'

'Of course; the lettings agency said it has its own jetty. Diving? Unusual activity for a family.'

'No, it's five young men. All very polite.'

'From Britain?'

'Yes, I think they're lawyers. Two said they were anyway.'

'Right. I'll have to see what the availability is like for next summer. Thanks.'

Back at the car, he climbed in with a shake of his head. 'No joy,' he said, handing the sheets back to Iona.

They made their way along the narrow lane until they reached a crossroads. 'Got to be straight on,' Jon said, crossing over more in hope than certainty. Eventually, it brought them back out onto the A5025. As they meandered through the gently undulating terrain they kept passing other turn-offs, some little more than grassy tracks. 'They'll all lead to something,' Jon announced. 'Farms, or other buildings. Need a bloody helicopter to search this island properly.'

Iona was nodding glumly when her eyes widened. 'Over there!'

Jon hit the brakes. 'What?'

She was pointing off to the side. 'The tortured pine. The one from the drone footage. That's it!'

The twisted upper part of the solitary tree was clearly visible against the sky. She's right, Jon thought. A lane was on their left and he turned into it. After about two hundred metres they could see a lay-by on their right. At its far end was a stile and, next to it, a green footpath sign that pointed across the fields. The tree was now in full view. It stood beside an outcrop of rock flanked by a patch of gorse bushes.

'So this is where they came,' Jon said, pulling in. 'I bet they parked right here.'

'They could be somewhere close,' Iona responded. 'Why else come all the way to this spot? Shall we wander over?'

Jon shook his head. 'It's too open. For all we know, they're in a property that's within view. We'll be far easier to spot than the other way round.'

Iona sat back. 'If they are, it's not one on this list. Next is an address in Amlwch itself.' She was flicking through the other sheets when her phone started to ring. 'Weir.'

'Put him on loudspeaker, will you?'

She did as he asked before accepting the call. 'Hello, sir. I've got you on speakerphone. I'm with Jon in the car.'

'Sir,' Jon quickly said.

'No problem.' His voice carried a faint metallic echo. 'We've got stuff happening thick and fast this end, I need to fill you both in.'

Iona glanced at Jon. 'Go ahead, sir.'

'The French have now provided some additional details. The boat they intercepted belonged to a charter company. The owner of that charter company was in his office, skull caved in by something big and heavy. On the boat, they recovered two handguns along with the surface-to-air missile. So these boys really meant business. Got all that?'

They both spoke together. 'Yes, sir.'

'Good. Next thing, we've had a possible sighting of Doku Zakayev back here in Manchester.'

Iona hunched forwards. 'Where was this?'

'In the vicinity of a residence belonging to a relative of Bilal Atwi. This was two hours ago. We anticipate having warrants for all seven properties connected to the family in another hour's time. The units in the Wirral have already been recalled. Jon? I want all Specialist Firearms Officers back here, you included. We're going to strike simultaneously on the properties in the early hours.'

Jon caught sight of himself in the rear-view mirror. His forehead was buckled by a frown. 'We now think they've doubled back to Manchester?'

'Correct.'

'But the vessel coming from France. That wouldn't have got here until late afternoon. Aren't we working on the assumption Doku was trying to meet it when it arrived?'

'We're working on the assumption word has got to him that the plan is fucked. Now he's trying to flee.'

Jon sent a dubious look up at the car's ceiling. 'Where did this sighting come from?'

'An officer in an unmarked, stationary vehicle.'

'And this sighting is solid? The officer who made it feels confident?'

He saw Iona's head turn. He knew the implication of what he was saying, but couldn't hold back.

When Weir spoke, his voice had tightened. 'As I said, warrants are due and I want all SFOs back here, Detective Constable.'

Jon closed his eyes. This was simply not right. If you're fleeing, why go straight back to a place you know the police will be watching?

'DC Spicer? Is that understood?'

He felt a finger prod his ribs and opened his eyes to see Iona motioning at her phone. Reluctantly, he said, 'Yes sir.'

'Good. Last thing, we found a dealer who sold a Rib with a two-hundred horsepower Marina engine and trailer, to a Mr Hassan Omari. The man paid cash and towed it away eleven days ago. Now, get yourselves home for a bit of a breather, then I want you in here ready for a briefing at ten tonight.'

'Yes sir,' Iona promptly responded. 'See you then.'

The call cut and Jon slumped back in his seat.

'You bloody pushed it there,' Iona stated.

He sighed. 'Yeah, well. Does it feel right to you? Because it certainly doesn't feel right to me.'

'I can't say. Not without all the information to hand.'

'He said it himself. Possible sighting.' He looked about. 'The Uncle brought the Rib here, to this island, I bloody know it. And this is where Zakayev will be, not back in Manchester.'

'What can we do? We have to head back.'

He clenched a fist, bobbed it up and down before him as if sizing up which part of the dashboard to punch. His hand dropped back into his lap. 'He said the briefing's at ten. If we go straight to the office from here, it'll give us time to check a few more properties.'

Iona said nothing.

'Are you up for that?' he asked hopefully.

'No, not really.'

'Come on, Iona. Two more hours, then we drive back. Who'll know?'

She turned to him. 'Two hours, and that's it?'

'Yes.'

'All right.'

'Nice one.' He checked the lane behind was deserted then pulled out. 'My guess is this loops back to the main road. The last one did.'

It swung to the right, and before dipping down, they had a glimpse of the sea through a gap in the hedge. They were no more than fifty metres from the water. They passed another lay-by then crossed a small humpback bridge. On the other side of it, a blue dumper truck was completely blocking the road. Jon came to a halt. A white van was further along and there was a digger scraping out a ditch in the field to their left. Stacked on the grass beside it was a load of bright green pipes. The dumper truck driver started pointing back up the lane. Jon twisted in his seat and began to reverse. 'Shit, should have just done a U-turn back at that lay-by near the pine tree.'

CHAPTER 46

She still wasn't hungry, but went through the motions anyway. Scraping the knife across the surface of the margarine, watching a rime of yellow build on the blade's edge then smearing it in a thin film over a slice of bread. Would he want any? It was hard to tell. Since the workman had knocked on the door, he'd become even more agitated. Now he divided his time between checking the Xbox and sitting at an upstairs window where he could watch the men digging the ditch in the field beyond the garden.

He wasn't convinced they were genuine. And when they'd backed the half-filled dumper truck onto the road, effectively blocking it, he'd almost bolted for the boathouse.

It had taken all her powers of persuasion to convince him the property wasn't under surveillance, that it wasn't about to be raided. Why would they mount a surveillance operation that was so obvious? Surely they had ways that were silent and impossible to see? How could they even know about this place? Uncle Bilal would definitely have used a false name when he'd rented it. They'd left nothing back at the flat in Manchester. They couldn't be traced to here. They were safe.

He'd stalked back up to his observation point; the five workmen were still milling about, attention on the excavation at their feet.

As she laid a couple of plates out on the table, she checked the time. Half-past-two. Their window of opportunity was steadily shrinking. In less than five hours his shift would come to an end. They'd never know her pain. It wasn't fair.

She heard his footsteps on the stairs and lifted a dishcloth. Delicately, she dabbed at her eyes while ramming her emotions back down deep. It didn't help the way he was treating her, either. She wasn't expecting him to fawn over her, but he could show some sort of affection, couldn't he?

The thud of his feet went towards the front room. Of course. The futile hope they'd responded to his messages. Hardly messages. Pleadings. Desperate, like the whining of a child who had been –

A guttural shout.

She half-turned her head, listening for anything else.

His exciting mumblings were just audible and she almost ran towards them, knife still in one hand. It couldn't be. Surely not now, not after so long.

There he was hunkered down before the TV screen, arms stretched toward the brightly lit glass.

She arrived by his side and said nothing. Hardly daring to believe. The doors to the cave had swung open and the dragon was waddling into a cavern lit by flaming brands bolted to the rock walls. A galaxy of gems winked from the craggy surface. Curled on the floor beside an open chest of gold coins was a yellow worm-like creature. A line of small purple spiky horns ran above its slanted emerald eyes. The tip if its thin tail twitched.

Doku halted his dragon and brought up an inner panel containing the Russian alphabet. She guessed his opening comment was some kind of coded phrase. The text vanished and, a few seconds passed before one appeared above the slender inhabitant of the cave.

Doku appeared happy with this. He pressed a button that caused the message to fade then typed in a second, shorter one of his own. When the response appeared his grip on the controller stiffened. She looked down at his face and saw his lips moving as he read the brief lines over and over. 'Prynesi mne ruchku.' He looked at her and mimed writing. 'Ruchku!'

This was bad. She knew this was bad. He'd looked...he'd looked almost scared. She rushed into the kitchen and swopped the knife for a pen, scrap of paper and the phone. Laying them before him, she stepped back. A new message was on the screen. A series of numbers. 49.563844/1.844308.

Carefully, he copied them out and she guessed they were coordinates. For the GPS device in the boathouse. He checked the numbers two more times before accepting the message. Immediately, the yellow dragon's head sank back to the floor and its eyes closed. Doku reached over and yanked the plugs from the wall. Everything went dead. He slid the Xbox out from below the TV and started to disconnect its cables.

She picked up the phone and spoke into it. 'What is happening?'

He looked blankly at her, as if her presence next to him had been forgotten. She offered the phone and, standing up, he took it.

The double beep seemed to take ages. 'We have to go.'
'Where?'
'Across the sea. To people waiting.'
'Is this the plan? For the helicopter?'
'No. This is a different plan.'
'Different?'

He stooped to pick up the games console and marched towards the corridor with it in his hands.

She pursued him. 'Different? I don't understand.'

With a shake of his head, he advanced towards the kitchen.

'Doku! Stop.'

With a grunt of anger, he slammed the Xbox down on the kitchen table, whirled round and snatched the phone from her. 'Something has happened. I don't know what.'

She shrugged her shoulders, both hands out at her sides.

'I don't know! We must get ready to go.' He gave the phone back, lifted the Xbox up and walked briskly across to the kitchen door. Outside, he made a bee-line for the garage.

She could only follow.

There was a toolbox on the shelving unit in the corner. He selected the largest hammer from inside it and methodically started to smash the Xbox open. The casing split and fractured and he continued raining blows down on its inner parts. Once all the components were pulverised, he threw the hammer aside, brushed past her and returned to the house.

In the kitchen, she called to him again. 'Doku, what did they say to you?'

He came to a stop, turned round and stepped back to her. Again, that look in his eyes. This time it felt like she was closer to being punched. But he dragged in a deep breath, unclenched his fists and took the phone from her fingers. He spoke slowly, waiting for the translation to sound after each sentence before adding the next. 'The helicopter plan is ended. The ship is not coming. Now we must cross the ocean. They will not wait long. As soon as it is dark we must leave.'

CHAPTER 47

Jon leaned his elbows across the bonnet of the car and looked off down the cul-de-sac. 'I'm wasting our time, aren't I?' The holiday rental had no privacy; it was midway along a row of bungalows and beach access meant crossing the narrow road they were parked on, walking down a series of steps to a gravel slope leading down to the sea.

'Well,' Iona replied glumly, 'it kind of counts as private beach access. Just not quite as private as we meant.'

The couple who'd rented the place – probably with a combined age of over one-hundred-and-sixty years – were in plain view, fast asleep in the conservatory that jutted out into the front garden.

It must be like an oven in there, Jon thought, and they were both wearing cardigans. The bloke's glasses had slipped down his nose and her head was tipped back, mouth hanging open. Bless them.

'How many more on the list?' he asked.

'Five.'

'Five – and it's almost four o'clock. We need to allow three hours for getting back to Manchester. Maybe more since we'll be hitting the rush hour.'

Iona closed her eyes and turned her face to the sun. Now its fierceness had faded, it felt so good against her skin. 'I wish I had a magic idea, Jon. But I don't.'

'How about this one: we wander into Amlwch and get an ice-cream? I'm buying.'

She tipped her head to the side, eyes still closed. 'You mean call it quits?'

He shrugged. 'I don't think we stand much chance traipsing around here, do you?'

'To be honest, no.'

'Come on then. There was a little place round the corner. We can eat them on that bench further along.'

As they set off along the pavement, Iona spoke down at her feet. 'Maybe if we'd had proper support back at the office...'

'Talking of which...' Jon took his phone out. 'May as well find out if there's any more news.'

He put in the number for Kieran Saunders' extension. 'Hi there, any juicy developments, mate?'

'Not much. Bilal Atwi's missing car has been located. Two streets away from the flat on Fairbourne Road. A little bay of lock-ups: he'd rented one off a resident in the adjoining flats.'

'How was that found?'

'A uniform doing door-to-doors. She asked if anyone had seen a silver Mercedes and the person said there was one parked in his garage. Belonged to a man called Mr Dajani.'

'So he was using yet another false name?'

'He was. Paid cash, wasn't interested in a receipt.'

'Anything of interest in the car?'

'It seems not, but they're still going over it.'

'Nothing else?'

'Just the briefing at ten – you're aware of that?'

'Yes.'

'Warrants are now in for all the properties.'

'OK, we'll see you later.' He pocketed his phone and glanced at Iona. 'Atwi's Mercedes has been found. Garage two streets from the flat in Longsight.'

'You said something about another false name?'

'Mr Dajani. He was certainly being careful with covering his tracks.'

They were now adjacent to the end bungalow. Its unlit rooms had an empty appearance. Jon's eyes lingered on the placard on the front wall. For Hire. The number at the bottom was for Menai Cottages and Caravans, Holyhead. 'That's the third name we know he was using.'

'True.'

'I don't suppose he used it for renting a property on those sheets?'

She checked through the photocopies the owner of Morgan Holiday Lettings had given them. 'Nope.'

They set off once more, but had only gone a few steps before Jon glanced back over his shoulder. 'Hang on a second.'

'What's up now?'

'Just want to try one last thing. The end property? It belongs to the other lettings company.' He walked back to the placard, keyed in the number at the bottom and his call was immediately answered by an enthusiastic-sounding female.

'Hello, my name's Detective Constable Spicer, I'm with the Greater Manchester Police. I have an extremely urgent enquiry: could you help me, please?'

'Erm...I can try.'

'Thanks. I believe you have about four properties in the north of Anglesey that come with private beach access. I'm standing outside one in Amlwch. What I first need to find out is if any of the remaining ones are currently booked. If any are, I need to know what name they've been booked under. I'm happy to hold.' He looked at Iona and winked. 'Worth a try, don't you reckon?'

She crossed her arms with a smile. 'You are like a dog with a bloody bone.'

They turned to the sea and watched as a thick slab of cloud inched across the setting sun. The world around them dimmed for a moment, then a small gap in the cloud allowed a single beam to shine down. It played slowly across the still ocean; an alien searchlight scouring the planet's surface for life. The lady came back on the line. 'Hello? Our property by Burwen is the only one currently taken. A gentleman called Mr Dajani has that on a three-month rental.'

CHAPTER 48

Doku was like an automaton, a programme in his brain controlling all movement. Reduced to an observer, Elissa followed him into the boathouse where he surveyed the Rib. The tide was in. Lined up against the back wall was a row of plastic jerry cans. She could tell they were full by the way the boat rocked as he lifted them in. Then he climbed aboard and began to sort through the gear in the stowage area by the outboard engine. As he moved about, the boat nudged against the plastic painters hanging at regular intervals along the wooden walkway. She thought of a horse, tethered to a post in a frontier town as its owner hurriedly packed provisions into saddlebags.

He looked up to see her standing there. 'Yedu.' He lifted a hand and bit down on an invisible piece of food, then waved towards the house.

She nodded. As she walked round to the cottage, she could hear the workmen laughing about something. The one who'd knocked on the door earlier appeared at the top of the driveway. 'That's us all done for the day. Your water should be back on.'

She stared blankly in his direction for a moment. 'Oh. OK – thanks.'

'Don't mention it. Probably see you tomorrow.'

She gave him a quick smile and carried on. Through the kitchen window, she could see them climbing into a white van. The engine started and the vehicle moved off down the lane. Still able to make out the blue dumper truck through the shifting leaves of the hedge, she walked to the end of the drive and checked they'd all gone. The vehicle had been backed into the open gateway of the field. The bright yellow digger was directly behind it, alongside a pile of sand bags.

Back in the kitchen, she looked numbly about. Food. That was it. How long would the crossing take? Should she boil up the packets of couscous? Would just snacks be enough? What about after they reached land? What would happen next?

She felt sick. Who would be waiting for them? She imagined others like Doku. Stern-faced men whose words she couldn't understand. Where would they be taken? Where would they end up?

She went to the fridge and removed the yoghurt pots and sliced cheese. There was a pack of pitta breads on the side. The cheese could go in them. They had muesli bars and packets of dried apricots. They would need water. She started going through the cupboards, searching for an empty bottle she could fill up. All she could find was a two-litre bottle of orange squash. She tipped it down the sink. The tap spluttered and grumbled when she turned it on. The bottle was half-full when the stream of water abruptly dwindled. She lifted the lever fully up, but it had no effect. Suddenly, it gushed again. Brown water flecked with dark flakes flooded into the bottle.

She was emptying it out when he appeared beside her. He slapped a palm on the table. 'Bistryei! Potoropis!'

His footsteps thudded up the stairs. The water was coming through clear once more. She filled the bottle, dried her hands on a tea-towel then started to slice open the pitta breads.

A minute later, he was back. He'd packed both their bags. Pausing in the doorway, something occurred to him. He dumped the bags on the floor and approached her. 'Tyebe nuzhno budet pokritsya.' He repeated the pointing gesture he'd used in the boathouse, a forefinger curling round the curve of the earth. 'Kogda priyedem tuda.'

She reached for the phone in her back pocket. Before she could take it out, he lifted the tea-towel from the table. Then he draped it over her head and pointed again. 'Kogda priyedem tuda.'

A hijab, she thought. He's saying I need a hijab. The implications of it were still mushrooming in her mind as he turned round and continued outside with their bags.

She pulled the damp square of cloth from her head, strands of hair sticking to the side of her face. He had taken all her stuff. Or had he? She climbed the stairs to check: the only things she'd taken out of her bag were the photos of her brother and parents. She'd propped them on the dressing table earlier that morning so she could look at them while brushing her hair.

They were both still there; he'd forgotten them. The last link to her family had nearly been left in a rented property in the middle of nowhere.

She crossed the room and swept them up. With the frames pressed tight against her chest, she sat down on the end of the bed. It was suddenly important to know what would have happened to them. In her mind, she saw whoever owned the property coming in to the check the room. Spotting two unfamiliar items and puzzling over them for a moment before realisation dawned. Would that person have handed them on to the police, evidence of who the last occupants in the property were? Probably. And what would the police have done? Shrugged and thrown them in the bin? The possessions of an enemy. Valueless, like Tarek's life. Judged as worthless. Just like her parents' pain. Worthless. Irrelevant. Ignored.

The anger was like a spot of crimson. Like the glow of the dying sun through the window. When she walked into the boathouse, her bag was on the walkway, ready for loading into the Rib. She picked it up and waited for him to look at her before she spoke. 'I don't want to come with you.'

CHAPTER 49

On reaching the humpback bridge, Jon dropped their speed right down. 'I can't believe we were here earlier on.'

Now the road beyond the bridge was clear: in the entrance to the field on their right was the yellow digger and other bits and pieces. No sign of the white van. 'Packed up and gone home for the day,' he murmured.

To their left was the holiday home's driveway. As they passed it, Iona's elbow was resting on the ledge of the door, hand up at the side of her face. She peeped between the gaps in her fingers. 'No sign of a car. A light in the main house is on.'

Then it was hedgerow once again.

'Let's continue back to the main road,' Jon said, voice tight with excitement. 'We can loop back round and approach it again from the same direction. I reckon we dump the car before that little bridge and access the field from there.'

'Not just turn round and drive back?'

Jon shook his head. 'I don't want to pass the property a second time.'

Five minutes later, they were on the stretch of road that led to the stone bridge. Iona looked uneasily at the countryside bordering the lane. 'It's still light enough for us to be seen.'

'We've got the hedgerow as cover, and I can see a drystone wall in the field. We'll find a decent spot.'

When they'd called base, Weir had said nothing at first. Iona could picture him, head bowed as he tried to accommodate this new piece of information. In the background, the low rumble of voices went on. Their senior officer came back on the line. 'Stay put, I'll call you back.'

Then came a ten minute wait. During it, the ragged cloud bank on the horizon continued to grow. If it doesn't get too big, there was going to be a spectacular sunset, Iona thought.

Her phone lit up with Weir's name. 'DC Khan, the only asset close by is the SBS team at Wylfa. We'll get them there as fast as we can. The police on Anglesey are being made aware of the situation: roadblocks will go up. But, for the time being, you two are on your own. We need eyes on that property. Find yourself an observation point and keep us informed. Understood?'

'Here,' said Jon, pulling into the passing point on their left. 'Let's see what toys we can use in the back.'

As they jumped out of the car, Jon popped the boot.

'Wife's date-of-birth?' Iona asked as he keyed in the four digit combination of the weapons' box.

'Fifth of November. Means I've never forgotten it yet.' He flashed her a grin as he slid the tray back and lifted the lid. 'OK, the only optic I've got is the scope for the MCX. By the way, what sort of firearms training have you completed?'

'Just the initial course.'

Not enough to be carrying a weapon in a public place, Jon thought. 'OK, you take this.' He prised the telescopic sights out from its niche in the foam lining and handed it over. 'What else?'

'Identification clothing?' Iona pointed to the black baseball caps and bibs marked with white letters that spelled POLICE. 'I don't want those SBS guys mistaking us for the baddies.'

'Good point.' Jon lifted them out and handed them over. 'Trauma packs?'

'Let's hope not.'

'Better safe than sorry.' Jon removed one of the square green medical kits, along with two pairs of fabric handcuffs. He then took out the belt and holster for the Glock and slipped his arms through it. Once the holster was positioned beneath his left armpit, he lifted the weapon itself from the tray. Pointing it away from them both, he checked the magazine was full. Satisfied everything was in order, he slid the weapon into the holster and secured the fastening clip. After relocking the box and the boot, he turned to her. 'All good?'

'All good.'

'Let's go.'

They went to where the dry-stone wall that traversed the field reached the hedge. Jon started bending and snapping branches to create an opening. Nettles stung his hands and wrists. Funny how adrenaline masks pain, he thought, checking the field beyond. The wall ran straight across the strip of grass to the far side where it appeared to merge with a line of rocks that formed a barrier between land and sea. Looking to the other side of the wall, the field stretched for about forty metres before ending at a high hedge at the edge of the holiday home's garden. The building itself was completely obscured from view.

Staying below the height of the wall, Jon slipped into the field and beckoned to Iona. Once she was beside him, he pointed. 'We advance along the wall to the other side. Those rocks running along at the water's edge? I reckon we can use them as cover to get a heck of a lot closer to the house.'

Bent double, they scuttled along the base of the wall. By the time they reached the far side, a sharp throbbing had set into the muscles of Jon's lower back. He dropped gratefully to his knees and assessed things again. As he suspected, the end of the dry-stone wall had been constructed to merge with the dark grey rock that broke through the thick turf. Peering momentarily over the wall, he could see the hedge that formed the perimeter of the garden also ended at the field's edge. Beyond that, the curve of the coast meant only the end of a jetty was visible. 'We'll need to get closer for any view of the house.'

He patted the jagged rock. The surface was coarse and the edges of the deep groves running across it felt sharp enough to open up flesh if you slipped. Keeping low, he moved cautiously across to look over the edge. There was a drop of about two metres, then a thin expanse of grainy sand that would be hidden from anyone in the house. Dotted with items of washed-up litter, the strip of beach led round in a gentle arc to an outcrop of rock that was markedly higher than that surrounding it. Jon nodded in its direction. 'That's where we need to be. Tucked in to the side of that.' He jumped down, feet sinking into the soft surface. Iona appeared a second later and he reached out to guide her foot onto a decent sized ledge.

She landed beside him and examined her palms. 'Talk about abrasive.'

Jon was looking at the water. 'Can't figure if the tide is coming in or out.' Gentle ripples were carrying a mass of milky bubbles into shallow depressions in the sand. Jon watched the water as it inched its way along an S shaped groove. 'In, I think.'

'Me too,' Iona whispered back.

Keeping close to the rock, they stepped round the many buttresses that branched out from its base. Barnacles and small snails lined the crevices. At high tide, Jon thought, this will all be underwater. The far side of the narrow inlet was bathed in a peachy wash of light. The whiteness of the boats out on the water seemed to sing out in the gloom. At the modest promontory, they climbed up to a cleft in the rock and looked through.

The front of the property was now revealed.

It was an old building with small, deeply recessed windows. A stone path hugged the side of the house that was furthest from them. A few steps led down to a wooden structure whose open-ended front had already been flooded by the encroaching tide. A light was on inside and the prow of a boat was just visible. The wooden walkway continued across the sloping lawn to a jetty, the legs of which were partially submerged.

Iona raised the telescopic sights and swept the house.

'Anything?' Jon asked.

'No. I'd say the lit room in the house is a living area. There are framed pictures on the walls and bookshelves.'

'No movement in there?'

'None.' She shifted the sights to the left and examined the boat house more closely. 'Just saw movement! A shadow on the far wall. That's definitely from a person! In there fiddling about with something.'

'Male? Female?' Jon asked, removing his phone.

'Can't say. It's just a shadow being projected onto the far wall. Hang on, they're straightening up. Moving, definitely moving – '

The side door opened and the silhouette of a male was framed for a second in the bright light. Then he stepped out onto the path, trotted up the steps and vanished round the side of the house.

'Was it him?' Jon asked.

'Male, early thirties maybe, dark hair cut short. That's all I got.'

'Was it him, though?'

'Probably, but I couldn't say for sure.'

Jon sank down out of sight and made the call. 'Sir? We're in position with a good sight line to the property. Probable sighting of Doku Zakayev.'

Weir cut in. 'Probable?' He sounded like he was on a car phone.

'Same appearance and likely age, but he was only in view briefly. It appears he could be preparing a motorboat. It's mostly hidden within a structure at the side of the cottage.'

'OK. The SBS team are in two vessels. They're five minutes away.'

'They're coming by sea?'

'Yes. This is a containment job only; once all means of escape are blocked off, we'll make ourselves known. The SBS team have been instructed not to enter the inlet.'

'Understood.'

'In case anything happens, what's your position?'

'Facing the property from the sea, we are about fifty metres to its right, at the water's edge. We're tucked in behind a section of rock that is slightly higher than what's on either side. And we're wearing police vests and caps.'

'OK, we stand no chance of being there for another hour. Anglesey police have blocked either end of the lane leading to the property and a dog unit is on the way from Bangor. They're going nowhere, Jon. Just sit tight and keep watch. You're doing great.'

'Will do, Sir.'

He adjusted his feet so he could turn to Iona. 'They've got the area contained. We just keep eyes on the property.'

'I'm happy doing that.'

Jon looked along the narrow stretch of water towards the open sea. Two units from the SBS would be lurking there in no time. Jon couldn't help smile: part of his training to become a Specialist Firearms Officer involved a session with Special Forces guys on Armed Interception. The soldiers just referred to it as ambush work, but language like that wasn't deemed acceptable for law enforcement. At one point, one of the soldiers jokingly referred to the police trainees as Pepsis. Jon had asked why. You're learning bits of what we do, came the reply. But you'll never be The Real Thing.

With every second that passed, dusk deepened. The boats out on the water had now lost their glow. On the opposite shore, only the upper third of the trees were still lit by the sun. The peace was only broken by the sea as it tickled its way across the bumpy sand, stranded bubbles fizzing and popping as the water felt its way closer to the rocks. How long, Jon wondered, before it would be lapping at their feet?

'He's coming back out.' Iona announced in a small voice.

Jon twisted his torso round and straightened his legs so he could see through the gap. The figure was on the stone steps. At the bottom one, he paused, attention on something in his hand. Suddenly, his face was lit by a murky glow that shone up from his palm.

'It's him, I'm certain,' Iona hissed.

'What's he holding?'

'Too chunky to be a phone. And the screen: the back light is green.'

'GPS,' Jon replied, reaching for his phone. 'Sir, definite ID on Zakayev. No sign of Elissa Yared as yet. He's just re-entered the boathouse with, I think, a GPS device in his hand. I believe he's preparing to leave. Iona? Any more?'

'I can see his shadow against the wall. He's moving around again, coming towards the front of the boat. It looks like – '

A motor started up, its throaty growl shattering the quiet. The revs fell away and the vessel began to ease its way forward out of the boathouse.

'It's him!' Iona said. 'He's wearing a red life-jacket, steering the boat.'

'Hang on, Sir.' Keeping the phone at waist height, Jon peeped over the rock then ducked back down. 'It's a Rib, I'd say over twenty-five feet long. Single engine at the back. Iona, anything else?'

'White lettering on the engine says Mariner 200. Doesn't appear to be anyone else – hang on, I can see another life-jacket. Could be a second person at the back.'

'Is it Elissa Yared?'

'Can't say. Whoever they are, they're lying down, by the looks of it. Now the boat's swinging round...'

Jon took another look. The light was too dim: Zakayev was only visible because he was on a raised seat behind the driver's console. In the shadow pooled at the back end of the boat was a variety of objects, none of them clear. The revs increased and the boat picked up speed, a rippling wake spreading out behind it. 'Sir, he's on the move.'

He could hear Weir relaying the information to someone else as the boat's engine began to roar and its front end lifted clear of the water. Shielding the phone's glow with his hands, Jon said, 'He's gone, Sir, heading for the open sea!'

'Half hour left, Howie. That's all.'

The Prince took his feet off the chair and smiled across at his radio operator who was standing in the doorway. 'And no call outs. Are you up to much over the weekend?'

'Off to our place in Abersoch. Just hope this weather lasts.'

The Prince examined the satellite image of the weather system displayed on the nearest screen. 'This high pressure isn't moving anytime soon. Though don't expect any wind for sailing.'

'That's fine. I got one of those sea-kayaks the other day. Me and the missus, we'll give that a go. How about you? Being dragged back to London as usual?'

'For once, no. We're just going to mooch about here. I'm trying to teach our oldest to swim, so plenty of splashing about in the shallows with him.'

'Where's your house, again? Close by, isn't it?'

'Near Rhoscolyn Head. Twenty minute drive, at most. That reminds me, I need to make a call. Excuse me.' He punched in the number for his Close Protection Officer into the desk's phone. 'Evening, Colin.' He swivelled his chair so he faced the window. The runway lights were now all on, dots of light like a trail of gems in the dark. 'Looks like I'll be ready for a get away at about seven-fifteen. Can you bring the car round? Oh, you're already there?' He looked across to the main buildings where the staff car park was located. 'That's great. We'll hand over and I'll be straight across.'

He cut the call and went over what needed to be briefed to the crew that was due to relieve them. With the warm weather and lack of wind, and no call outs for the entire shift, there wasn't much to report. He ambled through to the rest lounge. The second pilot and winchman were before the TV, game controllers in their hands.

The footage showed an aerial view of a city under siege. Downtown Los Angeles, by the look of it. Wrecked cars littered the freeway, many acting as anchors to churning columns of black smoke. People were dotted about, some sprawled lifeless on the tarmac, some running, some directing weapons skyward.

The helicopter banked to the side, white-hot slashes of tracer scoring the sky around them. Beeps sounded in the cockpit along with comments from other pilots.

Firing missile!

Good engagement!

You got it!

They passed over a tower block, gouts of flame spouting from holes in its roof. Sparks swirled up like fireflies. On the streets far below, more gunfire echoed. A harsh alarm sounded and a yellow diamond lit up on the control panel.

Enemy lock alert – incoming!

The only constant in all the chaos was the chop-chop-chop of the helicopter's blades.

CHAPTER 50

'Come on!' Jon jumped down onto the damp sand. Even though the motorboat was rapidly receding, the noise of its engine carried clearly across the flat water. He began running along what was left of the beach, occasionally jumping over narrow gulleys flooded by the advancing tide.

Iona called out behind him. 'Where are we going?'

'End of the inlet!'

They came to a knee-high outcrop of rock that continued right into the water. Jon picked his way over it and turned, expecting Iona to be well behind.

She flashed past him, landed on the sand with both feet and was off through the swirling shallows.

'Bloody hell,' Jon muttered. She was fast.

He ran after her, Glock thudding against his upper ribs with each step. After another forty metres, what was left of the beach dwindled to nothing. The open sea was now directly ahead and they clambered up the rock for a better view.

Away to the left, a blood-red smudge was all that remained of the horizon. A purplish mass of clouds bore down on it, as if determined to crush the sun's power once and for all. The Rib was now about a hundred metres out, its dark colour making it all but invisible.

Jon heard the SBS boats before he could see them. The first appeared to his right and he immediately recognised it as an ORC: an offshore raiding craft, armour panels giving it a clumsy appearance. Its twin inboard engines had carved a wake that stretched right back to the coastline. The second appeared from the rocks less than thirty metres to their left. Jon could clearly see the heavy machine gun mounted on its front end. Behind the gunner were the heads and shoulders of at least five other men, all wearing black.

'Ha!' Jon shouted. 'Deal with this, arsehole!'

'Look behind us,' Iona stated.

Jon glanced inland. A procession of blue lights pulsed along the lane. The cavalry really had arrived in force. He turned back to the ocean. The boat that had appeared on their left was powering across on an angle that would intercept the path of the Rib. The second vessel was rapidly closing in from behind.

Jon shook his head. 'Game over, pal. Game over.'

Zakayev, obviously realising he was on a collision course, started into a sharp U-turn, only to see the second boat directly behind him. He swung it round and started on a course straight out to sea.

'Where the hell is he going?' Jon asked. 'Scotland?'

The two SBS boats positioned themselves about fifty metres either side of the Rib and began to squeeze in. It was like watching a pair of lions hunting a gazelle. The Rib swerved one way, then the other.

By now, the lack of light was making it hard to see what was happening. A few more seconds and they would have disappeared from view. An amplified voice carried back to them.

Jon cocked his head. 'What did they say to him?'

'Couldn't make it out.'

'Whatever it was, he needs to do as he's told. Those guys do not fuck around.'

As the voice spoke again, Zakayev turned sharply and made straight at the boat to his left. A thin trail lanced out from the front of the Rib then ricocheted up off the ORC's armour. A bloom of white light shone briefly in the air before settling on the water.

'Distress flare!' Jon said. 'He fired a distress flare at them!'

The three vessels faded from view.

A second white dot lit the darkness, a horizontal comet which seared away to the side. The engines' tones changed again, one lifting into a whine. A burst of gun fire rang out. Someone bellowed defiantly then more gunfire and the whining engine cut. The two deeper-sounding engines also dropped in volume.

'Jesus,' Iona whispered. 'What just happened?'

They watched the life of the two white flares sputter out. The dark sea was silent. A spotlight then flickered into life, followed by another. The two beams converged on one point, but it was too far away for them to make anything out.

Iona passed the scope to Jon and reached for her phone. 'Sir? We just observed the Rib being intercepted by the two – OK, yes. I'll hold.'

Jon had directed the lens at the shifting blobs of light. The Rib was listing badly. One ORC was now alongside it. Silhouettes were bending over the side. He thought they could have been attaching lines to the vessel.

Beside him, Iona spoke again. 'Yes, Sir. Still here.' Her voice was subdued. 'No one alive? I understand, yes. See you there.' She lowered the phone and looked at Jon. 'We're to go straight to the police station in Holyhead. Rendezvous is there.'

Jon lowered the scope. ' Doku Zakayev and Elissa Yared?'

She shook her head.

CHAPTER 51

As they approached Jon's car they could see a uniformed officer standing beside it. By the time he'd heard them and shone a torch up the lane, their identifications were already raised.

'DCs Spicer and Khan,' Jon announced. 'Greater Manchester Police.'

His torch lowered. 'Right, this is your car, then?'

'It is,' Jon answered, looking past him towards the humpback bridge.

'I was told to wait here until you reappeared.'

'Thanks. The house has been secured?'

'It has. No one was in it, so they've withdrawn and are now waiting for forensics.'

'Feel free to join them; we're to proceed directly to the station in Holyhead.'

'OK.' The officer paused in the act of turning. 'Who was it in there, then? No one actually said.'

'We're not a hundred percent sure,' Iona replied. 'Working that out will be next on the list.'

The officer had noticed Jon's firearm. 'Was that gunfire just now?'

'Gun fire?' Jon looked around. 'I don't know, was it?'

The officer's face changed. 'I get it. Not allowed to say.'

They looked back at him with blank expressions.

'Evening, then.' He walked away.

Iona sighed. 'What does he expect? We tell him everything about an ongoing operation? As if.'

Jon unlocked the boot and keyed in the combination for the weapons box. As he put everything back in its place, Iona stepped from foot to foot. 'Just realised my shoes and socks are soaking.'

'Mine, too. Reminds me of playing out in the woods as a kid.'

'I bet your mum had a nightmare washing your clothes.'

'She probably did. But she preferred that to me and my brother charging around inside the house.' He climbed into the car and leaned his head back. 'I'm so looking forward to sleeping in my own bed tonight.'

Iona slumped into the passenger seat. 'We've got the de-brief, first.'

Jon looked at her with dismay. 'Is it likely to take long?'

She puffed out her cheeks. 'I really don't know.'

Jon started the engine, eyes settling momentarily on the dashboard as he started to turn the car around. 'Seven o'clock. If we're home by midnight, I'll be happy.'

They'd been on the unlit A5025 for a couple of minutes before Jon cleared his throat. 'I wonder how Elissa died. Zakayev or the SBS.'

'Zakayev? Why do you say that?'

'He was happy to get rid of that working girl, Kelly. If Elissa had served her purpose, why not the same? One less person to be smuggled back to safe ground.'

'So why have her body in the boat?'

'Dump her out at sea? Or she was still alive in the back of the boat, but restrained. With that tape he liked to use.'

'Maybe she caught a stray bullet,' Iona said. 'Quicker than being knifed and rolled overboard, I suppose.'

They continued on in silence and, when they reached Holyhead, Jon glanced up. 'Proper streetlights. Easy to forget how dark it is without any.'

They pulled in alongside a dogs van in the police station car park. The crop-haired officer standing beside it was about six-foot-three. Jon guessed he wasn't far off eighteen stone. 'Your animals in there?'

He nodded. 'Waiting on a possible tracking job at the north end of the island.'

The man's heavy East London accent took Jon by surprise. 'You've come across from Bangor?'

'Yeah.'

Vaguely aware of a faint thrumming noise coming from nearby, he said, 'I don't think you'll be doing any tracking tonight.'

'No?'

The news didn't seem to bother him. Jon guessed being a dog handler involved plenty of call outs where his presence was only a precaution.

The man glanced briefly at Iona as she got out of Jon's car. 'You're part of this operation?'

'Yes.' He looked at the rear of the police building, wondering if the noise he could hear was an extractor fan running at full speed.

'I'm guessing you're not with North Wales police,' the dog handler said.

The sound had shifted. Now it seemed to be coming from beyond the building. And it was growing more intense. Jon looked around. 'What's making that – '

'Sea King's been called out,' the dog-handler stated matter-of-factly. 'Some numb-nut, probably hiking in Snowdonia without a compass. Once it gets dark they always panic and call for help.'

Jon looked up into the dark sky as a huge yellow helicopter rose into view, lights winking at various points on the fuselage. Waves of intermingling sound rippled down; the roar of the engine and chop of the rotors fighting for supremacy as it began to turn.

The dog-handler stepped away from his vehicle, chin raised as it started moving off. 'Heading East. Definitely Snowdonia.'

'Where has it taken off from?'

'Valley.'

The way he said the word made Jon feel he'd asked something that barely merited a reply.

'Valley?' Iona said. 'What is Valley?'

'The airbase? Where the Search and Rescue is based?'

'An airbase?' Iona mused. 'Has it...has it been in the news or...have I read about it? Why does the name seem familiar?'

'It's where Prince William is currently stationed. You mean that?'

The comment caused her to visibly flinch. She looked at Jon. 'He's a Sea King helicopter pilot at that air base.'

Jon could only stare back as the realisation hit home. 'A quick word, Iona?' He got back in the car.

The passenger door opened and she jumped in, eyes fixed on his as her words rushed out. 'They were after him, not the younger brother in Afghanistan.'

Jon breathed in deeply through his nose. 'Hang on, we need to think this through.'

'Jon, Search and Rescue – not a combat helicopter at all. Not even army. That's why they were here on Anglesey. Christ, that might have been him we just saw flying off.'

Jon tapped a finger up and down on the gearstick. 'Quarter past seven. Weir's not due for another thirty minutes. Let's find out before we present a theory that makes complete prats of ourselves.' He lowered the window. 'Mate, how do we get to this air base?'

'Head left out of here. At the end of the road, you'll see a sign at the junction. You'll be at the main gates in all of three minutes.'

'Cheers.' He pulled out of the car park.

'What are we going to do?' Iona asked. 'Drive up to the barrier and demand to know if the Duke of Cambridge is on duty?'

'Unless you've got a better idea, because I haven't.' He could see the sign up ahead.

'How does it work with members of the Royal Family?' Iona asked. 'Will he have an armed escort or something?'

'For round here? No. He'll have a Close Protection Officer acting as his driver. Some bloke on a jolly, sitting round for most of the day with his thumb up his arse. All he'll have is a side-arm.'

'And the car?'

'That'll have anti-ballistic protection. Bullet-proof windows and reinforced doors. But all that's irrelevant if you're shooting at it with a fucking surface-to-air missile.'

A thought thudding home caused Iona to lift a hand to her lips. 'What if it wasn't the car? If they knew he was on duty, the target could have been his helicopter.'

Jon shot her a horrified look. 'Jesus fucking Christ, I hope we're wrong about this.'

By now they were on a long, straight road that hugged the edge of a large lake. They overtook a lone cyclist. A moment later, he appeared in the rear-view mirror, his front light rapidly blinking on and off, on and off. To their left was a deserted housing estate. When the gaps between the rows of plain-looking properties aligned correctly, it was possible to see what appeared to be floodlights beyond a perimeter fence. 'That must be it, just over there. I bet this is all accommodation for the personnel.'

A side road branched out from it and Jon's eyes snagged for an instant on the large blue dumper truck parked on the verge. In front of them, a distant pair of headlights came into view. Iona's phone started to ring.

She flipped it over in her palm to see the screen. 'Weir again. I'll put him on speakerphone.'

Jon's attention was on the solitary vehicle coming the other way.

'Hello Sir, how far off are you – '

'Iona, we just had word from the SBS commander. There was only one body in the boat: Zakayev's.'

The other car was now no more than thirty metres in front. Dark Blue. Jon recognised the make. Jaguar.

'Only Zakayev? What about Elissa Yared?'

'She wasn't there.'

'But I thought they said – '

'So did we.'

The car passed them at the point where they were alongside a streetlight. Jon got the briefest glimpse of the man at the wheel. White. Balding. Moustache. Barely visible in the back was another figure, also male.

His eyes went to the rear-view mirror as he touched the brakes. 'Think we just passed him.'

'Hang on, Sir.' Iona lowered the phone. 'Passed who?'

'The Prince.'

Iona twisted round. 'In there?'

'Yes. The guy driving had CPO written all over him.' Still looking in the rear-view mirror, his attention shifted to the cyclist. Pedalling slowly, the man was almost at the turn off for the side road where the dumper truck was parked. The large vehicle started to roll forward off the verge. Jon came to a stop, eyes now locked on the bulky vehicle. The mound of earth showing above the sides of the rear compartment must have added another few tons to the vehicle's weight. Its lights had failed to go on. Jon started to reverse, knowing something was seriously wrong.

As it reached the junction with the main road, the truck seemed to be slowing. It was at that point Jon knew where he'd seen it. Blocking the road just past the humpback bridge. 'Iona...'

Suddenly the truck lurched across the white lines. Missing the cyclist by inches, it crunched into the side of the Jaguar.

CHAPTER 52

Iona's shocked cry filled the car. 'No!'

Jon veered to the left, only just hitting the brakes in time to stop the car plunging down the short, sharp slope and into the inky water.

Iona was leaning forward, face turned away from him. 'It's reversing! It's reversing!'

Weir's tinny voice rang shrill from her hand. 'DC Khan, what's happening!'

Jon slammed the car into first then floored the accelerator, hands fanning to and fro across the wheel.

One hundred metres away, the dumper truck's rear wheels mounted the pavement and it juddered to a halt. The cyclist was climbing to his feet, one hand rubbing at his head.

Weir sounded like a munchkin on helium. 'DC Khan, talk to me! Are you there?'

'We have an incident, Sir!'

'What kind of incident! Talk to me!'

The stricken Jaguar was still on the road, but only just. Its front quarter, including the driver's door, was completely crushed. Jon doubted the CPO could have survived.

In the truck, the outline of a small head was rocking back and forth.

'Can't find the gear,' Jon announced. 'Maybe the impact – '

The heavy vehicle began to roll forward, but it had barely picked up any speed before connecting with the Jaguar again. This time, the truck's front bumper sank into a point half-way up the side of the car before it stalled.

The cyclist seemed to come out of his trance. Waving both arms above his head and yelling, he ran to the side of the truck and climbed up on the footplate.

'Oh fuck,' Jon muttered as their car surged closer. 'Don't do that.'

'What is happening!' Weir yelled again.

As soon as the cyclist pulled the truck's passenger door open, a blinding flash of white came from inside the cab. The man flew backwards, back of his head slamming against the concrete as a huge ball of light blossomed out from his chest.

'Flare!' Iona gasped. 'One of those – '

The man's top caught alight, flames quickly engulfing him as the ball of phosphorous blazed on. A veil of smoke started drifting towards the truck.

Jon slammed on the brakes, throwing him and Iona forward. 'Stay here!' He leapt out of the car, and as he punched the combination into the weapons box, the truck engine was coughing as the driver tried to restart it. Leaving the weapons box open, he sprinted across the asphalt, the weight of the Glock skewing the swing of his right arm.

Crackling and hissing, the flare continued to burn. The cyclist was now wreathed head to foot in blue flame and Jon knew nothing could be done for him. He circled the body and stepped through the curtain of smoke. The crazily-lit truck was directly in front. The passenger door had swung shut, but he could make out the person at the wheel.

Elissa Yared.

Shoulders hunched, she was almost hugging the steering wheel with one arm. The starter kept turning over, but the engine refused to catch.

He moved closer to the Jaguar, trying to assess it. The corner of the truck's front bumper was pinning the passenger door on his side firmly shut. His left palm slapped against the car's rear window and he bent close to the glass. The back seat was in shadow, but he could make out a figure collapsed across it.

To his side, the truck fired back into life. This time, the throb of the engine picked up slowly and steadily. Beneath his hand, he felt the Jaguar begin to judder. It started to slide sideways towards the drop.

He bounded across to the truck and stepped up on the foot plate. The door handle lifted easily up and down: a useless flap of metal. She had locked herself in. 'Armed police! Take your foot off the pedal now!'

She didn't react. Neither did the engine. The acrid stink of rubber was in his nostrils as he felt a bump. He looked to the side. The outermost wheels of the Jaguar were now off the road and on the verge. A little further and the bank fell steeply away to the water's edge.

Jon brought up the Glock. No window breaker attached to its tool rail. Fuck! He tried to smash the glass with the butt of the gun. It bounced back. Something was on the seat next to her. Framed photos? 'Elissa, take your foot off or I fire!'

Her head turned and their eyes met. Her lips were stretched back in a silent grimace, and he saw she was crying. Rage and fear. A stubborn child, a little girl, swept up in a tantrum. Knowing to stop but powerless to do so. The truck continued edging forward. Left hand gripping the cab's roof, Jon leaned back. He pointed the gun at her face. One more try. 'I will shoot you!'

She turned away from him and he knew her decision was made. The Jaguar was now starting to teeter. Fixing her ear hole in the sights, he went to take the shot. His finger would not move. Metal started to grind as he willed his finger to squeeze the trigger. Nothing. 'Jon,' he said to himself. 'For fuck's sake.'

The Jaguar's rear wheel was now off the ground, the gap below the car getting wider and wider –

A massive retort. Two more. Glass flying in as Elissa was flung violently forward, face connecting with the windscreen. More sharp cracks ringing out as her head bounced back, skull and neck coming apart, hands falling from the wheel as she slumped sideways against the far window. The lorry's roar lost power and the engine cut as it rolled back.

Gun-smoke churned slowly in the driver's compartment. Jon turned his head so he could see behind the cab, to where the muzzle flash had come from. Iona was kneeling on the mound of fresh earth, the barrel of the MCX still directed at Elissa's corpse.

EPILOGUE

'Oh my God, Jon.'

He glanced up from his recording of that week's rugby highlights. Alice was standing in the doorway to the front room with the morning's post. One letter had been lifted clear of the other items and she was rapidly wafting it beneath her chin.

'It's embossed. The Royal crest, I think. What if it's an invite to the palace itself?'

He attempted a smile as he turned back to the screen. 'Doubt it, Ali. More likely to be a signed photo.'

She flipped the envelope over, a couple of steps taking her to within reaching distance of the battered old armchair he refused to get rid of. 'No, it's a letter. Definitely a letter. From the offices of HRH The Duke of Cambridge, it says here. Who do we know that's posh? I'll need a hat and dress.' She raised her chin, words now clipped and formal. 'Oh Jon, the excitement is such that I may well piss my pants.'

He tapped the threadbare armrest, attention still on the television. 'Chuck it there. I'll open it in a bit.'

The letter stayed in her hand as her head tilted to the side. Her eyes moved to the screen then back to him and her voice returned to normal. 'Jon?'

'Mmm?'

'What's up?'

'Nothing. I'm just trying to watch this.'

She placed the rest of the post on the floor, swiping the remote from his hand as she straightened up. The footage froze. 'What's up?'

He leaned back, clicking a finger and thumb. 'Ali, I was watching that. Give.'

She crossed her arms, remote tucked out of sight. 'What's up?'

'What do you mean, what's up? I've got a window of opportunity here.' He jerked a thumb in the direction of the baby mat. Duggy was flat on his back, arms thrown out at his sides. 'Mini-monster will come back to life soon, Holly's at her dance class...'

In the corner, he saw Wiper's eyebrows lift. Even his Boxer dog wasn't buying it.

Alice crouched beside him and looked up into his face. 'Jon, it's from this country's future king and you're more interested in Newcastle against bloody Worcester. It's not even live.'

'It's a good match.'

'All the fuss from work? That's only been making you cringe – I can see it on your face when you get home.' She reached for his hand. 'Is this...is this because of – because you took someone's life?'

He tipped his head back and screwed his eyes shut. 'Ah, bollocks.'

'Jon?'

'Bollocks, bollocks, bollocks.'

'There was no other choice, Jon. Everyone – from your colleagues to the Royal bloody Family – agree on that.'

His chest swelled as he slowly filled his lungs. The words came out in a rush of air: 'I didn't take the shot.'

Silence.

'What was that?'

He opened his eyes and looked at his wife. 'Iona killed her, not me. I tried...I had my...' He took aim at the wall, suddenly in another place. 'I had her. Had her right there.' His right forefinger was crooked in. 'It wouldn't move. My finger would not move.'

The letter and remote control were laid on the floor, both now forgotten. She wrapped her hands round his. 'You didn't fire?'

He tipped his head back, eyes staying open this time. 'Not a fucking shot. Not one. I had the Glock, but Iona opened up with the MCX – destroyed the brain stem, stopped her dead. Just like you're taught. I was there like a spare part. I was a spare part. Couldn't do it, Ali. Couldn't fire.'

'But...' Her head shook slightly in confusion. 'Then how come – '

'Iona's not firearm trained. She shouldn't even have been carrying a weapon. Opening up like she did? There would have been...it would have been a shit storm. Massive shit storm. So we swapped. I went in the back of the dumper truck, trod where she trod, knelt where she knelt, put a hand in the soil, got it on the MCX, left a palm-print on the roof of the lorry's cab. We swapped.'

'And no one said it was really – '

'No one could see. Him – the Duke of Cambridge – he was unconscious. He doesn't remember a thing after the security check at the air base. The CPO,' he shrugged regretfully, 'history. Same as that cyclist. The nearest eye-witnesses were a way off. The marine flare had left a haze hanging in the air. Shadows, Ali, that's all we were.'

Alice stared at their entwined hands. She was quiet for a few seconds before rotating her wrist to glance at her watch. 'Need to go in a minute,' she said distractedly. 'Collect Holly.'

The comment almost made him smile. Life, he thought. Something happens and on it goes. Can't be stopped.

'So...so...' Alice was frowning. 'When were you going to tell me?'

'I hadn't made a schedule, babe. I knew it would come out when it came out.'

'I thought it was odd, you know? You'd ended someone's life and you didn't seem...I mean, there wasn't the effect I expected.' She looked up suddenly. 'How's Iona? Did she get offered counselling, like you? Jesus, the poor thing, is she having to pretend – '

'She declined counselling.'

'So she hasn't discussed it?'

He shook his head. 'Only with me.'

'Only with you? She hasn't told anyone else the truth?'

'Neither of us have. She wanted it that way, so that's how I've played it. Until now.'

'And is she OK? How is she in herself?'

He lifted his eyebrows. 'Iona? She's calmer than me. There's everyone at work treating me like this ice-cool pro. And I'm nodding along and I'm playing it down and I'm waving it off – and really I'm feeling sick. Then I look at her. And she's at her desk just typing away.'

'Jesus. What's her nickname again?'

'Exactly. If only they all knew. And now I feel like this huge fraud. They think I'm being modest: I'm not.'

'Jon, you kept at it. You did what you always do: you didn't give up. You never do. You were both there, but Iona happened to take the shot. Don't be so harsh on yourself.'

'Ali, we were both there, but only one of us fired.' He hunched forward, fingers now tight on hers. 'I couldn't do it. I'm an SFO and I could not fire my weapon.'

'Jon – first days in a new job. That's all it was.'

'And if you're wrong? If there's another time and I still can't?'

She raised herself up. 'There might never be another time. Not one that requires you to fire.'

'But if there is?'

She opened her mouth then closed it. Her eyes went back to her watch. 'I have to get Holly. We can talk later, OK?'

'OK.'

'Wiper? You coming?'

The dog shot towards the doorway, thin tail swishing from side-to-side. The front door shut with a gentle thud. He peered at the floor beside the sofa. Duggy was still stretched out, little pot-belly poking up at the ceiling. Smiling fondly, Jon retrieved the remote and turned his troubled eyes to the screen. He pressed play and the game resumed.

Printed in Great Britain
by Amazon